AUTHOR	CLASS
LESLIE, D.	F
TITLE	No.
CALL BACK.	FICTION RESERVE
YESTERDAY.	475045591

D0266604

Call Back Yesterday

BOOKS BY
DORIS LESLIE

Novels

FULL FLAVOUR
FAIR COMPANY
CONCORD IN JEOPARDY
ANOTHER CYNTHIA
HOUSE IN THE DUST
FOLLY'S END
THE PEVERILLS
PERIDOT FLIGHT
AS THE TREE FALLS
PARAGON STREET
THE MARRIAGE OF MARTHA TODD
A YOUNG WIVES' TALE
THE DRAGON'S HEAD
CALL BACK YESTERDAY

Biographical Studies

ROYAL WILLIAM: *Life of William IV*
POLONAISE: *A Romance of Chopin*
WREATH FOR ARABELLA: *Life of Lady Arabella Stuart*
THAT ENCHANTRESS: *Life of Abigail Hill, Lady Masham*
THE GREAT CORINTHIAN: *Portrait of the Prince Regent*
A TOAST TO LADY MARY: *Life of Lady Mary Wortley
Montagu*
THE PERFECT WIFE: *Life of Mary Anne Disraeli
Viscountess Beaconsfield*
I RETURN: *The Story of François Villon*
THIS FOR CAROLINE: *Life of Lady Caroline Lamb*
THE SCEPTRE AND THE ROSE: *Marriage of Charles II
and Catherine of Braganza*
THE REBEL PRINCESS: *Life of Sophia Dorothea,
Princess of Celle*
THE DESERT QUEEN: *Life and Travels of
Lady Hester Stanhope*
THE INCREDIBLE DUCHESS: *Life and Times of
Elizabeth Chudleigh*

DORIS LESLIE

Call Back Yesterday

HEINEMANN : LONDON

~~475045591~~

William Heinemann Ltd
15 Queen Street, Mayfair, London W1X 8BE

LONDON MELBOURNE TORONTO
JOHANNESBURG AUCKLAND

2040165706

First published 1975
© Doris Leslie 1975

434 41826 9

Printed in Great Britain by Cox & Wyman Ltd
London, Fakenham and Reading

To Christina Foyle

who also remembers

AUTHOR'S NOTE

All characters in this novel are entirely fictitious, but the incidents appertaining to the raids on London during the Blitz are drawn from my own experiences. I was a voluntary air-raid warden while waiting to be conscripted, but was passed medically unfit for active service when I was called up owing to an injury sustained while on duty in Civil Defence. I therefore remained in A.R.P. for the duration of the war.

I am gratefully indebted to Charles Eade who compiled *The War Speeches of the Right Hon. Winston Churchill* (1952) for the few excerpts I have quoted; also to A. J. P. Taylor, *English History 1914–1945*, and to Sir Robert Bruce Lockhart's *Comes the Reckoning*.

DORIS LESLIE

INTRODUCTION

In collecting these reminiscences of Noel Harbord I have reconstructed from her memoirs and her journal much that she had left unwritten. But she conveyed to me before she died that were her recollections to be published, they might be of interest to those who were unborn during World War Two, besides the many who served in the Civil Defence of London as did she.

Her script is somewhat haphazard and not always legible. At her request I have substituted fictitious names throughout.

I first met her at the private view of Sybil Barton's posthumous exhibition of sculptures. Although I profess to be no critic I was unimpressed by the majority of her exhibits; yet there were a few notable exceptions, in particular the bronze cast of Colin Harbord: one of Barton's earlier efforts.

As I left the gallery I just managed to save an old lady from slipping on the step into Bond Street. It was raining and the concierge on the pavement was hailing a taxi, not for her but for a couple waiting there before her.

I had noticed her in the gallery leaning on a stick – she was slightly lame – in front of the Colin Harbord bust: this of a man with a fine articulation of bone structure which was more delicately wrought than the usual Epsteinian style of her work.

She thanked me as I helped her up from a near fall and I asked, since she appeared to be alone, if she had ordered a taxi. She said she had not, but as she lived in Piccadilly she could walk that short distance. Whereupon I offered to give her a lift and drove her to her flat. She invited me in

I

and offered me tea. I was interested in her. She had an engaging personality, with a small, young–old face scarcely lined, a silvery crop of boyish curls, and eyebrows perpetually raised, as if in surprise, above eyes that were singularly bright and unfaded.

That was the beginning of our friendship. We met again several times afterwards and it was on my third or fourth visit when she told me she had written her memoirs.

'I did not write them', she confessed, 'with any idea of publication, only for myself to recall the events of yesterday – with time returned. And as you are a writer you might perhaps consider them worth while. But', she added, 'I would not, for personal reasons, submit them to the firm with which I was connected many years ago even though that publishing company has passed into other hands. . . .'

The memoirs are now published a year after her death.

ONE

'I didn't do it. I meant to but I didn't – I did not! Why can't you believe me?'

Those frenzied words of his rang through the corridors of memory in recurrent repetition, for to us who tread the downward years the past becomes the present and there is no life but memory.*

I see him now as I saw him then, his face deathly white, his hair greying yet still so childishly fair, one stray lock fallen over his forehead . . . he whom I married in the post-war years of World War One. He was invalided out of the Rifle Brigade having gained a commission from his school cadet corps.

The orphaned only son of wealthy parents, his father had been killed in a car accident in the early days of motors and his mother died shortly afterwards with money enough, at accumulative interest, to leave him a substantial income when he came of age. An uncle on the distaff side had been appointed his guardian but, living a bachelor dilettante existence in the South of France, he concerned himself little with his ward after he had left Eton and joined up . . .

From Colin's account of himself Noel learned that he spent his three or four thousand a year, a considerable income in those days and comparable to four times as much today, on anything and everything he fancied: objets d'art, books, first editions, pictures – he went in for the post-war ultra modernists (futurists they called them) – and antique

* From the memoirs of Noel Harbord.

furniture for his flat in Albany and the villa in Florence that had been his mother's.

Noel, an only child, was also orphaned. They had that much in common, but Colin could remember his parents, she could not. Her father of the Indian army was killed in a border skirmish and her mother came back to England and died when Noel was born. She was brought up by an aunt, her mother's half-sister . . . We hear that this aunt, Miss Rhoda Penfold, was 'an indomitable fifty, moustached, grey, gaunt and an ex-militant suffragette'. After Noel had been sent to three successive schools where she distinguished herself not at all, it was discovered she had a 'taste' for art.

According to her memoirs:

It seems I could paint, had an eye for colour but couldn't, or wouldn't, draw. Aunt Rhoda landed me at the Yew Tree School of Art in Chelsea. It was bombed in World War Two. She had a hideous house in Fulham bordering a slum that had once been open country. She also had a house in Kent not far from the coast where I spent most of my childhood.

As a beginner I was put into the antique class at the Yew Tree and I loathed the antique. I was then barely seventeen and the youngest of the younger ones in the women's classes.

Colin and I first met at one of those Art students' 'revels' as they called them, held in the Botanical Gardens at Regent's Park not far from where the landmine dropped about sixteen years later . . . I went as an Aubrey Beardsley pierrot and he too, coincidentally, each the facsimile of the other. But for that we might never have met; for having spotted me in the crowd he came up and spoke to me. That set us talking Beardsley. He had some original drawings and a first edition of Beardsley's one literary extravaganza, *Under the Hill*. From there we went on to the Yellow Book. He had the whole thirteen volumes of which Beardsley was art editor. He said his uncle, who had been his guardian, had known Beardsley and many of the 1890s coterie, including Oscar Wilde ... 'I sat on his knee when I was three or four,' he said. And: 'You must come and see my Beardsleys. I have them at my flat in Albany but the Yellow Books are in Florence.' Most of his money was his mother's, left to him in trust until he was twenty-five ...

Barton passed us and called to Colin: 'Join us later, Colin,' and to me: 'Hullo, Merry! Why aren't you dancing?'

She was a columbine with a harlequin whom I recognized, in spite of his mask, as Ashley, one of the Yew Tree men. We were all surnames at the 'Tree', men and girls alike. We never knew each other's Christian names or if we did we never used them. I was always 'Merry', for Merryon.

I had done pretty well at the Yew Tree, and was going in for the R.A. Schools. I wondered if Colin would let me do him as the portrait study for the R.A. Schools entrance exam. He was eminently paintable although his bone structure would have been better for modelling, but I was not going in for sculpture – nor, incidentally, did I go in for the R.A. Schools. Barton did. She was for sculpture. Barton ... So Botticellian with her pale, empty eyes, her egg-shaped forehead, her button mouth and what Walter Pater called the 'peevish' look of Sandro's Madonnas.

She and Ashley passed on to join the others who were jazzing on the grass in a clearing. We, Colin and I, sat on a seat under a cedar. Fairy lights had been strung among the trees lining the path where couples strolled in a kaleidoscopic pageantry, with the dark star-pricked sky above and the multi-coloured costumes below merging into the near and far distance like paints spilled from a palette.

The sounds of young revellers mingled with the syncopated blare of a jazz band. It was the joyous aftermath of those horrific years when most of us had never known what he had known.

They were singing while they jazzed to the saxophone:

'Yes, sir, you're my baby' . . . I asked him 'Shall we?' And got up. So did he but not to dance, saying:

'Sorry, but this' – he patted his thigh above the knee – 'is not in training yet. He's a new one, the latest model. I've only had him a week and I'm not quite used to him.'

I felt awful. I guessed what it was before he told me.

'Did you,' I began stupidly, 'lose it . . . in the war?'

He didn't answer that.

'This time, in a month from now,' he took his watch from a pocket of his white trews that clung to both his own leg and the other as if he had been poured into a skin, the other so well shaped you couldn't possibly have told . . . 'I'll take you to the Embassy Club. Do you know the Embassy? And Tim'll do his stuff.'

'Oh . . . Yes.' I tried to laugh it off because he had a laugh in his voice about it. He called it 'Tim' after his orthopaedic surgeon, Sir Timothy Dunlop, whose mechanic had fitted him with this 'latest model'. We walked to a marquee. You wouldn't notice it when he walked. It was only very slightly stiffer than his own. The marquee had filled to capacity with people clamouring for drinks and eats at a buffet. Colin found a table for two just vacated. He said, 'Sit and I'll forage.'

He foraged and came back with a plate of sandwiches, a bottle of champagne and two tumblers. He poured one for me and one for himself. I wondered how he had managed to get a bottle for they didn't usually go in for champagne at that sort of a 'do', but he had that way with him of always getting what he wanted.

While we ate and drank – he drank three tumblers to my one – we talked, or rather he talked. I listened.

At that first meeting I learned a lot about his early life. It was as if he unloosed on me much he had held within himself until he met someone to whom he could disburden. When afterwards – a long time afterwards – I asked him why he had given me, a stranger, such intimate details of his childhood, he said, 'But you were not a stranger. I felt I

6

knew you, had known you for ever, the moment I looked into your eyes . . .'

He had a vivid recollection of his earliest experiences, of all he had seen and heard to do with his parents during the first few years.

'I was very young – about four or five – after my father came back from Malta where he had been stationed.' (That too we had in common, both our fathers had been soldiers.) 'We lived', he said, 'in a great rambling old house in Suffolk. I had a Nannie whom I adored – and she got married and left and I had a series of governesses until I went to prep school. I hadn't a chance.' He refilled his glass and stared down at the bubbling wine. His forehead was lined with the thoughts he jerked out. 'You see everything was all against me. My mother always back and forth to Florence, where she had a villa. Her father had money and she was an only daughter. I never knew my grandparents. All of us seem to die young or youngish – except me who ought to have been bumped off in the trenches. Anyway –' He seemed to make an effort to say what he had begun to say or didn't want to say, and then:

'It was on one of my father's leaves, and Nannie at forty had left to get married with promises that I could go and stay with her and her husband. He was head gardener at some place near ours. They had a lodge there. So I was left to a daily nursery governess . . . One night my mother had come up as she sometimes did to kiss me goodnight. She smelt of wine or whisky. I can remember her as rather blurred, like a picture that has lain too long in an attic with dust on it . . .' He gave a shrug and his face lightened as he looked at me saying, 'I can't help telling you all this. You have a listening face . . .'

The gist of 'all this' he was telling me as we sat in that stuffy marquee with those pantomimic costumes all about us amid the hum and buzz of voices and the strains of jazz as accompaniment (How it is all revived as I recall it!) and I heard him say:

7

'I couldn't sleep. I often didn't sleep for she would wake me, kissing me goodnight – not that she really loved me as mothers are supposed to love an only child. She was brought up in and imbued with the aesthetic movement of the 'eighties and 'nineties and their reaction to Grundyism, especially living as she did among them in Florence for most of her earlier years. In the battle against materialism in that final two decades of *fin-de-siècle* she felt – as did so many others of their kind and time – a curiosity of life. William Sharp called it that in his one number of *The Pagan Review* written in 1892 promoting "the New Paganism". I got hold of this sort of thing before I went to Eton. My mother had it all in our library and I read everything I could lay hands on before and during my teenage years.'

Hearing him say this, not spoken so readily as I have given it almost word for word as it comes back to me, but with pauses and hesitancies in between, I said: 'You must have been a very precocious boy to have read and understood all this even before you went to Eton.'

'As an only child and orphaned, one is thrown upon oneself and one's own resources.'

'Yes,' I nodded, 'I know. I was an only child but I never knew my parents.'

'Maybe you were lucky.' A clouded look came into his eyes. He was obviously trying to pave his way for giving me what he forced himself to give me – why? Because, as he told me, I was not a stranger . . . He had always known me. And this was not just a flirtatious gambit to be followed up by something as near to going the 'whole hog', as the Yew Tree girls would call it, if they dared. Some of them did dare, but I never did. For I, not ignorant, was old-fashionedly innocent, a trifle shocked at the talk of the more sophisticated who inclined to brag of their whole-hoggishness . . .

He was saying: 'You'll think me a bore to be telling you all this but I have to get it off my chest. It's been held in too long and also because' – he gave a kind of choke, then cleared his throat – 'because although I've only known you for three hours, I mean known you here in the flesh, other than in my dreams . . .'

I saw the bottle he had brought was more than half empty. I'd had only one glass of it and that I hadn't finished. Decidedly, I thought, he's had too much. And then, more to himself than to me, he went on:

'It was Christmas Eve.' (I'm hearing him saying it all again as I heard it more than half a century ago) . . . 'My father was home on leave and he'd persuaded her not to go to Florence for Christmas as they usually did, leaving me in our house in Suffolk with the servants. My father cared for his home – that tumbled-down old manor house near Ipswich. But', he said, 'I sold it as soon as I could do what I liked with my property when it came out of trust. . . . I had been sent to bed as usual, and she kissed me good night and told me to hang up my stocking and Santa Claus would give me a present. I remember telling her, for I wanted so much to love her but I couldn't somehow – she was always in a hurry to be off somewhere or other or entertaining when at the Larches – our house in Suffolk. I never knew why it was called Larches. Perhaps because it hadn't any larches . . .' He had a laugh in his voice. I used to wait for it, that invisible laugh which was one of his endearing qualities. He had so many to make him all that he was and – all that he was not.

And while I was thinking that about him with one ear for what he said and another for what I am saying of him now . . . 'When she spoke about Santa Claus giving me a present, I told her there wasn't a Santa Claus. No more than there was a God . . . I'd been taught nothing about God, not since Nannie left. It was part of my mother's paganistic experimentalism or whatever had caught her up in those 'nineties of the decadence and Oscar's martyrdom.'

He fell into a few minutes of brooding, his forehead wrinkled, gathering the urge to be rid of long-withheld

9

repressions . . . 'I said to her,' he had found himself again to continue, 'I told her, "There isn't any God – it's all fairy tales about him sitting up there with Jesus on his right hand – and how could he have a hand if he's a spirit or a ghost?" '

I ached for that poor little lonely boy who wanted to love a mother who didn't want to, or couldn't, love him.

'Did she mind?' I asked when he paused again, thinking back to his thwarted childhood – 'mind that you had said you didn't believe in God?'

He shook his head. 'No. She was, if not an acknowledged atheist, an agnostic, or rather a free-thinker. She'd discovered Nietzsche and lapped up his iconoclast-ish-isms' – he had some difficulty in getting out the word – 'as a kitten laps up cream, that being part of the "movement" she went in for, and it must have been, as I see it now, partly responsible for the friction between her and my father . . .'

Another, longer, pause. I was very interested in these confidences, at least half of me was interested, the other half seeing him on canvas, that delicate structure of cheek and jaw bone and the white pierrot head and shoulders against a dark bluish background with the flare of oil lamps lighting the marquee. I would ask him to sit for me if we ever met again. I was mistrustful, over-cautious maybe, not sure if these self-revelations could be a tactical attempt to get me to 'go the whole hog'.

'About your mother,' I prompted him. 'You were telling me of a Christmas Eve.'

'Yes,' he released a bitten underlip. I guessed he didn't want to say what he felt he had to say, and that made me the more anxious to hear it.

'Yes, well she went downstairs after kissing me good-night – I can still smell her kiss with wine or whisky in it and I heard the piano being played, "The Blue Danube" – she could play anything by ear – and then I must have dozed off and woke to hear her shrieking. I knew it was she and not from the servants' hall. I couldn't hear what she said – not in words – but I heard my father shouting "Quiet – Quiet! You bitch!" I knew it was bitch, but didn't think it an insult, a compliment rather, because he had a spaniel, Molly, one of a pair of his gundog bitches and I had a mongrel Betty, a cross between a collie and a labrador. I adored her and she died of eating poison laid down in the stables for the rats . . . My second tragic loss, she and Nannie . . .' He gave a kind of shudder and refilled his tumbler. I put my hand over my glass as he began to pour more into mine. He drank his at a draught and refilled it; the bottle was now quite dead. And after yet another, longer pause, he went on: 'She was still yelling – I couldn't hear what – and then the sound of crashing glass as of something thrown. I crept out of bed and tiptoed to the drawing-room. The door was ajar. I looked through it and saw my father struggling with my mother – holding her hands as if to keep her off. She wrenched herself free and came at him with her fists . . .' He lowered his head, his underlip caught beneath a tooth. I knew he was reliving his childhood's terror of that scene which had lain dormant in his subconscious and now dragged up to be told to my 'listening face'.

'I can't' – his voice broke – 'I can't remember all that happened then, more than that she was still screaming at him and she had what looked like froth coming out of her mouth and her hair was all tumbled round her shoulders. And he seized her by the hair and swung her off her feet, both were shouting at each other and then . . . she fell. I went away and up to my bed and lay there shaking, terror-stricken. . . . I slept at last, but for ages afterwards I dreamt of it. I sometimes wonder if it wasn't all a dream or a nightmare. . . .'

He told me he had learned from his guardian, the uncle, that after his father got himself killed in that car crash his mother had gone from bad to worse and died of drink or – something else.

From other revelations, not at our first meeting but later, I heard that when he joined up just out of school, and he and his company went over the top, he killed a German in a hand-to-hand fight, stuck his bayonet into him. . . . I can never forget how he spoke of that killing, with a kind of horrified shame and yet a sadistic satisfaction, he who abhorred all blood sports, wouldn't shoot or hunt and had, I think, a greater love of animals than of humans; but he could tell with gloating reminiscence how he had killed that German. He told me he hated the Huns.

Looking back on all he had revealed to her of that scene between his parents on a Christmas Eve when he was five or six years old, it may, she says, have left him with psychological aggressive tendencies nurtured in a desire to protect his mother against his father who was equally representative of his unloved ego. . . . Could this have resulted in a repressed grievance against these two sources of his unwanted being? . . . 'I may be wrong,' she suggests, 'I have tried all these years to account for that which happened afterwards. Besides, what effect could that diabolical hand-to-hand fighting in trench warfare have had upon him and other young survivors of the First World War? They, their sons, the youth of the Second World War, "those few" who fought in the greatest of all battles in the air, the Battle of Britain, they knew nothing of that four years' holocaust . . .

'But I wander away in time. I am back again now in the 'twenties when I first met him and we talked, or I listened to him talk, while all colours faded out of things and then sharpened to the pinkening sky of dawn.

'On leaving the marquee we went back to our seat under the cedar and he drew me into his arms . . . Then, after my first instinctive recoil from his too stormy kiss, I dissolved . . . I suppose I did love him at that moment.'

*   *   *

They met several times after that. She went to his flat to see his Beardsleys. He had a manservant who had been his batman, named Latimer – which, she thought, was misspelt for Littimer as he reminded her of the Littimer in *Copperfield*, Steerforth's servant. She said he was eminently respectable and looked at her as Littimer looked at David, 'as if I were so very young . . .'

The aunt, as we are told, denounced an engagement. 'He has no job – one of the idle rich. A drone. As for you – do you really intend to be tied to him for the rest of your life and no freedom? None —' she declared, thumping a fist on the arm of her chair and repeating, 'None – unless you can prove adultery and cruelty! Hah! When we are sufficiently represented in what passes for Parliament in this man-governed country, which is still wearing its Victorian blinkers, despite a world war in which women played their part and risked their lives, when WE' – she capitalized it – 'are more than as now, resignedly permitted the vote *and* an occasional seat in the Commons, then we will dispense with the injustice of so-called "women's rights" that do not allow the dissolution of marriage for incompatibility, but must still prove adulterous association and physical assault . . . Bah!' Again a thump and a snort as of a horse prepared to take a jump. This aunt, Miss Penfold, was a good horse-woman and followed hounds when at her small country house in Kent.

'From there,' as the memoirs recall it, 'I was sent to Kindergarten and was summarily taught the three R's. Aunt Rhoda visited me at weekends when not engrossed with her "Cause" or serving her sentence in Holloway, hunger striking. During those earlier years I was left, as was Colin, to the care of servants but I had no beloved Nannie as had he to love or to love me.'

'Thank God,' fervently asserted Aunt Rhoda, when Noel told of her intent to marry Colin, 'that I was never forced to suffer the humiliation of divorcing the man I married —'

'What!' I interrupted in gaping amaze, 'You, Aunt . . . *married?*'

'Yes.' Aunt Rhoda drew herself up, looking more gaunt than ever and folding her arms and her lips simultaneously, while I stared in astonished disbelief. Married? She, whom I had always thought of as one of those withered-up old suffragettes who, as we at the Yew Tree believed, fought for what they called their 'rights' because they couldn't find a man to marry them.

'I', said Aunt Rhoda as if she took that thought from me, '*was* married, which surprises you. Married out of the schoolroom by my parents, your grandparents, when the be-all and end-all of a girl's existence was to be – married.'

By the disgust with which she uttered the word, with a grinding of her teeth, it might have been a synonym for murder. 'He was a wealthy fox-hunting squire, a neighbour of ours, and I,' she said, 'was put through all the nauseating performance of the ceremony conducted by the vicar at the altar, while previously to that and the engagement I had been duly presented at Court to the old Queen. And *that* for the girls of my day who were born in what was called "society" or of the landed, or aspiring to be landed, gentry was a ritualistic martyrdom, all part of the enslavement of marriage. But I, already aware, at seventeen, of the barbaric semi-purdah to which I was committed, bided my time, endured what is nothing less than legalized prostitution. *They* get paid for it and we were not, more than to be given a roof over our heads and in most cases a perennial suc-cession of children. Nor were we enlightened as to what copulation entailed. . . . However, I'll pass by the horror I sustained at my initiation in the bridal bed and also the misery of submitting to his demands, especially when he was drunk. I endured it for two years, became pregnant, had a miscarriage due to physical violence when I refused to cohabit with him. So –' Aunt Rhoda pronounced this with prideful emphasis – 'I left him. There was no legal separation, no divorce although I could, if I had sunk to the shame of it, have produced evidence enough of adultery and cruelty. I had my marriage settlement bestowed upon me by my parents (a dowry they called it in my days); braved the censure of them and him who made attempt to retrieve me and drag me back to my enslavement. Then he gave up, went his way and I went mine, which brought me to join the army in the war for our rights.'

'And now you have your rights,' I said, not yet recovered from the shock of knowing her married, I who had always known her as 'Miss', a spinster.

'Not enough rights yet.' Aunt Rhoda meditatively plucked at the hairs on her chin. 'And that is what I am coming to now.' Which she proceeded to propound.

'We are hoping eventually, when we have a majority voice as Members of Parliament, to enforce a law that all men prior to marriage must be medically examined to ensure that they have not contracted a venereal disease. Only by such medical precaution can we safeguard a woman from the danger of man's promiscuity and lustful appetites. As you are of age' (I was then just twenty-one) 'I cannot forbid this marriage unless your future husband shall undergo examination, but I do urge' – Aunt Rhoda pinioned me with her eye, a steely penetrating eye that seemed to bore such holes into mine that I blinked as if under a flashlight – 'and I must insist that he enters into matrimony with a clean bill of health.'

When, not without some misgiving, I told Colin of this conversation, he took it at first with astonished incredulity and then with hoots of laughter.

'Good Lord! I knew she was a crank but this', he spluttered, 'proves her barmy.'

Needless to say he was not medically examined and so – we were married.

It was a very quiet wedding, not in church, in a registrar's office. The aunt and Colin's uncle were the sole witnesses. They dispensed with the church service as much by mutual consent as by the aunt's suggestion or decision. Neither Noel nor Colin had more than the little religious instruction their schools had taught them, and Miss Penfold, a professed agnostic, expressed her disapproval of the marriage vows in which the woman must bind herself for life as the lesser half of the man who was sworn before God to cherish her, worship her with his body, and endow her with all his worldly wealth . . . 'Whether', she snorted, 'he was worth no more than a couple of beans, and the woman, his goods and chattel, must promise to obey him – Obey! Which entailed bearing his children, submitting to his lustful demands, regardless of her wish or desire. Bah! Don't talk to me about the sanctity of marriage . . .'

As Noel recalls: I didn't talk to her about it, but could not help a secret hankering for a wedding . . . A real wedding, never mind the nuptial vows, myself in a bridal dress instead of the fawn gaberdine travelling coat and skirt (they didn't call them suits in those days) and the customary ceremonious performance, Mendelssohn's wedding march and 'Here comes the Bride', with bridesmaids, presents, and a reception afterwards at the Hyde Park Hotel or Claridges, like Barton had when she married – not Ashley whom she ought to have married, having had an affair with him as the whole Yew Tree suspected though she would never admit it, always close as an oyster about herself. But she did go to Paris with him, ostensibly to view the Salon exhibition. No, she didn't marry Ashley, she married the son of a war profiteer who had made a fortune in munitions and got himself a knighthood. I saw her after we were both married when we met again in Florence and she brought with her – that other.

More about him later. I run too far ahead.

TWO

Those last years of the 'twenties were overhung with the shadows of coming events and disasters, including the general strike of 1926, of which these two knew nothing as they were in Florence at that time; and if they had known they would not have cared. They had money enough to enjoy what life could offer and it offered much to them, too much, perhaps to Colin. She soon realized he was recklessly extravagant, continually overdrawn at his bank. 'Spending,' as she wrote, 'on anything and everything that took his fancy ...'

It seems she had a small income left her by her parents, but which appears to have been quite inadequate for her own personal requirements since she was as little concerned with money or the want of it as was Colin.

Her aunt had paid for her schooling and all else from the accumulated interest of the capital left in trust by her parents under the guardianship of Miss (or should it be Mrs?) Rhoda Penfold.

This remarkable woman retained all her faculties to an advanced age and much that is here reconstructed from the salient events of Noel Harbord's life is gleaned from her relationship to Miss Penfold.

Having given up the flat in Albany as too small for the two of them they rented a flat in Grosvenor Street and spent the summer months there and the rest of the year in Florence.

It seems Miss Penfold expressed her disapproval of their mode of life.

'A pair of ne'er-do-wells', as Noel gives it on a day when the aunt descended upon them in Grosvenor Street. Colin had seen her alight from her car, she had been driving for years in and before the war, and he went off to his club to avoid her.

'As far as I can see,' said Aunt Rhoda seating herself in one of the Hepplewhite chairs Colin had bought – a set of six at Sotheby's – 'you will have to keep him as well as yourself. You would never have made a living at art unless commercial, so you had best make an effort to do something to earn an honest guinea instead of frittering it away between you on all this . . .' A wave of her hand and a disparaging snort at the furnishings of the drawing-room with its eighteenth-century antiques. What it all cost Noel never knew nor thought to ask. 'You would do better to sell it and invest what it brings which should go toward his overdraft . . . Oh, yes.' Miss Penfold nodded her head on which was perched a hat of green felt swathed with purple velvet, the colours of the bygone Suffragettes' Cause. 'I know,' the aunt continued, 'that he has a large overdraft.' How, Noel wondered, could she possibly have known that?

She did not tell Colin of her aunt's warning, nor pay much heed to it. An overdraft meant as little to her as it meant to Colin, but she did wonder if she might turn to some good account her training at the art school . . . Commercial art. What did that entail? Advertisements? Fashion plates? Designs for dresses in *Vogue* or the covers of women's magazines? . . . No. Never! Cut down expenses if they must or go on as they were going and damn the consequences. It was cheap enough living in Florence and the rent in Grosvenor Street had not yet been put up – but was likely to be, according to the landlord's agent.

Extract from the memoirs

Florence . . . How I loved our life in Florence, the Flower City as Colin called it. The villa that had been his mother's stood some way out of the city on the hills toward Settig-

18

nano. Our garden was set close to a vineyard and bordered with iris and the small courtyard with roses, their yellow and crimson petals falling to spread a carpet on the grey flagstones, for summer comes early in Tuscany. . . . From our windows we could look down across the olive groves to the beautiful church of San Miniato and beyond that the Arno glistening in the sun and to the city itself and the towering rose-hued dome of Brunelleschi. And in those dew-drenched mornings I would leave Colin still asleep in our bed, and would walk back under the fruitful olives and into the garden to bury my face in the roses and know the first quickening of *my* fruit – for I was pregnant after more than a year of marriage.

They returned to London in the autumn of that year for the birth of her baby, but it was not to be. She was taken ill on the Rome Express from Florence, and on arriving at Grosvenor Street the pain and vomiting persisted. Their doctor sent her for an X-ray which revealed acute appendicitis that necessitated immediate operation.

Yet it was unlikely, according to medical report, that she would ever have carried the child. 'Something', she says, 'was wrong with me, I couldn't quite understand what, which meant that if I did conceive I would lose the baby.'

'The sins of the fathers,' obscurely pronounced Miss Penfold, 'unto the third and fourth generation.' . . .

It seems that neither Noel nor Colin was unduly disappointed that they had lost their child. 'Although he', she tells us, 'had hoped for a son to be given all he had missed from his parents.' But she, who had never known either a mother's or a father's love and guidance, had no image on which to reproduce herself.

In the following year they were back again in Florence, and it is there that Barton now appears with that 'other' who is to enter the star-crossed lives of these two Harbords . . . 'Star-crossed' is her definition of what is to come and what had possibly gone before in their unloved and unwanted formative years.

Colin, as she records it, bought a car in Florence, a Fiat. 'Tim' did not prevent him driving, and on the day when I ran into Barton he had taken the car into the city to have the battery recharged. We arranged to meet at Doney's in the Via Tornabuoni. On my way there I crossed the Ponte Vecchio, that oldest and most beautiful of the bridges where the little jewellers' shops shoulder one another, sparkling with trinkets of all sorts, coral necklaces, white, red, pink, and rings of garnets simulating rubies set in carven silver and purporting to be genuine Benvenuto Cellinis which, of course, they were not for fifty *lire*. I stood awhile leaning over the bridge where there is a gap between the crowding shops, and waited there awhile to look down on Arno and thought that here in this very spot Dante might have seen Beatrice pass on one unforgotten day. Or Lippo Lippi might have sneaked out at night to meet a girl just here . . . so noisy with *vetturi* and the crack-ing of whips at the poor jaded horses, for the *vetturi* were the taxis then, yet the Bridge did not lose, for me, its unspoiled loveliness while I stood there on the Old Bridge and saw the ancient *palazzi* rising up from the glistening waters, their grey, sun-weathered walls just as they were seven hundred years ago. And high above the palaces and that river of gold which is Arno on a sunny morning, I saw the snow-capped Appenines circling the city in great amphitheatres. And while I stood entranced as I was, and always am, although I cannot often go back now to my beloved City of Florence, I heard my name called . . . 'Merry ! Is it Merryon ?'

I wheeled round –and saw her. Barton!

She was unchanged, yet why should she not be? It could only have been about three years since I had seen her. She was still that same Botticellian 'peevish-looking' Madonna-like Barton with those abstract lines of her face, and her transparent pale skin.

'Barton! How lovely! I didn't expect to find you here in Florence.'

'Why not? We all come to Florence sooner or later. Do you know Sinclair? This is Merry – Merryon. I can't remember your married name.'

'Harbord,' I told her, feeling, as she had always made me feel, a nonentity, she whose personality and that small one-toned voice of hers, seemed to hold some hidden force. No one, not Aunt Rhoda, nor Nielson, our Head at the 'Tree', whose criticism of my drawing used to reduce me to a jelly – not even Nielson could give me that 'inferiority complex', which in my day had not become a cliché to be used indiscriminately by suburbia among the late discoverers of Freud, whom Aunt Rhoda in her seventies had described, as I recall it: 'One of the two greatest evils of the twentieth century; the other being Hitler' . . . But Hitler was unheard of by us of the 'Tree' in the diminishing 'twenties.

'Of course. You married Colin. Have you given up painting?'

'More or less.'

'What are you doing in Florence? Sightseeing?' As if I were one of the loud-voiced enthusiastic Americans passing and repassing where we stood on the bridge, or guttural German *Frauen* ejaculating: '*Kolossal!*'

'No – I – we live here – I mean we have a villa at Settignano for the winter months.'

'Really?' Uninterested. She was examining my face, her almost lashless eyes half closed. 'You're more paintable than sculptural. And by paintable I mean that Nielson and' – she disparagingly named one or two of the less gifted students at the 'Tree' – 'made you sit for them. Pretty-pretty, isn't she?' To Sinclair.

He had not spoken until then, merely gave a casual nod of acknowledgement to her introduction. And looking over my head (for he was tall, about six foot two and immaculately tailored), he said: 'You mean she is no more "pretty",' he slightly stressed the word, 'than was Caro Lamb.'

'Because of the cropped curls?' discussing me as if I were not there, and at once deciding me to shingle, which was the latest fashion. I had always deplored my 'curly' hair and longed for hair straight as rain like Barton's, parted in the middle to enhance that enchanting Madonna-like look.

She turned and walked on leaving us together. He said, still not looking at me: 'Which way are you going?'

I told him I was going to Doney's – 'to meet my husband'.

'We are going to Doney's too.' At last his gaze left the distance and he stared full at me. 'So shall we?'

We went on together, he humming 'Tea for Two' from 'No, No, Nanette', which had been all the rage in London, and they still danced to it at Rajola's, the élite of supper and dance rooms in Florence.

We came over the bridge and saw Barton looking in at a window of the shop on Lung'Arno that sold and made such excellent shoes. I had bought a pair of snakeskin at a quarter the price we would have to pay in London.

As we came up to her Barton said in her toneless voice: 'Go on, you two, I'll join you at Doney's. I want those crocodiles.' Meaning a pair of crocodile shoes displayed on a velvet cushion, very small, and expensively priced even for Italy with the exchange high in our favour.

So Sinclair and I walked on to Via Tornabuoni, past the Palazzo Strozzi, unchanged through the centuries, where the flower sellers offer their heaped fragrances to passers-by. The beautiful narrow street was full of flowers, sunshine, strollers and loungers, all chattering, multi-lingual: German, American, a few drawling English, their voices coming from the back of their throats, and wearing their old school ties; the women in the latest shorter skirts below the knee. Among this usual motley crowd were the ubiquitous blue and silver-laced uniforms of officers from the garrison congregated at the door, their sloe-black eyes under the peaked caps searching the faces of all women under sixty, in particular the Americans, with whom to scrape acquaintance in hope of an heiress. So many with titles, Conte, Marchese, even though but distant cousins of the head of the family, offer themselves and are accepted with half a million dollars.

Not without some difficulty could we pass through the throng outside the doors, for Doney's was more than ever crowded, that day being a saint's day, and the garrison, or most of them, off duty. And once inside, there appeared to be no vacant place. However, Sinclair had seen a couple just about to leave a table in a corner.

'Here, quick.' He took my arm and we made for it just in time to prevent two officers from preceding us. Both backed and exaggeratedly bowed to me.

'*Signora, prego.*'

I thanked them, and Sinclair gave them a cursory look, his nose wrinkled as if at a smell. As we sat the two officers stared at me in the way I was accustomed to being stared at by Italian males, interpreting the movement of their lips to the usual '*Bella, Bella*', with which any woman passably attractive was greeted; and as they turned away: 'You are very insular,' I told Sinclair.

'Because I am not inclined to suffer too-obvious fools gladly?'

'By obvious fools do you mean the too-obvious gallantries of Latin men?'

'Who still regard women as their lawful prey or possible mothers of the species, like the slothful drones who gather the honey with which to stuff themselves while they wait in greedy anticipation of the nuptial flight when the lucky one may gain his mother, the queen, to be murdered when he wins her.'

I had nothing to say to that nor did he give me any chance to follow up the analogy between drone bees and

23

lecherous Italians because he had beckoned a waiter who dexterously managed to reach our table without spilling the tray of drinks he carried in obedience to another summons.

'*Subito, Signore.*' He deposited the glasses from his tray to a near-by table and returned to us, the empty tray under his arm.

Drinks were ordered, a dry Martini for me and a vodka for him. This was the first time I had seen or heard of vodka outside of Tchekhov.

'That's a Russian drink,' I said, guarding surprise, for although the Russian revolution was more than a decade past we still thought of Soviet citizens as 'those Bolshies', who since the round-up of Communists in the more recent General Strike were under suspicion as a menace to Britain.

'Yes, do you object?'

'No, why should I? But I have never seen anyone drink it before, I have only read of it.'

'It is as common as ale in Russia,' he said, offering me the dish of olives the waiter had brought with the drinks, 'and cheaper than lavatory paper there.'

'Have you been to Russia?' I was more interested in him now whom I at first had thought to be the typical static Englishman wearing his old school tie.

'Yes. Another drink?' Changing the subject rather abruptly.

I refused another drink and he called a waiter to bring a second vodka for himself.

Conversation flagged while I examined his face as I always did examine faces, reading into them something that could convey the personality of the subject were I to venture on a portrait. I found him paintable with his lion-coloured hair, his eyes deep-set, his cheekbones well defined, the mouth sensitive, almost womanish save for the firm modelling of the lips that looked to be grafted upon steel.

Taking the proffered vodka from the waiter he remarked, with a twinkle in his greenish-hazel eyes,

'Well, Caro? What is it you see that you regard me with such microscopic – or should I call it professional – intensity?'

Somewhat taken aback I fabricated an apology.

'I'm sorry. I didn't mean to stare. I wasn't thinking about you. I was thinking of something else.'

'So! I was unduly self-flattered.'

And seeing that twinkle deepen while I parried with an irrelevant riposte, conscious of my uncomfortable flush, 'Why do you call me Caro? What have I to do with Caro Lamb?' For I knew the delightful portrait of Caroline Lamb in her page's costume.

'You should know. From contemplation of her boyish angles, I turn to unthread her temperamental tangles.'

I didn't know whether to take this hastily improvised retort as a compliment or not, remembering Barton's scratch at me as 'pretty-pretty' which I certainly was not . . . But 'boyish angles'? Yes. I was angular enough, hipless, breastless, which suited the latest fashion from Paris that decreed busts and hips were out.

The entrance of Barton followed by Colin threading their way through the crowd at the bar brought to a halt his further contemplation of me.

She had a cluster of flowers in her hand; these she put on the table and sat in the chair vacated by Sinclair, who had risen to greet her and ordered a waiter to bring two more chairs.

All now seated, Barton turned her attention to Colin, who I noticed had never taken his eyes off her. I knew he had known her before our marriage although neither of us had seen her since.

'I've been telling Colin' – that she called him by his Christian name made me wonder how long she *had* known him before he and I knew each other, for we of the Yew Tree were always surnames, but of course Colin had

25

nothing to do with the Tree – 'I've been telling him,' she continued, sipping at her aperitif between puffs of the cigarette she accepted from Colin, 'that I want to model him.'

'We', I said, 'will not be in London until the spring.'

'Then you must come back next week with us. I simply can't wait until the spring. I've been waiting years to do a head of Colin.'

I glanced at him and suffered a slight shock. His eyes were still fixed on her but with a glazed look in them now and his whole body seemed to be tensed as if in an iron grip. . . . I had noticed him like this on one or two occasions lately when he would stop speaking and stay motionless for a few seconds and then suddenly become mobile again and go on talking or whatever he was doing as if nothing had happened.

It first occurred, or I had first noticed this in him, about a month ago at the villa. He had fallen off the ladder to the dove-cote where he had gone to count the chickens of our fantails. I didn't see him fall but he told me of it at dinner that night saying Mario, our gardener, must see to one of the rungs at the top of the ladder as it was loose.

'Did you hurt yourself?' I asked, alarmed.

'No, only a bump on my head – no worse than I've had a dozen times dropped on me from the roof of a dug-out.'

I thought no more about it after that, since he had made so light of it.

Needless to say we did not go back next week with Barton and Sinclair who, apparently, had accompanied her on this short visit to Florence instead of her husband, Richard Farrell. He, she carelessly explained, had to stay in London for some tiresome business conference, his father having retired as chairman, and Richard had been given the chairmanship.

'More money for her to burn, I suppose,' Colin remarked on our way back to the villa after that meeting at Doney's.

'She doesn't have to burn *his* money,' I reminded him.

26

'She has more than enough of her own to burn. She must have made a bonfire out of her one woman show last year.'

'Amazing,' he muttered. 'Quite amazing.'

'Why? She has an extraordinary talent, although I'm not so keen on her work as many people are. For me it is a cross between Epstein and Rodin – and not so much of either to be a pastiche of one or the other.'

'I don't agree.' I saw his hands tighten on the wheel with so fierce a grip that his knuckles showed white.

'Careful!' I cried, 'that was a near head on!'

He had accelerated at a bend and all but shaved a wing of an oncoming Bentley driven by a uniformed officer who, sighting me, stayed the much-discussed four-letter word in *Lady Chatterley's Lover* which he was about to hurl at Colin.

'Those bloody Wogs,' was all he said to that before he resumed: 'I find her amazing for the reason that her work is entirely inapposite to her– physically. I mean her fragile hands, her whole body so nymphlike and delicately formed. One cannot associate her with hacking at great lumps of stone with a carpenter's chisel to obtain such energy, such virility, which shows an Epsteinian influence rather than Rodin.'

I told him: 'I can see you paying twice your overdraft for that head she will do of you which I intended to do and didn't finish.'

He turned his right cheek to me. I could never get used to his driving on the wrong side in Florence.

'I can't think why you never finished it.'

'Perhaps because I was too engrossed with the original.'

He laughed his hidden laugh. 'You mean that ever since the Creator performed a surgical operation on Adam's fifth rib to make Eve, you and all women, Eve's daughters, have been trying to get back again where you belong.'

'Oh no. Don't delude yourselves. We and all of us, the Aunt Rhodas and Pankhursts and Co., have not fought all

27

these umpteen million centuries since we were hounded out of a Garden for taking from a tree an apple which we were forbidden to eat, and finally to win our independence only to be dragged back again into man's worshipful body endowed with all his worldly wealth, which is seldom enough to sit on a sixpence.'

'The woman tempted me, remember.'

'Yes, so like a man to hide behind our petticoats.'

'Which, in the first instance, if I remember rightly, was a fig leaf.' . . .

And if she remembered 'rightly' this short dialogue she would forget more important reminiscences and leave me to fill in the omissions in her scrawled manuscripts. Here and there I found copies of letters sent or received, and also extracts from a diary which she calls her Journal that she began to keep somewhere in the later thirties.

They went to the station to see Barton and Sinclair off to London on the Rome Express. Colin, bare-headed, waved to her where she leaned from the window, one of her hands lifted in a gesture that seemed to beckon . . . I gathered they did not wait until the spring to return to Grosvenor Street.

THREE

Barton's bust of Colin, we are told, took months to complete as she was engaged on two commissions, one of Lady Amersham, who had been a musical comedy chorus girl in the days of the old Gaiety Theatre during the late 'nineties when young peers would stand in wait at the stage door. Noel met her on several occasions. We hear that she was 'quite a character'. She had a house in St John's Wood.

Noel first saw Lady Amersham on a morning in early June when she came to Barton's studio to see the finished bust of herself. She arrived with two Pekingese, for she had walked the short distance from her house to Barton's studio which was also in St John's Wood, although their flat was in Grosvenor Square.

As recounted by Noel: She who had been Birdie Dobree (*née* Mabel Dobbs) still retained in her sixties much of the 'pretty-prettiness' attributed to me by Barton that had captured the infatuated Lord Marchbanks shortly before he succeeded to his father's marquisate of Amersham. Her husband had died a few years before his son and heir had married the daughter of a duke . . . 'Which reverts him to type by marrying into the peerage instead of the Gaiety chorus. He might have done better if he had,' she said with her chirping chuckle (no wonder she had been given the stage name of 'Birdie'). It's good for the breed to mix the blood. These boys of mine,' she lifted one of the Pekes to bestow a kiss on his black button of a nose, 'look to be bred out. I,' she added pridefully, 'was one of the first to marry a peer and half the House of Lords today are the sons of Us. Freddie was the first of his breed to fall by the way of the stage door but his son and the sons of the others, who like moths to a candle were lured to the footlights, have returned to their folds – if moths *have* folds. I know sheep have folds and all the peers I've known *are* like a lot of sheep and all the Amershams until my Johnnie, thanks to me, were chinless and most of them brainless.' Then, turning to the bust on the pedestal where Barton had placed it: 'Darling. You have made me look like a mentally deficient cherub. Is that how you see me? Freddie used to call me his chirruping cherub.' Again the birdlike twitter. 'And so did the fellow who's my daughter-in-law's father, the girl who might have been mine only we Gaiety girls didn't go so far then, and that's why they married us. They don't have to now, not since the war and women's rights. Did you know' – (to me) – 'but of course you didn't, you were too young, that I was one of *them* along with Sylvia and Christabel Pankhurst and Rhoda Penfold and that lot?'

I, who had been enjoying all this, broke in with:

'Rhoda Penfold! Did you know her?'

'Of course I knew her, and they all knew me. Made me speak at their meetings. Good advertisement. Marchioness of Amersham. Attracted huge crowds at the Albert Hall. Brought Amersham along with me too. Roped him in – he always did what he was told and I managed to get one or two of the fathers of the boys who now sit in the Upper House. Not any of the Commons. They didn't want us nor our vote, but we got under their skin like a running sore – and then when we showed up in the war doing men's jobs – well, they gave in and there we were and here we are! Yes, Rhoda Penfold!' She gave a reminiscent chirrup. 'Face like the back of a cab, voice like a fog-horn, but a fighter. Bashed a bobby in the eye when he grabbed her for breaking a window of a Regent Street jeweller's shop.'

'She is my aunt,' I ventured modestly.

'Is she?' Birdie opened her eyes – a faded periwinkle blue – to their widest. 'Good for you! I guessed you had *some*thing. Your aunt? So you'd have been roped in with us too

30

had you been old enough when we were on the march.' She got up in a whirl of summery chiffon. 'Come, darlings,' to the Pekes; and to me, 'You too. Come to lunch. I'm just round the corner. As for that' – she pointed a finger at the bust of herself – 'Johnnie's commissioned you' (this to Barton) 'to do it but I don't like it. Never mind. He pays.'

We hear much of 'Birdie' Amersham from both Noel's written and verbal reminiscences. We also learn more of Colin's uncle and former guardian than her verbal and almost illegible memoirs can offer.

This uncle, Archibald Tarrant, his mother's brother, rarely came to London from his villa at Menton and when he did he stayed at an hotel; but if no immediate accommodation were available in the height of the season, he would stay with the Harbords in Grosvenor Street.

Noel's description of 'Uncle Archie' gives us a clear enough picture of this 'left over', as she calls him, 'of the 'nineties', when as a youth he knew the leading lights of the *fin de siècle*.

Extract from Noel Harbord's memoirs

. . . Colin's uncle came unexpectedly to stay a night or two. He usually stayed at the Burlington but couldn't get his suite there that time because he hadn't booked it long enough in advance. He had to attend the funeral of one of his old friends who, like Archie, was a collector of fine arts. It seems some of his pictures and things, including his collection of snuffboxes, were left to Archie, which Colin thought should fetch a hell of a lot if he auctioned them at Sotheby's.

'Not that it would matter a damn to us,' he said, 'for although I'm his next of kin, he is more likely to outlive me than I him.'

Archie Tarrant always reminded me of some Elizabethan

31

revenant with his short pointed beard, his hair swept back from an unlined forehead. His hair, so shiny a black, may have owed something to the contents of a bottle. He had a small mouth, and little teeth stained by the smoke of his perpetual cigars. His speech was somewhat stilted in a carefully modulated voice and he was quite knowledgeable about his Tuscan Primitives.

After Colin had left us that night – he complained of one of his headaches and went to bed early – I had a long talk with Uncle Archie. I had never been alone with him for more than minutes on the few occasions he came to stay with us.

I don't know how we started talking about Colin's mother – I think I began it by saying how, coincidentally, Colin and I were both orphaned and brought up by an aunt in my case, and by an uncle as was Colin.

'But he did know his mother,' I said. 'I never knew mine.'

And he, pursing up his thin small lips, said, 'It might have been better if Colin had never known his.'

I was in two minds whether to tell him what Colin had told me about his early life, on that first time we met at the art students' ball, but instead I asked: 'Why do you say that?'

He took out his cigar-case and lighted a cigar before he spoke.

'His mother has left him a legacy which is less an asset than a liability.'

'Do you mean he would have done more with his life if he had not so much money to fritter away, as my aunt is always telling me?'

'I am not speaking financially,' he said.

I waited. I could see he was going to say more and he did.

'Has Colin ever told you of how or from what his mother died?'

'No, not exactly —'

Colin had told me she died of drink but I didn't like to go into that. I waited to hear it from him.

He removed his cigar from his mouth, and looking at me with his remarkably blue eyes – so startling a blue in his sun-tanned thin-skinned face – he said with slow deliberation, 'His mother was an epileptic.'

I experienced shock.

'I thought he did tell me that his mother,' I faltered, 'died of – of drink.'

'Which did not ultimately cause her death, but it is better that Colin should think so.'

'I see.'

I began to see. 'Is it – is epilepsy – can it be inherited?'

'Yes, in certain cases, it can. Her father and mine, Colin's grandfather, was an epileptic.'

And Uncle Archie was his son . . . Was that, I wondered, why he had never married, because of the family 'legacy'?

I left it at that, not wishing to probe further for fear lest I probe too deep.

*   *   *

As a result of the uncle's disclosures concerning the family 'legacy' we learn that Noel kept a guarded watch on Colin. But as time went on there appeared to be no immediate cause for anxiety. She had obtained further information from the uncle who consulted a friend of his, Sir Jeremy Gore, the eminent neurologist, and was heartened to hear that long lapses between any minor or major attack could indicate a more hopeful prognosis. As there had been no evidence of either she decided not to watch for or worry about any alarming recurrence. Besides she was beset with more insistent concerns, as suggested in these extracts from her written reminiscences.

. . . Barton had finished with Colin. I mean she had finished with his head if not with him. He spent an unconscionable time in her studio having nothing better to do . . . Not only spending his time but spending his money – on her? How right Aunt Rhoda was to keep on at me about his and my extravagance although I did cut down expenses wherever I could. I gave up Molyneux and bought reach-me-downs off the peg at sales. Colin's overdraft didn't bother him and it ought not to have bothered me, but having got his permission to ask our bank what his balance was I found him overdrawn to two and a half thousand. 'But the only way to live these days,' he said when I tackled him about it, 'is on an overdraft . . .'

Of course Aunt Rhoda had something to say about that.

'He'll find himself in Queer Street,' she said, 'and where would you be then?'

As that required no obvious reply, she went on with, 'You've made your bed and must lie on it together – on a feather mattress.' And then was off upon another tack, sniffing like a hound on scent.

'I understand that Barton woman has finished the bust she did of Colin and is exhibiting it at the New Art Gallery. Is it any good?'

'All Barton's work', I told her tactfully, 'is good.'

'Umph.' Or some such sound between a snort and a grunt preceded her next remark. 'He spends too much of his time in her studio when he should be looking for a job. Not that he could ever find a job, being totally unemployable. But he can't live for ever on an overdraft. As for that mantis of a Barton . . . Yes, I said mantis. A praying mantis. A creature that is entirely carnivorous in habit but does not actively pursue its prey. It waits patiently until a fly comes within its reach. One of the most remarkable and less common of the species has a flowerlike shape and an allur-ing colour. You should study entomology. There is much to learn from insects that is apposite to woman and to *man*.' She said this with another of her snorts. 'Take bees. Or ants. One wonders if the Creator originally intended the bee or the ant to be made in His Image. Especially the bee, for its intelligence is equal if not superior to that of man. It is the *female* of the species who controls the hive which is her world. Invests its finances, which is the honey she gathers, and who *works* – builds their cities and makes their laws not by mere instinct but by superhuman intelligence – and mark you! – the male, the drone, is solely bred for procreation. Read Maeterlinck.'

It may be this oblique allusion to Barton likening her to a mantis that, while it tickled her sense of humour, wakened in Noel some dormant suspicion regarding Colin's continued visits to the studio long after Barton's bust of him had been finished.

They had not gone to Florence in the previous autumn; the villa, at Noel's insistence, had been let furnished. To this, in view of the current economic crisis, the uncle, Archie Tarrant, agreed.

'It were better to draw in his horns. But,' said he, dryly, 'one might suggest he apply the withdrawal to – the singular.' A facetious innuendo which was lost upon Noel.

It was after the New Art Gallery exhibition that her suspicion of Colin's relationship with Barton became a certainty when further revelations were supplied by Lady Amersham.

'I hate to tell you, darling' (telling it with anything but hate), 'that I called unexpectedly on Sybil.' (How apt a name for her, notes Noel, whom I have always known as Barton. . . . Sybil. A sorceress. Complementary to a praying mantis, to which primitive tribes attribute occult or supernatural powers.) . . . She had looked it up in the Encyclopaedia.

'And', continued Birdie, 'I saw – having called unexpectedly – you know that Sybil always leaves the door of her studio unlocked so that anyone can go in unannounced – I saw the pair of them, Colin and she,' a chirruping titter accompanied the remark, 'in flagrant delight!'

Noel had herself well in hand to say, with nonchalant

35

humour, 'How were they flagrantly delighting, and to what extent?'

Whereupon Birdie proceeded to enlarge:

'Of course she may have been using him as a model for the nude or, tee-tee, the semi-nude because of his leg, poor dear. But she also was —'

'Spare me the details, *please*,' Noel laughingly implored. 'Although I am sure Barton would strip as well or better than any, er, professional. I remember when we were students at the Tree, I wanted to paint her in the altogether for my R.A. life study.'

'You don't mind me telling you, do you, darling?'

'Mind? Why should I mind what I already knew?'

This she assured herself was no prevarication. She *had* known but had avoided the precipitance of a crisis.

We have her reactionary impression after she realized that which her pride refused to acknowledge. What Birdie had told her was only hearsay, yet it could perhaps be accepted in a divorce court as evidence . . . Divorce! How ghastly! As if I ever would . . . Think of the hideous publicity . . . And what proof of cruelty if cruelty plus adultery is still demanded as a woman's means to an end of marriage . . .

Her mind ran round in circles. Colin! How could she possibly submit him to the loathsome humiliation of divorce to cite – laughter verging on hysteria seized her – a praying mantis! 'Flower-shaped and of an alluring colour' . . .

And now she was confronted with a curiously detached observance of the situation, the thought uppermost being that she should feel so little hurt. Did this mean that she had never utterly loved him, that the shared comradeship and connubial intimacy of their few years of marriage had become a habit, not an urgent need? She faced the fact, and surprised herself to face it, that she had never experienced the complete sexual satisfaction of intercourse. But surely sexual satisfaction was not love in the sense of an all-

36

absorbing passion, the merging of body and soul as romantically portrayed by the poets . . . No. Love must be more than the mating compulsion of monkeys and lions or bitches or birds or any lower forms of life; of amoebæ in ditch water. . . . What sort of a fool has called ditch water dull when it teems with the activities of male and female created He them right down to the most primitive organism . . . Or bees. How right Aunt Rhoda was to compare the bee to a higher intelligence that used the drone only for procreation. Colin, therefore, was only obeying his compulsive instinct by mating with Barton – one must look at it biologically – yes, with Barton even as with me . . . How commonsensical can one be if not obsessed with 'love'. And what *is* love? As Pilate asked, 'What is truth?' Well, what is it? Seeing all sides of oneself, one's ego in the right logical perspective? Or does it mean that I'm not in love with Colin and never have been, so I don't really care if he is an adulterer in the Biblical sense of the word. I suppose I'm waiting to find a man whom I can love wholeheartedly and who will love me . . . If such love exists.

However, after all this mind-searching, she decided to 'have it out' with Colin and we can believe the scene, which she cursorily gives us, went in this wise.

He had come in late from his club, where he had dined. He often did dine at his club, particularly since their cook had been away ill and Latimer was on holiday. So he must go to his club and get a decent dinner instead of the burnt offering of a chop cooked by herself.

She had gone to bed early and was sitting up reading Roger Fry's *Characteristics of French Art*. It was a warm September night. She had not drawn the curtains and looking up from the illustrated page she saw the frail slip of a new moon through the window . . . A slight shiver passed over her. Unlucky to see the new moon through glass, so they said . . . whoever 'they' were. She watched a star unveiled from a drifting cloud and, still a little shivery, went to close the window and draw the curtains. A chauffeur-driven Rolls coupé drove up, Colin got out and spoke to someone inside. 'Tomorrow then,' she heard and saw him glance at the chauffeur's immobile back as he leaned forward to say something to a person unseen.

She closed the curtains, returned to bed and continued scanning the pages of Roger Fry's book but saw nothing of the superb illustrations. So! He had gone with her somewhere which required evening dress . . . That much, through the window, she had seen of him in a dinner jacket, but he had left her earlier in the evening in a lounge suit. He must have changed either at his club or in his dressing-room here after bidding her goodnight. But what did it matter if he *had* taken Barton to a show or – wherever? It was her car, she knew, but maybe her husband was with them . . . her husband, Richard Farrell, a mere cypher in the Barton entourage, seen at her cocktail or dinner parties, unrecognized by some, unknown by many: or if she entertained at the Savoy or Claridges, he would be conspicuously absent . . . So it was unlikely that Richard would have accompanied his wife tonight wherever she had gone with Colin. Farrell, the complaisant husband, may or may not have had his own extra-marital interests, as had possibly fifty per cent of the men whom Barton knew in what was called 'Society', and who rampaged through the nineteen-twenties in the company of the Bright Young People. They, now in the 'thirties, had settled down to marriage or whatever was the next best or worst choice of a career for them.

'Is that you, Colin?' Noel called, hearing him in the *en suite* bathroom turning on the tap of the basin and brushing his teeth.

She waited.

He came in wearing his latest pyjamas, those she had given him for his birthday.

'Where have you been?' she asked, as she put Roger Fry on the bedside table.

'To my club, as I told you, because you didn't want to cook dinner for me.'

'Why did you go there in a dinner jacket – or change into one? You don't usually dress for dinner at the club.'

'Why shouldn't I?'

He switched off the light by the door and prepared to get into the bed beside her.

'No,' she moved away from him. 'I'd rather you slept in the dressing-room. I have a cold and don't want you to get it.'

'What's all this?'

He stood beside the bed staring down at her, who had turned from him that he might not see the trembling of her lips. It was going to be more difficult than she had anticipated. They had their rows, trivial differences, as with all married couples, but these were usually on account of his extravagance when he would buy various objets d'art and antiques which were often fakes. But now, for the first time, she must force herself to question him, to assert her rights as the wronged wife . . . No! Not that. Those old shibboleths, as in the case of Victorian husbands when women must accept that man, as the superior being, could ignore their marriage vows and enjoy extraneous relationships with a mistress, permanent or temporary, or with a prostitute, were now exploded. But woman was man's equal now. She had the vote, she could voice in Parliament her rights and her wrongs whether opposed by a male majority or not.

She steeled herself to say:

'I know you have been out with Barton. Where? I saw you come back in her car.'

'Yes. We went to the Ballet.'

'You didn't tell me you were going to the Ballet with Barton.' She was still turned from him, addressing the curtained window.

'Is there any reason why I should tell you?'

'Yes, every reason.' She turned to him now, sitting up.

Her nightdress, open at the throat for coolness, had slipped off her shoulders. She was conscious that her rapid breath lifted the transparent chiffon with the beating of her heart.

'I know that you and Barton', she said, steadying her voice, 'are having an affair.'

She searched his face, seeing half of it, the upper half dipped in shadow from the bedside lamp that dimmed his eyes and lighted his tightly compressed mouth. . . . He gave her no answer but she saw a muscle move in his jaw, and he swallowed after what seemed to be minutes yet could only have been seconds, before he spoke.

'If by an affair you mean have I been to bed with her – no.'

'It is of no consequence where or when you and Barton performed' – her sense of humour, ever an ally *in extremis*, put into words what Birdie purported to have seen – 'and probably most uncomfortably on the floor or the model throne in her studio, but I hope she is better at it than I.'

She stifled a gasp of laughter that changed suddenly to alarm as she saw the effect upon him of that jibe at her own expense. He was deathly white and swaying where he stood: then to her horror he fell and lay where he had fallen, motionless.

She scrambled out of bed and knelt beside him. So still he lay, she feared. O, God! not that! Fumbling for his pulse she felt its hurried beat, but at once his eyes, fast closed, were open . . . Of course! He'd been drinking . . .

'What on earth—' he spoke in his natural voice, put a hand to his head and got upon his feet. His face, so white, was flushed. 'What happened?'

'You fell.'

'Did I? Can't think why.'

'You must be plastered. Do you remember what I said?'

'I do. And I'm not plastered. . . . It had to come out sooner or later.'

'Are you in love with Barton?'

She surprised herself that she could ask him that while relief overswept her at his return to norm from what she had thought to be his sudden death from heart failure. She recalled that the cook's father had 'been taken' (as was told her) 'all of a sudden like' from a heart attack.

'In love?' He was pulling back the bedclothes to get into the bed. "I suppose I am.'

'I asked you not to sleep here. I have a cold.'

'Now do be reasonable. You can't expect me or any man you may have married to be entirely monogamous. Man is inherently a polygamous animal.'

'I'm glad you admit to man's animalism. Does it equalize the promiscuity or polygamy of man to that of tom cats?'

'You are being rather absurd about this, darling. You've imbibed too much of old Rhoda's sex-starved antagonism to man's natural demands, which is the result of psycho-sexual sublimation.'

'I suppose Barton has put you up to this sort of Freudian jargon. She'll be having you analysed next. I know she went through a course of it. As for Aunt Rhoda and sex-starvation, she, on the contrary, had too much of man's "natural demands" and so she walked out on her marriage. Do you want me to walk out on mine?'

'Don't be a bloody fool.'

'I could, you know.'

'Could what?'

'Divorce you.'

'Is that a threat or a promise?'

'Neither. Aunt Rhoda didn't demean herself by divorcing her husband and nor would I; anyway you haven't knocked me about yet so I wouldn't have enough evidence.'

He took her in his arms. She wrenched herself free.

'You can't have us both. Or is that what you want? If so

you won't have me. Go to her then and let it run its course until you get over it.'

'Like measles?'

'Well, isn't it?'

'I haven't,' he said, drawing her close, 'got over you yet.'

'No. *No!*' He smelt of drink. Revolted, she pushed him away, and was across the room and making for the door.

There she turned. 'I've just this to say. As far as our marriage goes it is from now on a marriage in name only. I don't share our marriage *or* our bed, wherever it may be, with Barton or anyone else . . . What are you counting on your fingers?'

He said with a comical lift of his eyebrows:

'I'm reckoning up exactly how many times I've committed adultery since I married you.'

She was staring at him in startled incredulity mingled with shock at this brazen admission.

'Don't', he said, quizzing her, 'look as if I'd admitted to murder or theft. I've neither stolen nor killed – at least not since I murdered an enemy Hun – I'm merely stating a fact as given in the Word of God, that he who lusts after a woman, that is to say when he sees one who appeals to him as bedworthy, he has committed adultery in his heart. So according to my reckoning there are at least a dozen women I've had a hundred times – in my heart – while married to you.'

'I am not amused,' she spoke coldly, controlling the hot temper that rose at his teasing. 'It is immaterial to me if you have had, as you put it, a dozen women a hundred times in your heart or anywhere else. What does concern me is how you intend to go on living on an overdraft, and also how to meet your commitments. If men must work and women must weep and as you'll never work and I'll never weep —'

' "The sooner it's over the sooner to sleep." ' He finished

42

it for her and stretching an arm switched off the bedside lamp, leaving her in darkness.

*   *   *

While the Harbords seem to have been unaware of, or unconcerned with, the economic crisis of the 'thirties and the threat of world disaster, as yet the merest shadow on the political horizon, we find that Noel set about determinedly to put *her* world to rights.

After she had pronounced her ultimatum, offering Colin his choice between herself as wife or Barton as mistress, and as he appeared to have accepted her decision that their marriage should end in so far as they would live together as husband and wife in name only, she decided that, since he, the man, would not work and she could not weep, she must make an effort to recoup their dwindling resources.

It is about this time that she started intermittently to keep a diary or journal which gives a record of the years before and during the Second World War. Here we see from her scribbled notes that she takes up the threads of her broken marriage – which seems not to have broken her life. Instead it brought her to a fuller understanding of herself and her potentialities.

I had been sleepwalking, she confesses, and was only half awake. Although I thought I was in love with Colin when I married him I had never intimately known any other man. In the 'twenties, when I married him, the Bright Young People, daughters, sons, brothers of the boys who had laid down their lives in four years of war, had never been involved in nor suffered from post-war recuperation for we were in our nurseries or the schoolroom when the world was shattered. But I, of their generation, was not of them who would congregate to overcrowd the *mise en scène* of daring and adventurous excitements, of treasure hunts, of contraband intrigues and the hysterical defiances of parental autocracy. Despite the rigid observance of Aunt

43

Rhoda's 'Right to Might', that asserted the independence of woman versus man, I had been as far removed from the hedonistic exploits of my young contemporaries as if I were walled up in a convent.

All this self-analysis would seem to elucidate her discovery that she was neither hurt nor humiliated by Colin's admitted liaison with Barton; or, as she suspected, with any other woman – one of the dozen or more whom he teasingly had counted on his fingers.

Yet, as she recounted, something he had told her after they agreed to live their lives together without any marital obligations on either side made her realize that what he had from Barton he could never have from her.

He said: 'It is as if all I had missed in my mother I found in her.'

I was staggered. That Barton could even remotely resemble a matriarchal image suggested he was trying to excuse his infatuation for her with the Oedipus complex of Freudian patter in which I knew Barton indulged. But he was dead serious when he went on to say:

'She reminds me of all I remember of my mother. Even physically she resembles her – that indeterminate fragility of feature and form but with an inner force that is shown in her work. This', he said, 'I saw in my mother when a child and I had that awful glimpse of her transformed' – he shuddered, closing his eyes as if he could visualize behind his lids that which remained a latent reality, re-enacted – 'transformed', he repeated, 'into a raging virago.'

I said: 'I can never see Barton transformed into a raging virago. And as for inner force, she has the same —'

I almost quoted Aunt Rhoda's definition of the mantis waiting in patience to seize and devour its prey.

'The same what?' he prompted, breaking in on my pause.

'It doesn't matter. I've forgotten – No, I've just remembered – something Barton told me once when I went to see the finished bust she did of you and —'

44

'I didn't know,' he interrupted, 'that you had ever been without me to her studio.'

'There's a lot you don't know about me, but this you had better know about Barton, that she said, having just done with her latest man of the moment, she doesn't attempt to hush up the names of her seducees —'

'Her what?'

Ignoring this I went on: 'And she said: "If there is any seduction to be done, *I* do it." '

He was fiercely red, gnawing at his underlip.

'So if she has been filling you up with her Freudian stuff to account for her seduction of you I think you had better see her as she is – a predator, and not a Botticellian Madonna slightly the worse for wear.'

With which I left him visibly appalled.

Later that evening he came to me while I was doing my face before dinner. He stood behind my chair and spoke to me in the dressing-table mirror.

'Don't you mind that I am – that Barton and I —'

'Go on, say it.' In the glass I smiled at him encouragingly.

'That I and Barton are – well, have found each other.'

'You mean that you are in love with her and are finding excuses to account for it as a quite inane "Mother Complex". As for not minding, why should I mind? I don't regard myself as the injured wife. I would never make a scene and go down on my knees imploring you not to leave me for another woman – any woman. I tend to regard marriage like buying or renting a house. We can always let a house if we don't want to sell it just as we can let a husband or wife if we want to.'

'For God's sake!' he had turned a sickly white. His eyes were dazed, his mouth twitching. He seized me by the shoulders, forcing my face round to his. 'What are you saying?'

I was alarmed. Surely he couldn't take in dead earnest what I had said in joke.

'What I meant – No, don't!' jerking my head away from him for he had caught my throat in both hands and was squeezing it tightly. 'Don't throttle me!'

He let fall his hands. There was an ooze of blood on his bitten lip.

'You make me see red,' he muttered.

'Because I see reason? Listen. I don't really mind about you and Barton. I think it will do you all the good in the world to have, as it were, a leasehold with another woman. You and I have had as much as we want of each other – at present. Go away with her. Go to Florence or anywhere abroad. Her husband wouldn't care. He goes his own way, which is not hers. Besides he's used to her various – what you might call – rentals. Be her seducee. You hate that word, don't you? But it really does fit her. All her men are seducees except —'

I stopped, remembering Sinclair. I had never seen him since we met him in Florence. I had heard vaguely from Barton that he had something to do with publishing.

'Except?'

He had quite recovered his momentary lapse of temper – or what?

'That Sinclair man who was with her in Florence. I think he had never been a seducee. She may have tried and failed. Anyway it's a long time ago and she may have had other – interests.'

'I can't understand you.' I saw him in the mirror frowning, angrily puzzled. 'You are entirely different from the girl I married and loved.'

'If you ever did love me.'

'Of course I loved you.'

'Yes, as so did I love you, but neither of us was adult then.'

'What do you mean – neither of us adult? I was in my later twenties and had been through the war and lost this.' He slapped his thigh – 'and you were no child. You were twenty-one.'

46

'I was twenty when we met, and still adolescent, a late developer or arrested development if you like, and only when I lost our baby did I begin to grow up. And you' – I turned to him and took one of his hands to lay against my cheek – 'you have never grown up. That's why you are still looking for your mother, the mother you never had, at least you never had a mother's love and you think you have found it in Barton because she possesses you as you wanted to be possessed by your mother. But I've never been possessive, have I?'

'If you are not,' he said passionately, 'I am. I'd not hand you over so easily – so readily – as you hand me over to Barton. Is there anyone else – any other man that you have found as a replacement for me?'

'I wish there were!' I passed a comb through my hair. It was bobbed now, page-boy fashion.

Colin said: 'When I first saw you I told you – I know exactly what I told you – that I had seen you in my dreams before that night when we met at the students' ball. Do you remember?'

'Yes,' I rejoined callously. 'I remember. Did you say the same thing to Barton? Is it your usual method of approach?'

'No!' he cried outraged. He knelt beside my chair burying his face in my knees. I felt his whole body shaking. 'It was you – always you. What I feel for her is entirely apart from you. Don't you understand?'

He had lifted his head. His eyes implored me to understand. I stroked back a lock of his hair that had fallen on his forehead. His hair was still childishly soft and fair, with hardly any grey.

'My dear, you poor little boy —' He was so like a little boy asking forgiveness for having been caught stealing forbidden sweets. 'I do understand. You don't know what you do want. All *I* want is that you should grow up and not always be searching for your mother's apron strings. I've never had apron strings, not having an apron for you to cling to.'

He got to his feet. 'I see,' he said, in a slow dull voice, 'that you only say this in self-defence because I've hurt you. I have hurt you, haven't I?'

'No, not dreadfully. Not as I ought to be hurt.'

'If you loved me,' he persisted, 'you would be hurt.'

'Darling, I do love you —'

Even as I said it doubt crept in. Did I? (O, this love! Why is there only one word for love in English? To love and cherish as in the marriage service. You can love oysters or asparagus or a dog or a man, all with the same word!) . . . I achieved a crow of laughter.

'What's so funny about it?' he asked roughly.

'I was thinking that there ought to be more words in English for the definition of "Love".'

'It's the same in French or Italian, isn't it?'

'Not in the same sense as inanimate objects or things to eat, or God. But what I was going to say is that if you really want to go away from me to her — yes, I mean it, and when you have finished with her or she has finished with you, then come back here to me.'

'I thought it was understood I should never go away, as you put it, from you to her and that we should be, to all intent and purpose, as we are now.'

'Except that we don't co-habit, as they would have it in a court of law. We can live here or anywhere else like brother and sister.'

'As the Pharaohs lived with their sisters?'

'Not quite. Incest was a royal prerogative in ancient Egypt.'

'You've got it all taped, haven't you?'

I could see he was furious. His pride had been damaged. He would have me in tears, begging him not to go. I felt I should apologize for taking it so matter-of-factly, giving him my approval and my blessing that he should have his fill of Barton or until she sickened of her fill of him.

48

I said: 'I know it isn't usual for a wife to agree to her husband's infidelity but, you see, I don't think of you as unfaithful. We didn't take any marriage vows. We were not married before God, only before a registrar, all legalized and formal. It didn't take five minutes.'

He was biting his lip, feeling the strain of all this and holding himself in before he let himself out, then:

'Damn you!' he shouted and went, or rather bolted, from the room.

FOUR

Extract from the journal of Noel Harbord,

Grosvenor Street

[undated]

I have discussed with Archie (I can never call him uncle, he is so utterly un-avuncular) about our arrangement, that is to say our non-cohabitation, ostensibly married and living under one roof, which may not be our roof for long. The rent of this place has been put up and we are financially put down . . . I asked Archie if he could get me in touch with one of his publisher or author friends. He knows many people with names in the art or literary world; none of those, of course, whom he knew when he was young in the 'nineties; they have all gone west except a few ante-diluvians who are scattered in the South of France or Rapallo, where he now has a villa, having sold the one at Menton.

I wondered if I could get a commission for the illustrations of an author's works, either new editions of Jane Austen, the Brontës or Sterne, or some recently discovered star; or book jackets for novels – period novels for preference. I know I'm not much good at anything other than portraits, but I told him I would take a course in black-and-white at the Yew Tree if he thought I had a chance of earning something to help Colin's overdraft.

I didn't like telling Archie much about that, he would think I was trying to get him to stump up. I'm sure he would, if he thought we were at lowest ebb as we are now, only I'd never let on to him about it. And I wouldn't even have mentioned that I thought of doing book jackets or illustrations. I let him think I was just bored because of

Colin and I having agreed not to differ about Barton, and the rent to be raised again when they renew the lease.

He said, taking the inevitable cigar from his case: 'So you want to join the ranks of the working or workable women?'

'Needs must when the devil or the bank manager drive.' I spoke jokingly about it saying, 'I think Lucifer must have been the Manager of the Celestial Bank Company Limited and afterwards transferred to the other branch, lower down!'

I wasn't going to hint at more than that concerning our present finances, with *our* bank manager hammering away at Colin to pay off another thousand of his overdraft or else – Is that how bankrupts are made if the bank comes down on them? So I laughed it off, avoiding his searching look at me from those very blue, still remarkably blue, eyes although he must have been well on in his sixties.

'I understand,' he said, stubbing out his cigar in an ashtray – we were in his suite at the Burlington where he always stays when he comes to London – 'that Colin has sold out his Bloemfontein shares. I would have advised him to hang on to them had he asked me. It is the worst possible time to sell anything on the stock market, unless government stock which has picked up since the election which brought Baldwin back again. And now that Italy has launched her threatened attack on Abyssinia, a fellow member of the League —'

'Do you mean the League of Nations? I'm mentally deficient about politics,' I said.

'Which is just as well. You are only following the National Government's trend in what Winston Churchill called the years that the locusts have eaten.'

'I did see something in the paper the other day,' I was trying to excuse myself for being so completely non-existent about current political affairs. 'The Foreign Secretary, Hoare, isn't it? who met the French Premier while on holiday in Switzerland to propose a settlement between them that they should give a large slice of Abyssinia to Italy.'

'Which', said he, 'will cause Hoare's resignation and replace him with Anthony Eden as Foreign Secretary, and that will save Baldwin from party mutiny. But it is only the tip of the iceberg. . . . Now, as to you, if you wish to be a wage-earner in the working world of art as illustrator or whatever, I cannot foresee much lucrative advantage in that direction. Yet if it will offer you some interest other than the placation of your or Colin's bank manager, I suggest I take you to Marriott. They are always on the lookout for an artist who can offer them good book jackets for their latest best-selling author.'

'I don't want to do book jackets for any tripist bestseller,' I told him tartly, 'and I don't know if I *can* do book jackets. They have to be done in watercolour and my medium is oils, which I much prefer.'

'Just as you will; but if you want me to make an appointment to see Marriott's managing director I can arrange it. How is Colin? Have you observed any symptoms that might be attributable to his, er, his legacy?'

'I wouldn't know what symptoms to look for. He drinks a lot but seldom gets tight. He can hold his drink. He does sometimes look rather dazed and not all there, and once, just lately, he fell and lay so still I thought he'd had a heart attack but he was up in a minute or two and had forgotten all about it.'

He nodded. 'Just so. Jeremy Gore told me to ask you to report anything disturbing, but if there are such slight indications and only at long intervals there is no cause for immediate anxiety.'

She admits to feeling 'rather guilty' that she had not given much thought to Colin's condition which Archie had told her was an inherited tendency, and she goes on to record:

52

... So when I left him at the Burlington, I went off to the London Library, managed to get a book on general medicine and looked up epilepsy. It didn't tell me anything more than what Sir Jeremy had told Archie of Colin's condition. Anyway I haven't seen anything to worry about yet and hope I never shall. I am wondering if I ought to warn Barton to look out for symptoms. It is quite agreed that I have accepted his 'affair' with her. It is an understanding between the three of us that we should not enforce our connubial obligations on either side. Barton's stolidly complaisant husband has never interfered with her extra-marital adventures. Whether he has any of his own doesn't matter. All that interests him, according to Barton, is that he is reaping the harvest planted by his father in munitions. Archie says Labour's chief grievance against the Conservatives is what he calls 'Labour's Love's lost' because they are bitterly opposed to rearmament, particularly at a time when Germany is under this Hitler who Archie says is 'a demoniacal fanatic' risen from a house-painter to get himself the Chancellorship of Germany. Archie seems to have taken up politics in as big a way as he took up the Tuscan Primitives, 'an art fancier' as Colin used to call him, as if he were a breeder of canaries. I understand he was that, too, at one time, and had an aviary in his garden at Menton. Anyway we are, as he says, 'perilously near to the tip of the iceberg with Baldwin contentedly smoking his pipe among his prize pigs' – (I don't know if he meant his prize Cabinet pigs!) . . . Aunt Rhoda has *her* opinion of Baldwin and Co. too. (I wish I knew more about politics!) She calls the Conservatives 'a lot of damned ostriches. Heads in sand.' And she agrees with Stafford Cripps (the first I've heard *his* name) who, according to her, spoke of the League as the International Burglars' Union Association which may involve Labour in a capitalist and imperialist war. . . .I can't understand any of this and when I asked Archie with who labour – meaning the working man and not the Party – would be involved in a capitalist war – all he could say correcting me was: 'With *whom* not with *who*. Your knowledge of correct English is exceptionable.' . . . We were in a taxi when he told me this with his usual dry sarcasm on our way to Marriott, the publishers to *whom* he had said he would introduce me with a view to getting them to offer me a book to illustrate, or book jackets. I hadn't much hope.

Further extracts from her Journal

[undated]

Yesterday Archie took me to Marriott. We were shown into a grand waiting-room by an equally grand receptionist who appeared to be not at all impressed with Archie's pointed imperial (as I believe they called his little beard in his young days) nor by his attractive drawling voice when he asked for – I didn't catch the name. I was looking at the rows of their latest best-seller displayed on a shelf along the wall. I hadn't read it because I was put off by the reviews and even more by the author of *Love's Ecstasy* (what a title!). I met her at one of Birdie's cocktail parties. An extravagant blonde, dripping with mink and pearls, and when Birdie introduced me saying in her twittering voice, 'Here is a budding R.A., if only she would take herself and her work more seriously. You should see the portrait she did of me . . .' The portrait I did of her was a commission from Johnnie (her son, Amersham) and he gave me £250 for it. I know she put him up to it for I had told her we were in the red, not intending her to take me at my word . . . And this Love's Ecstasy person gushfully embraced me, leaving a smear of lipstick on my cheek which I never noticed until I was back home, and she said 'Darling! How *wonderful!* You must paint *me!*' . . . I refrained from telling her she was painted enough already . . . And now looking at the rows of her Ecstatic latest I wondered what sort of stuff Marriott *did* publish. I had always thought of them – for they advertise extensively and their books get rave reviews – as discriminating publishers and was surprised they could stoop to Ecstatic Love!

However, after not too long a wait while 'Miss' (I presumed her a 'Miss'), having asked if Archie had an appointment in a tone that suggested he had come to offer a manuscript that had been rejected by a dozen other publishers, and being handed his card without any answer whether he had or had not an appointment, she took it and, head in air, went away. She came back again, a trifle less refrigerated, to say that Mr Sinclair would see him in a few minutes. . . .

Sinclair! I was stunned. How could I possibly have guessed that the Sinclair I had met so briefly – is it nine or ten years ago in Florence? – could be a director or something connected with this particular publisher, unless it were his father or an uncle or relative of the same name. . . . I was still wondering about it and rather excited too at the prospect of meeting him again, if he were my – no, Barton's – Sinclair, when 'Miss' answered a buzz from a phone on her desk and said a trifle less icily: 'Mr Sinclair will see you now,' and rose from where she sat, took us to a lift in the passage, pressed a button and shot us up to be shown into a room with a brass plate on the door, inscribed J. L. Sinclair.

We went in and it was . . . Barton's Sinclair!

To some of us there comes a moment of significance when our life's span converges to one given point upon the compass of our destiny. Such moments may be almost inconspicuous on the milestones that mark our way along the road from birth to death . . . A chance encounter, a trifling incident, the meeting with one whom we never thought to meet again can be of ultimate importance in the shaping of our lives . . . One might believe all history is founded upon trifles: a game of bowls, the blind eye of a hero, the necklace of a queen, a scrap of paper, such as these have become traditional in the winning of great wars, the ending of a dynasty, the shattering of worlds. . . .

So when I faced J. L. Sinclair in his managerial office to discuss whether or not I might submit my sketches for the illustrations or a jacket of one of his author's books, I could not know that this meeting after – how many years? – was to be the turning-point of my whole life. . . .

J. L. Sinclair, M.C., M.A., the M.C. having been awarded to him in World War One, greeted me with:

'But this is wonderful! I had no idea that Archie's nephew's wife – was you!'

Thus it came about that she was commissioned by Marriott, publishers, to design a book jacket for a novel with a seventeenth-century Restoration setting by W. R. Yates, the then most popular historical novelist of his day. She submitted a rough sketch for it in watercolour but requested that she should be allowed to do the finished design in oils. She received the consent to this from the editorial department, and also a personal telephone call from J. L. Sinclair, inviting her to luncheon with him to discuss further commissions. He told her his editor was impressed with her design for the jacket of Yates' forthcoming book. And so . . .

I met him, she related, at Claridges. I was not at my best, for besides a streaming cold I had barely recovered from a ghastly scene with Colin. This due to the latest and final threatening demand from his bank manager that he reduce his overdraft or, if not . . .

In order to raise enough ready cash to placate Lucifer, I sent for Sotheby's to see and value some of Colin's antiques. A Queen Anne corner cupboard and a hideous figure of Wen Ch'ang Ti Chu, supposed to be the God of Literature, in yellow and green robes sitting on what looks like a lavatory seat and dated 1659. I never cared for it but he had bought it in St James's and paid the earth for it. And

56

I also showed the very polite young man from Sotheby's a Sheraton writing table in sycamore, all of which should keep Lucifer appeased for the time being . . . But when Colin found out what I had done (which I admit was inexcusable without consulting him, yet needs must, as I had told Archie, when the devil drives) he flew into an alarming state. He raged at me, threw his arms about and himself on to the settee and let forth a frightening retrospect of what he had confided to me when we first met long ago at that artists' revel. . . . He had rarely referred to his childhood since then and never to the first fight he had seen between his parents, although he occasionally spoke of similar scenes he had witnessed, and so young too, in which his father and not his mother had been the assailant. Both of them drunk, as he in after years had realized, when his father brutally assaulted her, and she, yelling like a maniac, rushed to attack him; and the worst of these scenes, as he recalled them, were to do with money. . . . She, accusing him of stealing her money for she had more than he who was always overdrawn as was his son . . . 'But you,' he shouted at me turning a mottled red, 'what right had you to steal my property? Mine! Mine! It was *mine*! Yes, you've stolen it to sell . . . !'

He was beside himself. He seemed to be suffering from some internal conflict . . . 'That sod of a dealer you brought here unknown to me to buy my most cherished pieces!' He looked to be fighting some invisible assailant. There was blood on his underlip. Then he fell back, making grunting, gasping sounds. . . . This was the first time I had seen any definite symptoms of what I took to be his 'legacy'.

I tried to contact Archie but was told he had left his hotel the day before. I knew he intended going back to Rapallo for the winter. So I rang Sir Jeremy but his secretary said he had been called to a consultation in Scotland. I left it at that and found Colin had got over his attack or whatever it was, and had gone out leaving me a hurried note . . . 'Sorry darling but you really shouldn't have done that especially getting rid of Wen Ch'ang Chu . . .' I presumed he had rushed off to Barton to tell her all about it. I wondered if she had ever seen him in one of his attacks of – temper? After all this it is not surprising I was a bit off colour when I lunched with J. L. Sinclair.

She recalls little of significance at that luncheon between these two who met and talked across a table in the crowded restaurant of Claridges, more than this from her Journal:

Luncheon with J. L. S. to discuss illustrations for a book Marriott is publishing on Tuscany dealing chiefly with Florence and the towns of Northern Italy. He said his chief editor had been so interested in the sketches I submitted for the Restoration novel that he had shown them to Grierson, author of *Rambles in Tuscany* (I don't like the title and told him so but he took no notice of that). And he said Grierson was keen that I should do the illustrations in colour for it. I told him Colin and I had met Grierson when we were at Settignano. This would mean I must go to Florence to make some sketches there, and to Lucca, Pisa and wherever else Grierson wished to 'ramble'.

The result of this meeting was that she stayed in Florence for three weeks, including a few days in Lucca and Pisa, leaving Colin in London with Barton. They had let the villa at Settignano and so she stayed at a hotel in Florence until she had completed the necessary sketches for Grierson and Marriott's approval. She returned to Grosvenor Street in November 1935.

*   *   *

In the New Year that, to a politically initiated few, looked to be on the verge of disaster with Hitler and Mussolini kennelling their hounds of war eager to be unleashed, Britain was plunged into mourning.

As recently as the previous May the King had celebrated

his Silver Jubilee amid a nation's enthusiastic rejoicing. This surprised him who, as he drove through the shouting streets of his capital, is said to have remarked: 'I had no idea they thought like this about me. I think they must really like me.' . . . So modestly unassuming was he, conscientiously consigned to his monarchical duties, anxious only that his successor should observe the same essential duty to his people and his country to which he had dedicated himself throughout his reign. Unswervingly had he weathered the storm that rocked his kingdom and the world in those four agonized years of Armageddon; yet even at the end of his life rumours had reached him of his heir's involvement with the woman for love of whom he was to sacrifice his Throne, and which may have hastened his father's death.

His passing on 20 January marked also the passing of an era that was the beginning of an end for better or . . . for worse?

Gloom hung like a black cloud over his Kingdom and over London, for, as Noel describes it: 'All of us here wore some token of mourning during those subdued six weeks . . . Little did we guess that mourning would be universal for the loss of those dear to us and others unknown to us in the doomed years ahead.'

Grierson's book, *Rambles in Tuscany*, published in June of that year, captured the imagination not only of those who, nostalgically, had known Italy before Mussolini had cast his ugly shadow on its beauty, but of the reviewers. Noel's coloured illustrations came in for their share of recognition, for Grierson had declared against any photographic reproductions. As the result of encouragement from the national and provincial press Noel was approached by publishers other than Marriott for her work. Two of these, Kell and Wrotham,* she accepted and kept two more in reserve when her contracts for these were completed. 'Which', she records, 'have offered me enough

* See *Fair Company*.

to keep the wolves and Lucifer from howling too loudly at our door . . .'

We now learn that Barton having, seemingly, had her fill of Colin, was hunting fresher game. That Colin had not yet had his fill of *her* is evident in the scribbled notes of Noel's journal: 'I wish he could find a replacement for Barton because without her "maternal image" that he mistakenly believes she represents, he is moody, irritable and flies into unreasonable tempers with me over nothing . . . But we still preserve the brother-and-sisterly relationship that is in no way related to the Pharaohs! . . .'

There were times when she feared for him. He was drinking far too much – and although he could, as she says, 'hold his drink', she felt it must have an ill effect on what was called his 'legacy', which Tarrant told her could be stimulated by excess of alcohol and also by the deep-seated impression in his sub-conscious since his early days when he had witnessed those scenes between his parents as he had decribed to her.

His chief grievance or aggressive instinct, which seemed to be gaining hold, was against his father as destructive of the image he had built in his mind of the mother whose love had been denied him.

Further memoirs

It was when I had sent in my finished design for another of Yates' historical novels which was also to be published in America, and they, too, were very keen on my work and were using the Marriott book jackets, that J. L. S. rang me up. He asked would I care to go that evening to the ballet to see *Les Sylphides* if I was not otherwise engaged. He had tickets given him by one of his co-directors who was unavoidably prevented from using them – his wife was having a baby, which had not been expected until next week.

'I had hoped,' he said, 'to have taken my old uncle who

loves the ballet, but he is in bed with a cold. So if you could accompany me? ...'

I couldn't help but think he must have tried to get anyone other than me as a last-minute 'accompaniment' rather than sit alone beside an empty seat. I was half-inclined to tell him I had a previous engagement, but I could not resist *Les Sylphides* so I told him that although I had arranged to dine with – I fabricated – 'with Barton, I could put her off'. I deliberately named Barton because I wanted to hear his reaction to that mention of her, not having heard *her* mention him since we met in Florence; nor had I ever seen him at any of her cocktail parties. Not that I ever went to many of them, but we were still apparently on good terms, I having so readily accepted, no doubt to her surprise if not to her disappointment, our pact.

He fetched me in his Bentley. Colin was out and Latimer showed him in. I almost wrote Littimer for he, although politely deferential, would still regard me as did 'Littimer' regard David, as 'very young'. Nor could I bring myself to ask him if he had ever observed any symptoms of Colin's 'legacy', for besides that I knew he resented our marriage, he would not have enlightened me, even if he could, as to his master's disability. He was as loyal to Colin as was his prototype to Steerforth.

J. L. S. and I arrived at Covent Garden just as the curtain was rising. And as always I sat entranced, watching this most lovely ballet, drenched in the movement and the music of Chopin, and not until it was all over and we filed out was I aware of anything else, nor that J. L. S. was saying:

'We'll go to Rules for supper.' Not will you or won't you, just taking it for granted that as I was his employee, engaged to design his book jackets, it was his prerogative to invite or to order me to sup with him.

I had been to Rules sometimes with Colin but was not quite out of my trance even when a menu was offered by a bowing waiter who welcomed J. L. S. as an habitué.

'Oysters for a beginning, I think,' he said . . . And afterwards an omelette for me, a tournedos for him, and wine (which I didn't want, having started with sherry). And when we had finished eating – I had Crêpes Suzette, and he had cheese – I saw Colin with Barton and Arthur Toye, whose production of *Hail Fellow* had now reached its centenary performance, which he had not only produced but played the lead in.

'Her most recent acquisition,' murmured J. L. S. He had also sighted the trio.

I said, 'I haven't seen you at Barton's nor with her anywhere since Florence.'

'No.' The curt monosyllable was followed by, 'Nor have I seen you anywhere since Florence until you walked into my office a few months ago – for my undoing.'

That remark, so lightly spoken, brought from me an equally light reply with the reminder of his impromptu. 'To undo – or untie – *your* temperamental tangles?'

'Your memory is almost as good as mine but I see you have not lost your boyish angles.'

He passed me toast Melba.

'Was it', I asked, 'an impromptu?'

'I confess', his eyes engaged mine with a laugh in them, 'I cribbed it from one of our authors. I am a susceptible plagiarist from too close contact with infection.'

'Do you plagiarize when, or if, you write?'

'When I write, though I do not publish with my firm, my work is culled from those who have gone before. Not dead but retired.'

This ambiguity befogged me. I was about to inquire into it when Barton approached us.

'James! And Merryon! We three to meet again. May I join you?'

She beckoned to a waiter, commanding: 'Another chair.'

J. L. S. (so one of his names was James) had risen to give her his place beside me on the cushioned seat.

He offered her a liqueur – 'or if you have not already supped — ?'

'I have,' and turning she called across the room, 'Arthur, Colin! Come here. We'll be a *partie à cinq*.'

They rose and came to us but she threw up her hands, fluttering them. 'This table won't seat five. We must go on somewhere else – to the Embassy or back to my flat – No! to the studio.'

So to her studio and we in her Rolls . . . J. L. S. sat wedged between herself and me, Arthur Toye and Colin opposite us. She chattered incessantly. This unlike her because when I was with her in company or, as in the past, alone, she would talk but little. Perhaps she had never had much to talk about with women and had always been better than I at conversation in the presence of men, speaking in her small one-toned voice that insinuated much unsaid. Now, however, she was full of some talk or gossip to do with the Prince of Wales and his interest in an American woman married to a naval officer.

I didn't pay any close attention to this as I was uncomfortably conscious not only of the proximity of J. L. S. but also of a spirituous waft of breath from Colin in front of me and – from another source. Not from J. L. S. We had both taken the least part of a bottle of Château Lafite and I took no liqueur, nor did he. I had remarked upon this, saying, clumsily: 'I see you are disinclined for drink.' Why, I wondered, did I feel so inept at words with him? Not that on the few occasions we had been together I had any words – I mean ordinary or even *extraordinary* words, always having kept strictly to business. His reply in the slow, measured, teasing voice with which he would speak to me, as did Latimer, making me feel very young despite my thirties, was: 'I am not addicted to Bacchus, unfortunately, as he covers a multitude of sins. It is quite a mistake to believe *in vino veritas*. For veritably *in vino* one seldom speaks the truth.'

And listening to Barton, who was holding forth about

the Prince and Mrs – I didn't catch the name – I wondered how far *in vino* she was gone for, if she spoke truth, it was certainly somewhat near to *lèse majesté*.

At the studio we were regaled with more drinks which I refused. J. L. S. and Arthur took moderate whisky while Colin and Barton drank 'no heel taps' from a bumper of champagne. I could see that this was having its effect on Colin. As for her, I had noticed on other occasions that she could take her drink but had never seen her the worse for it until now. Her voice, usually so low and monotoned, was high pitched as she showed us her latest bust of Toye, commissioned by him to be placed in the foyer of the theatre he had leased as actor-manager for *Hail Fellow*, that was running a full box-office course and looked likely, he said, to reach its second century.

'It isn't yet completed,' Barton told us, standing before it, her eyes narrow in contemplation.

'It's not in the leass – least like him,' Colin was saying between a hiccup. 'Not the leass – Looks like an Epshtinian clown.'

'Darling,' she put her arm round him, 'you don't see Arthur as I do – does he, Arthur? You *are* a clown – not Epstein's – *my* clown – like Pagliacci; the clown who has a secret sorrow ... Wha' d'you think of it, James?'

'What I always think – or *have* thought,' he corrected himself, 'of your work.' He was seated on the edge of the model throne, and taking his cigarette-case offered one to me who still stood, for there was nowhere to sit – every chair and the settee was littered with drawings, sketches for her sculptures, and copies of various catalogues of her own and other exhibitions.

'And what is it,' she said, 'that you are always – or used to be, having had nothing to do with me for – God knows how long – ultra cynical of what I do or cannot do.' Which coherent remark called forth from him, lighting my and his cigarette:

'Cynicism is the hair shirt of the hypocrite.'

'Ah! You are self-confessed! The super-hypocrite.' And turning to me. 'You, my pretty-pretty, don't you believe a word he says. He's an adept at epigrams cribbed from his authors, just as he's an adept in sed-seduction. But he'sh – *he's*,' she said carefully, 'he's never seduced me. If there's any seduction to be done – I do it!'

I saw Colin leaning against a wall, his arms folded, come at her threateningly.

'You've worn out that old cliché of yours – you – you —'

He stopped and lurched against the model throne. Then to my horror he stumbled and fell, knocking his head against the base of the platform. J. L. S. was on his knees beside him, and to me who stood there, my cigarette dropping ash on to the clay-bespattered parquet, he said: 'I'll see to him.'

Barton called out. 'Don't fuss over him, James. He's done this before when he's plastered.'

I stubbed with my toe the cigarette on the parquet and I too knelt beside him. There was spittle on his lips, his teeth were tight clenched with blood oozing out. J. L. S. said quietly, 'He has bitten his tongue. Stand away,' he ordered Barton and Toye who had come crowding close.

'Don't play the fool, Colin!' This from Barton, and to me: 'He's plastered.'

His eyes opened. He had heard her and said in his normal voice: 'I'm not plastered. You are. What happened?'

He got up and passed a hand through his tousled hair.

I, still kneeling, said: 'You fell and you're drunk.' And to Barton: 'If you've seen him like this before, why didn't you tell me?'

'Why should I?' She shrugged. 'Since we have shared him, you should know all there is to know about him. But I'm through with him now. He bores me. I'm not his wet nurse any longer. He', she laughed shrilly, 'is breast fed enough. Time he's weaned.'

I could have struck her for that, my nails itched to claw that smile from her smudged Botticellian face . . . My hand, half raised, fell to my side. I looked at Colin. Had he heard that – did he mind? No! He was laughing, thought it funny, enjoying it. He went to her and took her in his arms and bent his mouth to hers to be kissed.

My God!

She kissed him lingeringly, smoothed back his hair. 'This wants cutting, darling,' she said, and to us standing there, 'Go now all of you! I'm staying here. I'm in the mood to get more done of my Epsh – Epsteinian clown. How right you are, Colin. He *is* a clown. He clowns his part in "Hail Fellow" juss' as he clowns his parts with me . . . Now, then, now *then!*' As Colin made a dash as if he were going to hit out at Arthur who had his back to all of us and was examining a Dürer on the wall. I had seen it often here and coveted it madly. She did tell me once that she would give it me or leave it me in her will . . .

'Don't be a baby, Colin. Arthur!' – He turned to her, the famous comical grin on his weak-jawed face adored by his fans. 'You must stay the night. I want to do something to this thing of you with its stick-out teeth which is looking lop-sided – or am I lopsided? I must have you sit to me in the morning. The rest of you – home! You can go back in my car unless James has his here!'

James had his there. He had sent it back to his flat from Covent Garden with the injunction to call for him at the studio in an hour's time.

We drove with Colin to Grosvenor Street. He was, or seemed to be, cold sober now.

'Won't you come in for a last nightcap?' I asked J. L. S.

'Yes, do,' said Colin who appeared quite to like him. I remembered he had told me long ago in Florence when we first met him that he thought him 'a decent sort', high praise from Colin, but only, I think, because they both wore old Etonian ties.

J. L. S. made a politely conventional excuse, bade us goodnight, and went his way. For some time after that I had no occasion to see him. I was hard at it on a book jacket for Kell and Wrotham who had approached me, having discovered I was not under contract with Marriott for book jackets or illustrations, and had offered me the jacket and frontispiece for another period novel. I was kept pretty busy for the remainder of that year, which enabled me to pay off something of Colin's overdraft, sufficient for the time being to placate 'Lucifer'.

So, as Noel records it in her memoirs, during that year which began with the death of George V, and the succession of his son, Edward VIII, neither I nor any of our immediate circle were aware of the series of events that were moving to a dramatic monarchical crisis.

He who, as Prince of Wales, had charmed the ladies of suburbia no less than those of the Court and had been immensely popular with the industrial classes and the miners, was proclaimed on the day of his succession by the Heralds with a woman at his side: an American whose name had been linked with his both during and after his father's lifetime. But the majority of the British public hardly knew of her existence and those who did know, and of the present King's interest in her, had learned her name, and that was about all, from the American Press. However, through that same source of the New York columnists, the as-yet-uncrowned King's association with a Mrs Wallis Simpson was to become of nation-wide significance.

That the King spent all his free time with her and had invited her on his Mediterranean cruise enchanted the gossips and set rumour speculating . . . Did he want to *marry* her? Never! An American? Not that the people of Britain would have objected to an American Consort for their King – his popularity had not yet sunk to zero – and a daughter of the American Ambassador would not have been dismissed as unsuitable as a Queen for their King but – a woman with one husband living and a second about to be divorced! As if he, never mind how much he defied convention, tradition and his father's memory, would dare outrage public opinion and his subjects' sense of that which they expected him to uphold!

It was Birdie Amersham who first told Noel of the rumour circulating around this Mrs Simpson and the King's infatuation for her.

'My dear! I've met her – she', chirped Birdie, 'is a friend of —' she mentioned a well-known socialite – 'or *was* because no woman is her friend now. They are all green with jealousy that the Prince – I can never get used to calling him King – has fallen for her in a big way. He means to marry her and why shouldn't he? Or rather she means to marry him. She is quite determined. Divorce be damned,' continued Birdie, non-stop and asserting the Rights of Women which she, surprisingly, had so strongly supported. 'There is no reason why not, other than the Church and that old Act which one of his great-great-grandfathers, George Three, was it, brought in when his son, not then Prince Regent, was chasing after an actress, Perdita as she called herself or *he* called her, which forbade or made it impossible for a Prince of the Blood to marry a commoner although his ancestor a hundred times removed – Henry the Eighth – married four commoners, divorced his lawful Queen, cut off the heads of two others and got rid of all five of them – one died in child-birth of course, and number six outlived him. You see I know my history! I read Yates. You have done two delightful book jackets for him. I loved his book about the girl Henry called his rose without a thorn. Poor little beast! He cut off *her* head, too,' she rattled on. 'So if one King can marry *four* commoners, even though two of his wives were princesses and Anne of Cleves so hideously fat in a fair wig the sister of a Dutch or German, was it, royal Duke? So why shouldn't this King marry a commoner?' . . .

It was now general knowledge, the talk of the men and women in the street as well as in Belgravia and Mayfair drawing-rooms, that the King intended to marry Mrs Simpson in defiance not only of public opinion but of the Prime

Minister, Baldwin, who was faced with a formidable crisis that seemed likely to divide the nation. The King had an ill-assorted army of supporters both in the industrial and mining districts and with certain Press Lords, Beaverbrook, Rothermere, besides Sir Oswald Mosley, 'that awful Fascist', as Birdie called him. She took the keenest interest in what looked to be the sensation of the century and Baldwin was confronted with a stern choice duly and unrelentingly presented to Edward: Renunciation of Mrs Simpson or – abdication!

The King was in a quandary. He wanted Mrs Simpson as his wife (she had him well in hand), but he also wished to remain King.

Baldwin was adamant. I must say despite his detractors, and they were many, including Archie Tarrant, that Baldwin, confronted with a situation with which no Prime Minister ever had to deal in British history, came out of it with conspicuous success. There was no wavering, no indecision. He consulted the Dominions and had their unqualified support.

We at home were on tenterhooks. Not that I cared much one way or the other. Always a Royalist – one of my ancestors on my father's side, according to Aunt Rhoda, fought for the Restoration of Charles the Second. He was a member of the Sealed Knot, the secret service in the cause of the King and had a barony conferred on him from Charles in recognition of his endeavour to secure his return to the Throne. But this has nothing to do with the Abdication bombshell that descended upon the country during that last week of December, 1936.

The headlines in all the papers blared it. We went in a fever of excitement that swelled to its head with the King's broadcast. Colin and I listened to it on our wireless as we called the radio in those days.

His speech has been floated into sentimental legend, that he renounced his Kingship 'for the woman I love'. It went down well with those of his feminine subjects who shed tears of sympathy for him and 'the woman'. Not so Colin. Hearing it, he exploded and burst forth with 'The ******' I forbear to repeat the epithet he used, but the gist of his remonstrance against the King's surrender of his duty to his country was:

'Thousands – millions of his fellow servicemen, for he was supposed to have been in the army – not to fight, just to look on in safety behind the lines – went to their slaughter. Gave their lives for their country and their King – blindly obeying their officers, and he, whose representative he was supposed to be, shirks it! Hands his kingdom over to his brother who never wanted it – is not prepared for it. And I—' he got up and went to the wireless that was still speaking in the voice of the King. I thought he would smash the instrument. His face was distorted, white to the lips with beads of sweat on his forehead. I feared for him. Was he about to have one of his attacks? . . . 'This!' he banged his fist on his thigh – all that was left to him of what once had been his leg – '*this* I gave for you and the country you've deserted!'

He made a dash for the wireless still broadcasting the speech heard throughout the world. He had seized a heavy paperweight from my writing desk between the windows as he passed, and as if it were a cricket ball he flung it with all his strength at the instrument that stood on a small table. It toppled and fell, still broadcasting, but now it was only an indistinct gurgle before it stopped. He must have smashed the battery.

'Colin! What on earth!' – I sprang up and went to him. He turned. There was blood on his lower lip as, pushing me away from him, he shouted:

'That's what we did to deserters. No! Not that – *that* can be mended – no! We shot them!'

He stumbled, caught at the window curtain, one of its drapes fell with him. He lay where he had fallen. I saw spittle dribbling from his mouth. His eyes were glazed and staring. I ran to the door calling for Latimer.

He came at once, so quickly I believed he must have been outside listening. He had his own wireless so he may have been on the alert to hear Colin's reaction to the speech.

'He' – I knew I must have been pale and spoke hysterically – 'He is – is ill. He fell – he threw —' I stopped.

Latimer was on his knees beside Colin. He raised his head and wiped the froth from his lips. Those glazed eyes closed. He looked as if he slept. Some colour had returned to his face, so white and strained.

'Oh,' I whispered to Latimer, 'what *is* it? Have you seen him – like this before?'

'Yes.'

The monosyllable was spoken without any expression either in his voice or his face as he bent over the prostrate form of Colin, and with ineffable tenderness smoothed a lock of his hair that had fallen over his forehead.

'How' – I made my lips firm to say – 'how often?'

He answered nothing to that. He was still looking down at Colin, whose eyes opened, and as if entirely unaware of anything that had happened, he got up, put a hand to his head, saying:

'I must have been asleep. Did I or didn't I hear that – that bastard speaking?'

'There has been an accident to the wireless, sir,' Latimer told him calmly. 'Mrs Hodson' – he named the cleaning woman who came mornings for the 'rough' – 'must have dislodged it in dusting. I noticed that one of the supports on which it stands is loose.'

'Better get it seen to, then.'

Colin had forgotten all about it.

This, I understood from Archie to whom I reported the incident, was usual in what he called *petit mal*.

'Latimer,' I said, 'knows of his – his lapses. I'm sure of that. He was his batman in the war.'

'He didn't' – Archie paused – 'have lapses before or during the war. They have developed later.'

'Can one do anything about it? Is there a cure – a

treatment? Could Sir Jeremy do something for him? Will he' – I shivered – 'go on having these – fits, are they? – for the rest of his life?'

'Possibly.' Archie stubbed out his cigar in an ashtray that I had put beside him on the table. He had come to my phone call, being here in London at the time.

'Should he go and see Sir Jeremy?' I urged. 'Surely he could give him something to prevent these – occurrences?'

'He does not advise bromide or drug control, not unless the attacks become more frequent. He considers that there is a risk of the patient becoming tolerant – that's to say necessitating an increase of the dosage which may produce toxic effects. Don't look so alarmed, my dear. These, er, lapses, are not at present serious and far more common than you may imagine and more disturbing to the onlooker than to the patient. I understand from Jeremy that some of the greatest would-be aggressors – for aggression may be a symptom of epilepsy – are known to be of epileptic character if not subject to the actual attacks. Napoleon and Caesar were reputed to be epileptics, and Jeremy suggests that this fellow Hitler with his maniacal persecution of the Jews and anti-Nazis is a possible epileptic.'

I could hardly take this discussion as reassuring although I think that Archie meant it to be; but I did feel somewhat eased of gnawing anxiety as to Colin's 'legacy', which is how I always thought of it, if some of the greatest figures in history could be considered sufferers from this same – disease or whatever it was. As for Hitler and aggression, one might well believe *him* an epileptic, if aggression were a 'symptom', for one heard ghastly tales brought by Jewish refugees from the German Chancellor and the awful horrors perpetrated in concentration camps. Some of the most brilliant lawyers, doctors, scientists were among those who had escaped from Hitler's 'maniacal' persecution. I wondered if Colin's tendency could also be maniacal? Not necessarily, if some of the most traditionally important historical men of genius were similarly afflicted . . .

But I had more now to occupy my mind than the unhappy incident of the wireless attack. Sir Jeremy, to whom Archie reported this latest incident, decided that for the present at any rate Colin should not be brought to consult him since he never remembered his 'lapses', and it would do him no good to be reminded of them. Get him interested in some occupation, was Sir Jeremy's advice. Consequently Archie suggested that Colin should start an antique business.

He surprisingly took to the idea. Disinclined to undertake any work or occupation for monetary advantage, and because he considered himself a connoisseur of antique furniture and objets d'art, he readily agreed to Archie's proposal. Our flat in Grosvenor Street was overcrowded. During the previous years he had gone in for bouts of buying; he spent hundreds in junk shops and at Christie's and Sotheby's, and my attempts to decrease his overdraft with my book jackets and illustrations defeated its ends. It became apparent that we could no longer afford to continue living in a Mayfair flat. Our lease was running out and to renew it the rent was certain to be greatly increased.

Archie, who owned some property in the Marylebone district, offered us what had originally been a small eighteenth-century house of which the ground floor had been let as an antique shop. The lessee had recently died, his lease finished and unrenewable anyway, and the stock had been sold as part of his estate. The floor above was tenanted by a Miss Gibbon.

'I let her have it', Archie said, 'at a moderate rent for she had little to live on more than she earned as secretary to a solicitor. I understood from my agent who collects the rents that she is in arrears. It seems her employer has also recently died and she is now out of a job. She might be useful to you, Colin, as an assistant. She seems an intelligent girl. I've met her once or twice. Her association with a solicitor might be of help to you in a business capacity.'

'But does she know anything about antiques?' objected Colin. 'If not she'd be no use to me.'

'I think she knows quite as much as you do about them,' Archie reassured him. 'I saw some good pieces when I visited her flat. Her father was a member of my club, the Fine Arts. He was killed in a plane crash a couple of years ago.'

'There seems to be an abundance of deaths around this Miss Gibbon,' I said. 'Have you any more houses to let in that part of London?'

Archie Tarrant, who seemed to be, as Noel tells us, 'their saving grace', had one or two more houses and not only found them a flat near to the antique shop but took over the rent of the Grosvenor Street flat because he said, in view of conditions in Italy under Mussolini, he intended selling his villa at Rapallo.

So it came about as we have it from Noel's memoirs both written and verbal, that another milestone was passed along her 'journey' as she recalls the episodes and incidents of her life reviewed from long distance in time where, she says, 'There is no life but memory'....

And now we find Colin installed in what looked to be, if not a flourishing business, at least an absorbing occupation. Some of his antiques acquired during their married life were deposited in the panelled showroom of the ground floor on display to would-be buyers. These for the first months were few but by the end of that Abdication year he had recuperated with the help of Miss Gibbon any losses he might have sustained.

'She', Noel tells us, 'was immensely capable.' She managed all his business affairs, both buying and selling, and knew as much as or more than he about antiques, having lived with them in her father's house all her life. Her father had been a man of means until the 1914 war and unfortunate speculations landed him in the bankruptcy court and left her insufficient to be independent. She had taken a degree at Cambridge in history; and her father's death – her

74

mother having died some years before – decided her to train at a secretarial college: and now in her later twenties she found herself assistant to Colin Harbord, acting as his manageress and general factotum.

We have a description of her from Noel's 'Journal'.

This Miss Gibbon, Colin's secretary, saleswoman (I'm sure she'd hate being called that, *he* calls her his aide de camp) is, in appearance, vaguely reminiscent of Barton. She has that negligible quality that masks a certain dominance. She has the same mouse-coloured hair parted in the middle and smoothed over her ears, and the same 'peevish' Madonna-like look, but there resemblance ends, or maybe never was. It is only because Barton has got under my skin all these years, that I see in Viola Gibbon a similar indefinable charm, a substitute for Barton – as possibly Colin sees her. I may be entirely wrong about this, but I do know he relies on her and that she has made that venture of his, urged on him by Archie, if not a paying concern at least not a loss – so far.

As for the one-toned voice of Barton, *her* voice is nothing like it. Despite that she is small and looks pale and frail, she has a voice that rings loudly. Quite out of keeping with the rest of her . . . I wonder why I am spending so much time and ink on her?

* * *

We hear very little of 'J. L. S.' for the next few months, chiefly because he was in Australia attending to the Marriott company in Melbourne, and also because Noel had been temporarily 'tied up', as she calls her latest contract with Kell and Wrotham, who had offered her higher terms than Marriott. This occurred after Sinclair had left for Melbourne. She admits she rather dreaded his return. His second in command, Ayling, one of his directors, had taken, as he put it, a very poor view of her 'backsliding' from her commitments with Marriott.

75

'I have no commitment with Marriott,' she told him who, having taken her out to lunch and regaled her with oysters, had her at a disadvantage to repudiate this accusation except in the most innocent attempt at righting a misunderstood wrong. 'I only signed with you,' she said, 'for a current book – I mean its jacket. But Kell and Wrotham have signed me up in a three-book contract for their jackets.'

'I didn't quite get away with it,' she confessed. 'Ayling took it hardly, and I was sure he reported by airmail to J. L. S. in Melbourne that I had "backslid" on them' . . .

We had now come to the New Year of 1937. The Abdication was almost forgotten with the succession of George VI who, after Baldwin had removed his brother from the Throne, fulfilled to the best of his limited ability the kingship that had been thrust upon him.

Delicate and nervous, afflicted with an impediment of speech he none the less endeavoured, and with ultimate success, to follow his father's example. Little could he have foreseen that his reign would be blasted by the most disastrous conflict between nations in the history of the world.

The parting speech of the ex-King had been received by his millions of listeners with mixed feelings. The majority, in especial the men, preserved a noncommittal silence while many of the women wept and held the memory of their 'Prince Charming' in their hearts. He went from England with no regretful send-off from those of his subjects who had deplored his choice of the woman for whom he deserted his kingdom.

So he married her, the ceremony being performed by a Church of England clergyman, and thereafter the fallen King remained an exile, having been created Duke of Windsor with the title of Duchess accorded to his wife. But that of Her Royal Highness was denied her, greatly to her, and possibly the Duke's, resentment.

Baldwin, who had so successfully dealt with this constitutional crisis, survived in triumph until the Coronation of George VI in May 1937. We have Noel's account of the procession which she, with Colin and Miss Gibbon, his 'aide de camp', witnessed in company with Sinclair, Ayling, and others of his staff.

J. L. S., who had a flat in Piccadilly, invited us there to see the procession. We had a good view of them as they drove past.

We heard from Birdie, who knew everything about everybody and because her son Amersham had married the daughter of one of Queen Mary's ladies in waiting, that the Dowager Queen had said: 'The Yorks will do it well.' . . . They did do it well not only at their Coronation but in the catastrophic years to follow . . . There was no sign, no cloud of that which lay in store for them and all of us as we watched that splendid procession. Those two, so young they looked – he in his robes just a mere boy although in his forties; and she so smiling and happy because he, her husband, as we learned from Birdie, an unfailing source of information, had managed, by diligent practice and patient tuition, to overcome his stammer enough to enable him to broadcast his Coronation speech to his Kingdom and the world.

Through the beflagged and shouting streets drove the magnificent coach with those two inside it looking as if they had drifted back from our childhood's dreams of a King and Queen in a glass coach, a fairy tale come to life . . . How romantic can one be and how stupidly naïve did I feel when I expressed something of this to J. L. S. while I munched *pâté de foie gras* sandwiches. He had provided a sumptuous luncheon on a buffet table where we could help ourselves at intervals . . . So long ago it seems, so much has happened since then, and the daughter of those two in their beautiful state coach is now, God be thanked, our Queen . . .

I am trying to recollect exactly when, or how much

77

longer after the Coronation, I became aware that Colin and his *aide de camp* Miss Gibbon were having an affair. That is to say Colin was obviously in love with her even if they had not actually become lovers.

Knowledge came to me with a letter that I found, he was always dreadfully untidy and careless about his correspondence, at least any that came to the flat, for of course since the advent of his 'aide' all his business correspondence went to the shop.

A crumpled piece of paper was lying on the floor in his dressing-room. He slept there – had slept there ever since we agreed not to co-habit, and he had never attempted to assert his marital rights. He had no further use for me that way. Recognizing his scrawled writing I picked up the letter, smoothed it out and, without any intention of prying, I began detachedly to read it as I might have read a fallen scrap of newspaper. But after the first few words I realized that he had written this letter meaning to post it or drop it in her letter-box in the flat above the shop and had forgotten or mislaid it.

I gave it back to him later but I remembered enough to quote from it almost verbatim:

Beloved, How am I to express in these clumsy words all that you are to me? That I am nothing to you – or am I? – fills me with doubt akin to joyful anticipation. That you are not indifferent to me I feel sure yet whether your sympathy and apparent response to what you must realize is my love for you for I do love you and never thought to love again. [He then enlarges about me which as far as I recollect went something like this] . . . As for my wife I have conveyed to you have I not? that for some time past Noel and I have lived apart although under the same roof . . . Is there any hope that you and I can come together not as man and wife but as lovers in the truest sense, for marriage is not for lovers. I, who am married, know the bitter disillusionment of the marital bond which is not the ecstatic love [he must have got hold of that from the *Love's Ecstasy* woman described by her publisher Marriott as 'Queen of the Romantic Novelists' . . . Oh, J. L. S. How could you?] . . . which [he goes on to say] is not the ecstatic love I feel for you that is the love of Dante and Beatrice or Paolo and Francesca . . .

There is a lot sickmakingly more of it which I skipped with the feeling as if I had sneaked on to some schoolboy's first calf-love letter. Colin! . . . He was still and ever would be a boy, seeking the mother love he had never had. Why did I not supply that mother love he sought? I never did. I never could. Although when we first met in another life at that students' ball he did give to my 'listening face' his childhood's terror glimpse of his parents fighting, a mutual state of violent aggression. But I had sensed that in confiding to me, then a stranger to him, I was not a replacement for the mother image . . . I was and have always been merely an abstract figure, one to whom he could soliloquize his inner thoughts as if I were an article of furniture. There is nothing in my physical appearance to suggest, as in Barton or Miss Gibbon, a Madonna-like replica.

And revisualizing Miss Gibbon on the few occasions when I have seen her hovering over some 'pretty piece' or displaying to a gushing American woman a (doubtful) set of Wedgwood plaques which Colin had acquired depicting George the Third, his Queen Charlotte, and their son, the Prince of Wales, I could see her in her spectacles – she would often put on a pair of horn-rims that sat uncomfortably on her little snub nose – and I laugh in reminiscence. She was, I thought, far less a mother to him than a school marm. He must be mightily impressed with her degree, M.A. Newnham, or should it be Cantab after her name as J. L. S. has it after his? . . . He seems always to be cropping up in these memoirs of the long ago. And that brings him back to me now . . .

79

I had not seen him for some months. Not since the Coronation. He had gone away again. Not to Australia this time, to Munich thence to Frankfurt for the Book Fair. He had interests in Western Europe as I discovered and – this according to Archie who had known him for years – he had got a double first in Modern Languages at Cambridge with intent to go into the diplomatic service. And that is all I knew about him then.

FIVE

For the remainder of the Coronation year we hear nothing from Noel or her pending domestic crisis that preceded the world cataclysm which began with the flight to Munich of Chamberlain, successor as Premier to Baldwin, in his attempt to mediate with Hitler on the matter of his Czechoslovakian aggression. She was absorbed in her work with Kell and Wrotham and not until the following entry in her memoirs do we hear:

Colin had left a note for me pinned to the pillow of my bed: 'Have gone to Paris with Viola'.

And that, laconically, was that.

Not a word as to what he had done with the shop, whether closed, the stock sold, or if he had abandoned it now and for ever, 'with Viola' . . . Gone, to Paris. Did he intend to open another antique shop in Paris? Or was it an escape 'with Viola' from me?

I rang for Latimer.

He had come with us to our flat, or rather maisonette of five rooms – it had been six rooms but we turned the smallest into a second bathroom for Latimer, and Archie has let it to us at what he called a peppercorn rent, meaning almost nothing at all. It was in a side street off Marylebone Road within five minutes' walk of Colin's shop. I knew Latimer felt it to be a derogatory descent from the sublime of Albany and Grosvenor Street to the ridiculous, as he regarded our new abode which is very nearly a slum. A hundred and fifty years ago it bordered upon fields and had an uninterrupted view of Hampstead's heights, obliterated now by Madame Tussaud's and Baker Street Station. But with 'Littimer'-like forbearance he endured it as he endured all to do with Colin, even his marriage to me.

'Did Mr Harbord tell you he had gone or was going to Paris?'

'Yes, madam.' Looking through me as if I were a pane of glass, his face expressionless as always when he spoke to or answered a question from me.

I walked round to the shop and saw the young man whom Colin or Miss Gibbon (Viola, I could never think of her as Viola) employed as part-time assistant should she be otherwise engaged, for Colin often sent her to sales if he could not himself attend an auction at some country house.

The young man with hair too long, a ring too large, a velvet jacket and an ingratiating smile greeted me with:

'*Good* afternoon, Mrs Harbord. You see me in charge here. Mr Harbord and Miss Gibbon have flown over to Paris for an important sale at Fontainebleau. The executors of the late Comtesse de Chatelet who was an American and had a *mar*vellous collection, and her executors are auctioning some of her pieces. Mr Harbord showed me an illustrated catalogue. *Too* marvellous. I *hanker* for a pièce de résistance − an enamelled striking clock with gold motifs by Fabergé. If he should bid for it I think he'd be quite *broke* if he got it. It'll fetch *thousands* . . .'

I said mendaciously, 'I knew Mr Harbord was going to Paris for that Fontainebleau auction but I don't think he'll come back with − the clock.'

I left him to it and when I got home having forgotten my latchkey, Latimer let me in, saying:

'Mr Tarrant has telephoned, madam, and asks will you please to ring him when you return.'

I rang him and said:

'Colin has gone to Paris with Miss Gibbon ostensibly to attend an auction at Fontainebleau.'

'I know. He rang me up this morning before he left to

82

catch the plane. It seems he is selling the business as he cannot meet his creditors.'

'Good lord! This is the first I've heard of that. *Selling* it? Why?'

'Because he cannot make it pay and so hopes to avoid liquidation.'

'But I thought the Gibbon was running it for him and that she is doing well with it.'

'Unfortunately, no. She was buying or persuading him to buy *too* well and unwisely.'

'That pansy they have there —' I began.

'That what?'

'That boy who stands in for her, he told me they have gone to Fontainebleau to an auction of some American woman whose executors are selling her stuff.'

'That is as maybe, but unlikely with intent to bid as he has not enough money to buy since he has so much of his stock unsold.'

'Or,' I persisted, 'he may be having a sort of honeymoon with the Gibbon – isn't a gibbon a species of monkey? – I know he is having an affair with her. Our marriage packed up some time ago so he may be hoping to give me evidence for a divorce.'

'I think not. He is probably finding Miss Gibbon a substitute for that sculptress friend of yours with whom he got himself entangled. Would you want to divorce him?'

'Of course not. Divorce is beastly – washing one's dirty linen in public.'

'In your case,' I could not see but I guessed the thin smile which accompanied the remark, 'it would be the washing of your *clean* linen in public.'

'Well, we are as good as unmarried already so it would be no question of publicly washing either our dirty or clean linen . . . Goodbye.'

No sooner had I hung up than the phone bell rang. I lifted the receiver and heard:

'I've been trying to get you for the last twenty minutes.'

It was J.L.S.

'I'm sorry. So you're back from Frankfurt?'

'And Munich.'

'Is there also a Book Fair in Munich?'

'Not a Book Fair. Another kind of fair on the outskirts of Munich at Godesberg, where the side shows are of immense interest to a multi-lingual crowd of fair-mongers who group around the arch showman and chief exhibitionist, Herr Hitler.'

'You aren't selling books to Hitler, are you?'

'No, any book of ours if by a Jewish author that I would have sold to a publisher in Berlin, would have been burnt on a scrap heap along with other books by other Jewish authors.'

'Do you mean they won't publish *British* Jewish authors in Germany?'

'No, and we have to declare that any of our authors whose work we send to a German publisher for translation has neither one parent nor a grandparent of Jewish blood.'

'I can't believe it!'

'There is a lot you can't believe and much that I could not have believed had I not seen and heard what I *have* seen and heard. And because I have published works by certain German or British Jews, I would have found their books on a scrap heap had I brought one of them with me, only I might have been exonerated as the publisher of a Jew because I had an Aryan German grandfather.'

'Are you then – a quarter German?'

'I am. My second name is Ludwig.'

Which accounts for the L. I thought, and said:

'Is that why you are such a good publisher? The Germans are good at most things.'

'Or were until they went bad under Hitler. I am named after my grandfather on the distaff side. Will you dine with me tonight?'

'Oh . . . No. I – It is so sudden.'

84

'Is it? I'm a sudden sort of person when I want a thing – or to do a thing. I'll come and fetch you at eight o'clock.'

I rang off. I went to my room and stared at myself in the glass. Yes, he is sudden. Too sudden. Taking me for granted – a 'thing' – and as if I were waiting to come to his call. I don't think I'll go with him . . . He doesn't say where. Is it black tie? I'll not dress. I'll go as I am – no, I'll wear my old Molyneux, the last I'm ever likely to have because I'm in the red now, having almost paid off Colin's Lucifer and he'll be coming down on me to get him out of this latest mess . . . with his gibbon . . .

I dined with J. L. S. at the Savoy Grill.

Of that dinner her memoirs of 1938 give enough account to reconstruct this meeting with J. L. S. on his return from Germany, which later appears to be of consequence.

Having ordered for her and himself he began with what she felt to be a grievance against her 'desertion', as he lightly described it – 'for having signed yourself away from me. I had decided, and so had Grierson, to contract you for another of his Tuscan Rambles, and as Kell and Wrotham have snaffled you, there is no alternative but for us to take over —' he mentioned the name of an up-and-coming young artist who had designed the jacket for a first novel that had made a smash hit here, and simultaneously in America.

Nibbling toast she said lightly:

'That's too bad, isn't it? Yet as Kell and Wrotham offered more for my work than Marriott pay me, I too have no alternative but to accept.'

She tried, she said, to keep it on a strictly business level, which was not easy; he was evidently veering towards a more personal approach. 'It is too long,' he said, carefully negotiating a lobster claw, 'since I have had an opportunity of seeing you outside my office. I observe the smallest crease between your delicately surprised eyebrows that indicates an anxious preoccupation.'

85

'What do you mean', she was not looking at him but into the as-yet-untasted glass of Montrachet, 'by surprised eyebrows?'

'I mean just that – surprised, as if you had awakened from some dreamless sleep to be confronted with the puzzling reality of life in a strange new world in which you are unable to participate.'

'And why should you think I am unable to participate in life's realities or the strangeness of a world which isn't new at all? There is nothing new under the sun. I am no dreaming idealist,' he roused her to retort, 'no self-imposed ascetic – an escapist from the uncertainties and crises that are going on today. I read an excerpt of a speech Churchill made in Manchester recently when he said it is his duty to rouse the country to the ever growing danger.'

'Ah, so you are not too dreamily aware of the devastating horrors that threaten our'– (sardonically) – 'happy little island?'

'I read the papers,' she retorted, 'and not only the book-page advertisements.'

The waiter offered cutlets. They sat in silence for a while, then:

'And perhaps you are not too dreamily aware to know that I'm in love with you?' ...

This passage ends abruptly here.

* * *

In the few months that followed Sinclair's startling announcement, Noel's reminiscences are less concerned with herself and her personal affairs than with the critical conditions that prevailed in Britain and throughout Europe during that last year of peace.

Baldwin, now retired to the Upper House, had been replaced by Neville Chamberlain as Prime Minister in the new National Government. Noel appears to have learned the little she records of political and current affairs at home and abroad, from Archie Tarrant, 'who', she writes in March 1938, 'is convinced that war with Germany is inevitable'.

Hitler, having entered Vienna, had incorporated Austria into Germany, and Tarrant gave it that Czechoslovakia was next on the list, an opinion shared by Chamberlain. 'But', said Tarrant, 'Chamberlain can't do anything about it since neither Britain nor France can help the Czechs against Hitler's aggression, in particular as our Air Force is lamentably wanting. To take the offensive,' he said, 'would be like attacking a tiger with a pea-shooter.'

The name of Sinclair, or J. L. S., does not appear significantly in her journal until May 1938 when:

J. L. S. has gone to Prague. Nothing to do with publishing, or so I believe, although he did tell me that two of Yates' books have been accepted for translations by a Czech publisher, but I am sure that these frequent visits to Central Europe and Germany are not always to do with Marriott's business. I tried to pump Archie about it as he has known J. L. S. for years. Before he became a publisher and after he came down from Cambridge he was in the Foreign Office. Has he gone back to the F.O. as a side line to publishing, I wonder? And if so in what capacity? I can get nothing out of Archie. He is close as a clam, which makes me all the more curious.

And then later:

Today, June 10, 1938, J. L. S. rang up. He is back from wherever he has been. Suggests driving to some quiet place on the river tomorrow, Sunday. London, he said, is too full of tourists and foreigners. (I suppose he has seen enough of foreigners abroad.)

And: 'Tomorrow, Sunday', he fetched her in his car and drove to that 'quiet place' on the river a mile or so from Datchet. He had a house there but did not live in it of late,

87

having let it, yet he still used the boat-house and had telephoned to have a boat ready for him. He had also brought a picnic basket.

Of that day's outing we hear:

It was a marvellous warm day, the sort of summer day one can only have in England when away from the crowd as we were. He rowed into a backwater where there was not a soul in sight, no sound more than bird song and the plash of oars. He moored the boat to a jutting snag under drooping willows. I said, and my voice sounded loud in that still warm air, though it was scarcely above a whisper: 'Why do they call them weeping willows? Do they weep? . . .' A silly remark – just something to say because I felt he had quite a lot to say which I was almost afraid to hear, yet I longed to hear it.

Thinking back on it now I recall that since the night we dined at the Savoy when he said he was in love with me, he had never spoken again of anything personal at all. I could only presume he had been merely flirtatious, which is hard to believe because he is no boy, in his forties. We had met, of course, since then, but only professionally. I had finished my book jackets under contract with Kell and Wrotham and was engaged on the coloured illustrations for a new edition of Jane Austen that Marriott was issuing. I enjoyed doing these, not in oils, in water colour and pen and ink, a new venture for me. The editorial and art department are very keen on them. I have finished *Sense and Sensibility* and am now starting on *Pride and Prejudice*.

After I had said that, stupidly, about weeping willows which called for no answer, he came over to where I sat in the bows. There was hardly room for both of us on the seat. He said:

'I know it's a bit of a squash but as we are going to have lunch here I can't pass things to you from the other side of the boat.' The picnic basket was at my feet.

'I'll see,' he said, 'what my fellow has got for us.'

There were portions of chicken, asparagus with a jar of melted butter, a bottle of vin rosé, a thermos of coffee, and fruit, strawberries, peaches . . . While we ate he remarked, casually:

'I ran into your husband in Paris.'

'Oh ? . . . Yes, he has been in Paris for several months.' I was equally casual. 'So you have been in Paris, too ?'

'*En passant*, on and off. Does that mean,' he paused with a chicken bone in mid air, 'that you and he are at the parting of your ways?'

I waited about half a minute before I answered that, surprised I could answer it and tell him what for so long I had held within myself.

'Our ways were parted years ago only neither of us knew it . . . It was never me he wanted, nor I him. I could never have been for Colin what he was searching for all his life. Nor could he have been for me what I was searching for.'

'I know that,' he said quietly. 'But do you know what you *are* searching for?'

'The unattainable, I suppose.'

'Which few of us ever attain. I thought I had attained it when I married.'

'You' – I managed to articulate – 'you are – married?'

'Yes, but we too have come to the parting of our ways.'

'Are you', I had to know, 'divorced?'

'Not yet. I haven't given her cause and she is not concerned with a cause. She is quite self-sufficient and as far as I know unattached as was I – until you happened to me. Yes, you!' He turned to throw the chicken bone into the river. His arms gathered me to him. My mouth was full of strawberries; he kissed it, strawberries and all.

'You', he was out of breath, 'are all I've ever wanted from the moment I saw you on the Ponte Vecchio in Florence. I wanted you then and I want you now, but you,' he said fiercely, 'you must want me as much as I want you – to marry!'

'Marry?' I drew away from him. Bewilderment, doubt, suspicion, struggled with all that I – yes, that *I* wanted as much as he said he wanted me . . . 'How can we marry? We are both married.'

His reply to that was:

'Divorce can be arranged,' as if he were arranging another outing on the river.

'No!' I started up rocking the boat; the dish of strawberries on my knee upset and they were tumbled at my feet. 'Not divorce – never! I couldn't do that to Colin. It might —' I stopped. I was going to say it might kill him, but that would need explaining to J. L. S., about his legacy.

'What might it do to Colin?' he prompted, stooping to pick up a handful of strawberries to drop them in the river. They floated away, little blobs of red. 'Pity about these,' he said, 'just as you were enjoying them. But that's the way of life.'

He pulled me down beside him, produced a silk handkerchief from the breast pocket of his grey flannel suit, cupped my chin in his hand and with the handkerchief he wiped my mouth. 'All strawberry stained,' he murmured, 'like a child caught stealing the jam. What I love about you, Caro, is your adorable *young*ness. Life, with all its hazards great or small, leaves you still the child unsurprised at fortune's or misfortune's slings. You dodge them as they come and pass them by. The only surprise you show is – here.' His lips hovered above my eyebrows. 'I think that you, like children, have in common with animals, the higher animals, dogs, horses, that instinctive acceptance of life's vagaries which bears no grudge against fate, or what you will, that decides our destinies for, as Walt Whitman says as far as I remember:

"I think I could turn and live with animals, they are so placid and self-contain'd. . . .

They do not lie awake in the dark and weep for their sins,

They do not make me sick discussing their duty to
      God ..."
who they take as they take life, or what life has done to
them, for granted.'

His mouth came down to mine.

So this, I thought, is love. Reality . . . But marry him?
No! I'll never marry him. I wouldn't want to lose him, and
to marry – to be legally bound body and soul, would be – to
lose.

We hear little more of her personal contact with Sinclair
during the remainder of that year, 1938. It is now evident
that she, as were many others, was alarmedly aware that
Britain stood on the brink of war. The French were mobiliz-
ing an army of 600,000 reservists and in continuous consultation with the British general staff; while Hitler was
making conciliatory speeches that he would never act
against Czechoslovakia if he were certain that Britain and
France would not intervene.

'He's bluffing,' this from Archie Tarrant to Noel who, she
said, devoured the newspapers and was all ears for the
wireless, with an anxious eye and ear to Colin in Paris – if
he were still there with his 'gibbon' from whom she had
dropped the 'Miss' and thought of merely as Colin's anthro-
poid appendage. 'The French', said Archie, 'are not likely
to be taken in by Hitler's pledge that Czechoslovakia is the
last of his territorial claims in Europe. The French say he
is bluffing and they will call his bluff, which is more than
Chamberlain is likely to do.'

'Why', Noel asked, 'are they digging trenches in Hyde
Park? Is it because they – the Ministry of Defence or whoever is supposed to look after Londoners in the event of
war – believe that Hitler will drop bombs on us? And why
are volunteer A.R.P. wardens calling on houses with gas
masks? A girl came to the flat yesterday and wanted to fit
me with one.'

'A necessary precaution,' Archie said. 'Hitler wouldn't

hesitate to gas civilians if he decides not to keep his pledge, which is to maintain peace in Europe. And Chamberlain, who is more easily persuaded than France as to Hitler's "good intent" – (save the mark!) – flies off to Munich armed with the dove of peaceful negotiation. I can see them,' Archie's smile slid sideways, 'sitting on the terrace of Hitler's hide-out at Godesberg, drinking lager and discussing amicable relationships between ourselves, the Nazis, and Mussolini, Hitler's shadow. So concerned is our gullible Neville that he lets forth – did you hear him on the wireless? – "How horrible, fantastic, incredible it is that we should be digging trenches and trying on gas masks here because of a quarrel in a country between peoples of whom we know nothing." He'll soon know a good deal more than nothing of the peoples and Hitler,' said Archie from behind a screen of cigar smoke. 'Chamberlain has convinced the Commons that Hitler's word is to be trusted. If you take my advice,' he told her, 'you'll join the Civil Defence. You and all of you who are sound of wind and limb might be useful in defending London's less able citizens who cannot defend themselves against air attack.'

A certain minority shared Archie's pessimism, but for the most part the general opinion was that Chamberlain had brought the current crisis to a successful finale. He gave out that Mussolini was acting as mediator with the result that Hitler agreed to a four-power conference. In the Commons the news was greeted with cheers. The tension relieved, some of the more emotional sobbed. The Liberal leader blessed Chamberlain with tears running down his cheeks.

Again Chamberlain flew to Munich to confer with Hitler and brought back with him a statement that the agreement symbolized the desire of our two nations never to go to war with one another....

That scrap of paper signed by both Hitler and Chamberlain was waved to an excited crowd waiting outside Ten

Downing Street by the Prime Minister who called to those below him up-gazing at the window where he stood:

'This is the second time that there has come back from Germany to Downing Street peace with honour. I believe it is peace for our time.'

'Peace for our time!' Those words were echoed in the hearts of Londoners and throughout the British Isles. Peace! They had the Prime Minister's word for it, had seen the paper in his hand that declared no war with Germany, no war in Europe in our time.

But what of Sir John Anderson, Lord Privy Seal, in charge of air-raid precautions, issuing gas-masks – millions of them to householders at vast expense, what of it? A necessary precaution as discussed by the man in the street and in the pubs, as any one of us would secure our homes against burglars and fire with bolts and locks, and fire extinguishers ... Of course there could be the off chance that this Hitler would go mad, was the opinion over pints of mild and bitter – if he isn't mad already with his persecution of the Jews. Refugees who had escaped were coming over here in shoals welcomed by us, offered homes and jobs, poor devils ... Yes, there was always the chance that Hitler, despite his promise to leave the Czechs alone might descend on *us*. After all look how he has kept his word not to attack Czechoslovakia ... Yes, and what now!

Only five days before Hitler had devoured Czecho-slovakia, Chamberlain had given *his* word from Hitler that Europe was settling down to 'a period of tranquillity' ...

As soon trust Hitler as a rattlesnake was the opinion over the pints and in the clubs.

'Do you believe it?' Noel asked Sinclair. 'I mean that Chamberlain thinks we can trust Hitler?'

She had brought him her latest Jane Austen illustrations.

'I do not, for I know,' he said, 'what I know.'

She did not inquire how or what he knew but she had drawn her own conclusions about his frequent visits to central Europe and nearer home too. He had been in the

Foreign Office – was he still in the F.O.? She forbore to question him but she could guess that his activities abroad were not wholly confined to buying or selling the foreign rights of his authors' works. She is reticent concerning her relationship with Sinclair, and not until the return of Colin from Paris is there any indication that she and 'J. L. S.', as she refers to him in the memoirs, were lovers.

It was on a morning in the spring of that fateful year, 1939, when she was at work in her studio; this, the room that had been Latimer's who had given in his notice the day after Colin left for Paris. Whether he followed Colin to wherever he had gone she did not inquire nor did she care. She was thankful to be rid of the highly respectable Latimer who still regarded her, as always in the past, as 'very young', and with secretly veiled insolence. She tolerated him for his devotion to Colin and had every reason to believe he had accompanied him when he went away. His room, an attic on the top floor of the maisonette, had a north light with a view below of dustbins, and above of rooftops and the windows of houses in Harley Street.

She heard a ring at the door bell and then:

'Where is madam? Where is my wife?'

And the answer from the daily woman who 'did' for her: 'She's in the stewdioh, sir.'

As her memoirs record it:

I heard him on the stairs. He was at the door, his hair all rumpled, his face strained and pale. I got up and went to him.

'Why didn't you let me know you were coming back?'

'I wrote.'

'Yes, you wrote – once or twice. You've been gone almost a year. Is your gibbon with you?'

'No.' He swayed and caught at a chair back to steady himself. I said:

'You're ill.'

'No – not now. I have been ill —' he put a hand to his head and sank into the chair I pulled forward for him. 'She sent me to a psychiatrist quack who charged the earth and parked me in a nursing home – a sort of loony bin.' He spoke in jerks.

'Where is she now?'

We were talking as if he had never been away, or as if it were the most natural thing that he should have left me for another woman, and had come back to take up our lives where they left off.

'Who —' I asked, and I too sat, on a stool at his feet, 'who paid for this sort of – loony bin and your quack? Did he try to analyse you?'

He answered both questions in their order.

'Archie sent me cash from time to time. He sold the stock at the shop to pay the creditors and I suppose he produced whatever he thought I would need to keep us both – I mean Viola and me. Thanks to you my overdraft is almost paid off. I didn't worry about you —'

'Obviously,' I interrupted. 'You never did. I've been your banker and your stooge for years.'

'I know. I' – again his hand went to his head – 'I'm a swine – no use to you and never was.'

'That's not your fault. It's as much mine as yours that I failed you, or we failed each other. I suppose the gibbon supplied my deficiencies as Barton did. So what have you done with her – I mean with Gibbon?'

'She's done with me. She got a job as a secretary at our Embassy in Paris and chucked me out of our apartment. Sick of me, I suppose. She told me to go back to you where I belong.'

I said:

'So now you are back we'll have to see what's to be done, but do understand this – we'll have to be as we were when we decided to live together but with no obligation on either side.'

95

'Not' – a wintry smile came across his face – 'not even as brother and sister like the Pharaohs?'

I patted his knee, his own knee. 'We've always been brother and sisterly but not like the Pharaohs. We're much more like real brother and sister than they were. Both of us have been searching for our parents, or in your case for your mother. I've never had a mother so I can't miss what I've never had, and your mother wasn't as you wanted her to be.' I looked at him searchingly. 'You're thinner. You've lost a lot of weight, haven't you? Did they give you enough to eat in that place? And did you have a private room?'

'Private, of course. Archie sent me the money for that too.'

I thought: And Archie never told me. Didn't want to worry me, I suppose.

'How long were you there?' I asked him.

'About six weeks. A doctor, another psychiatric chap used to have me on a sofa and ask questions, made me tell him all I could remember of my childhood and those scenes between – you know – what I told you. That psychological stuff is a lot of balls. Oh hell!' He clapped a hand to his trouser pocket. 'I forgot – the taxi! He's still waiting.' He pulled out a wallet. 'Damn, I've hardly any English money. I paid for my breakfast on the plane in francs. Can you — ?'

'How much?'

'I don't know. I'll go and ask.'

'No, I'll go.'

I took a wad of notes from my bedroom drawer and went downstairs.

The taxi man was reading a mid-day evening paper while he waited. Headlines in black capitals shouted at me:

THE PRIME MINISTER'S ASSURANCE TO POLAND

I pointed to the paper.
'What's all that about?'

'We're siding with the Poles now against Germany. As if we 'adn't enough on our plate! Always buttin' in with these flamin' furriners wot comes whinin' to us fer 'elp an' we gives it 'em. I was in the war, one o' Kitchener's army an' I'm bloody well – s'cuse me French – not goin' to 'ave any more of it. 'Sides I'm over age.'

'We've been promised that there'll never be another war so it doesn't matter if you're over age or not ... How much do I owe you?'

'Well, I bin tickin' up 'ere for arf an hour or more an' then there's the mileage – say three quid.'

I counted out three pound notes and handed them to him with half a crown.

He eyed it surlily.

'I get sixpence for a mile an' it's ten miles from the airport.'

'All right.' I gave him another half-crown and disregarding his glare returned to Colin.

'You'll be here indefinitely, I suppose, unless your gibbon wants you back again?'

'Don't you want me back again?'

He was doing his little boy act – to make me feel the same protectiveness I always felt, as if I were his elder sister instead of his wife more than eight years younger than he. I recalled what J. L. S. had said about my being unsurprised at life's hazards and my acceptance of life's uncertainties, bearing no grudge against fate or people, like children – or animals ... All this flashed through my mind while I told him:

'Your dressing-room has been kept ready for you, but what about Latimer? This – my studio – is his room.'

'I left him in Paris. He came to me there. He is settling with an agent who has let our apartment. Viola has taken an apartment near the Embassy.'

'So Latimer will be coming back here then?'

'If you don't mind.'

I thought, I haven't got to mind. I'll have to rent a room

outside unless I turn my bedroom into a combined studio, but it hasn't a north light . . . I said cheerily:

'Of course I don't mind.'

It is understandable that Sinclair did not take kindly to Colin's return; it did, however, solve the problem of finding a studio. At his suggestion he placed at her disposal an unused staff room at his Piccadilly flat, 'which', he said, 'used to be the cook's but as I have only one man servant and a daily now, and my man – my ex-batman – is a better cook than any woman I've had, you can use her room as a studio. It has a good north light.'

And so we have it that from the arrival of Colin from Paris with a resumption of their brotherly-sisterly relationship she had access to Sinclair's flat where she could work, in that 'good north light', undisturbed.

It is now that we learn from her recollections:

I suppose I ought to have felt guilty but I didn't, because I did not think I was committing adultery. What we had together was absolutely right. I was never committed to Colin to love, honour and obey. We were married in five minutes by the registrar. I can see him now. He looked like a goat with a little goat's beard, and I only realized when he said 'put the ring on your wife's finger', that I was Colin's wife, I mean his legal wife, not his wife in the sight of God. Besides, didn't He forgive the woman taken in adultery and tell her to go and sin no more . . . I am no man's wife and belong to no man except J. L. S. He would keep harping on divorce. He wanted to marry me – I mean really marry me – not just as we were – lovers, loving and being loved. He said: 'You can, you know, get a divorce from Colin. He has been living openly with this Gibbon woman in Paris. Then you and I —'

I told him as I've always told him that I'd never put Colin through all that beastliness. And that what we have together is too good for marriage. 'I'm not going to risk losing

98

it – or you. Besides, you are still married to your wife. So how could we have a divorce unless she will divorce you? And who then would she cite? Me?'

'Of course not. All can be arranged without compromising you. And she is now as anxious as am I for a complete termination to our marriage. She has found another man. She came over in the boat with him from New York where she has been living these last few years. As a matter of fact he's a fellow I knew in the F.O. She left the States because of this European war scare.'

'Oh!' I cried. 'I hate all this talk of divorce. You and she and I and – No! Get yourself divorced if you want to but leave me out of it. We go on as we are or not at all.'

This was the first of any rows we had, not just a lovers' row. It might have led to the parting of *our* ways except that he feared to lose me, as I feared to lose him. So he gave in. Never, he promised, would he mention divorce to me again, but he could let himself be divorced by his wife if she wished it . . . 'As to evidence,' he said, 'that also is easily arranged between my solicitor and hers.'

I covered my ears . . . 'I don't want to hear any more! I suppose you mean' – I was really het up about this – 'that you are supplied by your solicitor with a woman for you to sit up all night with her and go to bed in the morning for a chambermaid to see, which can be evidence. Can you wonder I loathe divorce?'

So they left it at that. And, surprisingly, Colin expressed himself pleased that Sinclair had allowed Noel a room in his flat for her work. He was also a frequent visitor there. He would drive her to Piccadilly on his way to his club or Christie's or Sotheby's, still interested, if not to buy, to watch a sale. It is evident that at this time he had no suspicion as to the relationship between Noel and Sinclair more than a publisher's interest in her work.

'He is making a good thing out of you,' Colin told her. 'Every review of a Marriott book that I've seen lately writes of the delightful or excellent or whatever adjectival gush they may load on a book's jacket, rather than the book, possibly because they – these reviewers – are for the most part disgruntled authors who can't get their stuff accepted by any publisher worth while and hope by buttering up a book by one of Marriott's authors and their jacket designs, they may have their manuscript at any rate *read*. I understand from Sinclair that about ninety per cent of MSS. sent to them are turned down, for they can tell, or their readers can, whether a book is publishable after the first twenty pages.'

Sometimes Colin would be invited to dinner with Noel if Sinclair was entertaining an author or two. And on one occasion we hear of an awkward, at least she gives it as an 'awkward', contretemps.

J. L. S. had invited a German author – a Baron von Swinehoff, or some such name – I can't spell it – whose book about his experiences as a flying ace in the war, the First World War, of course, Marriott was translating. He was quite well known in Germany and over here too as a writer of distinction, novelist, biographer, and an authority on aircraft.

I thought him rather attractive, not at all German or Prussian, more French, and he spoke perfect English.

It was after J. L. S. had been discussing the first Zeppelin brought down at Potters Bar in Hertfordshire, and talking about Zeppelins in general and how we were supposed to have been experimenting with the same sort of thing over here after the war, but as far as I could gather it hadn't materialized because, as J. L. S. said, 'We haven't your particular brand of experience', and I said (how could I have been such an abysmal tactless fool), 'How strange that we three and you should be sitting here discussing your exploits as one of Germany's top flying aces —'

'*The* top flying ace,' J. L. S. broke in trying to stop me, and I didn't stop. I went careering on. (No wonder he loves and teases me about my 'youngness'. He won't be likely to love me for it now! And there was I saying, in all innocence, if you can believe it!) – 'When only twenty odd years ago you were dropping bombs on us from your – or rather *our* enemy aircraft!'

J. L. S. elevated his eyebrows, and I saw Colin, to whom anything German is anathema – I am sure he wouldn't have gone to that dinner if he had known a German was to be the guest – I saw him clench a fist on the table and half raise it as if he meant to use it not on me, though I deserved it, but on the 'Hun' as afterwards when we got home he spoke of him, and went for me, dropping, as he said, that 'almighty bloody brick!'

Well, it was all that and more . . . For the 'Hun', the Baron, gave me such a dirty look when I uttered the unutterable that I could have bitten out my tongue. Colin bit *his* tongue for me. His face was tense and had whitened, usually the presage to an attack. . . . He muttered an excuse, got up from the table and made for the door.

I too excused myself and went after him, leaving J. L. S. to make the least of it to the Baron – something about Harbord having just got over the 'flu to account for him rushing off like this. He knew, for I did tell him, of Colin's legacy . . . Another reason why he was always pestering me to have a divorce.

I found Colin in the bathroom being sick. I waited in the adjoining bedroom till he came out. It was not an attack but the effect of what I had said and his hate of all things and people German, partly due to what he had been through in the war, and the loss of his leg but chiefly having bayoneted a German, since, for all his hate of them, he felt himself to be a murderer.

When we got home soon after that, Colin couldn't leave my 'almighty bloody brick' alone.

He came at me while I undressed. 'The fellow's a Nazi, and Sinclair knows it. He's not in the F.O. for nothing, always flying back and forth to Prague and God knows where. He was in Munich only a week before Chamber-lain's "Peace with Honour" stunt.'

It was news to me that J. L. S. had been in Munich. I knew he had been there last year but not lately – and that he should be engaged in what might be our intelligence department as a side line to publishing, or in publishing as a side line to that . . . I was still wondering about it when Colin said something else to startle me.

'I suppose you know that Sinclair's second name is German?'

'How do you know?' I felt a chill go through me as I spoke.

For how *did* he know . . . ?

'There's a lot I know that you don't know,' was his answer to that. 'He is half German himself.'

'Only a quarter. His mother was half German and was born here. His father was English right back to the Normans.'

'So you know that too, do you?'

Then he went to his room and left me still wondering . . .

She was not kept wondering for long. The day after that dinner at Sinclair's flat when she dropped her 'almighty brick', she tackled J. L. S. in his office ostensibly to submit her latest sketch of the frontispiece for *Northanger Abbey*, having finished the first two of the Jane Austen series. And, as she recalls it:

'I didn't know,' I told him, 'that you had been to Munich again this year. I knew you were there last year – nor did I know that you are still in the Foreign Office. Archie told me you *were* in the F.O. when you came down from Cambridge, but —'

He glanced up from the drawing to interrupt: 'This is charming. I like the bow-windowed shop.'

I snatched the drawing from him.

'I don't like it. I'm altering it. It's too over-crowded . . . I know I made an inexcusably silly remark last night to that Baron von Thingummy about his being a flying ace against us in the war and he gave me a dirty look for it which I well deserved, but Colin made a great thing of it when we got home. He hates the Germans and now he seems to think you're one or rather half a one. I told him you're only quarter German on your mother's side and that the Sinclairs have been entirely British ever since they were Normans when they were St Claire. That's right, isn't it?'

He got up from his desk and went to the window that overlooked the square. Marriott has had one of those Regency houses for the past century. The trees were glowing with the jade green of early June. I left my chair and followed him.

'You do know something, don't you? – about what's going on between us and Germany and Hitler – more than you'd know from just being a publisher. I read the papers and reports of Churchill's speeches – *he* ought to be Prime Minister. He would never have trusted Hitler with that scrap of paper. I don't want to ask you anything you don't want to tell me, but I'm not *quite* the fool you think I am!'

He swung me round to say in his teasing voice:

'You should know what I think you are, which is all that I want and all that you are and all that you aren't – which is no fool.'

'And which,' said I, 'is clear as mud!'

'But,' he went on, 'I'll tell you this —'

And he told.

'Poland is the fly in our ointment. You read your papers so will have learned that we're in one hell of a mess over Danzig. The Poles are standing on a time bomb and they look to us to dispose of it and in so doing to dispose of Hitler, which won't be so easy unless we dispose of all Europe with him.'

I clutched his arm.

'Does that mean a European war – in spite of Munich?'

'It's a case of heads we win' – he took a coin from his pocket and tossed it up – 'and tails we lose.' The penny turned over and rolled into a corner. 'The oracle has spoken! or rather – it won't speak and nor will Hitler yet.' Slowly and expertly he kissed my mouth. 'So,' he said, 'in case of – accidents, I suggest you join the A.R.P., and get Colin to do the same. You may neither of you be needed but if you are and as he is not eligible for the army with only one leg —'

'He'd be too old anyway,' I interrupted.

'We might even be asking for the maimed and the halt and the fifty-year-olds – not that he is near fifty yet, but if Colin is an Air Raid Warden he can go on hating Hitler and his Nazis with all he's got . . . Come, we'll go out to lunch.'

And no more was said of war or anything else except ourselves.

* * *

During those summer months events precipitated Parliament to guarantee Poland against Hitler's aggression. And now the Government was reluctantly impelled towards an alliance with Soviet Russia – 'to draw Hitler's fangs,' as Archie Tarrant put it, 'and so protect Poland and the smaller states from a savage mauling'.

But negotiations between a military alliance with Russia, France and Great Britain were doomed to deadlock. Yet while Chamberlain professed profound mistrust of Russia he agreed that Soviet assistance was desirable and he wanted to maintain his 'Peace with Honour' at all costs, which he believed could only be maintained by a military alliance between Britain, France and Russia.

'Our arch-optimist Neville,' was Archie Tarrant's opinion on the current crisis when he invited Noel to dinner at the flat he had taken over from the Harbords in Grosvenor Street. 'We are far too altruistic in taking other peoples' and other countries' troubles and finances to ourselves.

Poland has already borrowed millions from us with no hope of repayment, and now demands that we save her from the Nazis.'

And still the British public in general, apart from a few in particular, went serenely about their affairs. The younger generation continued hectically to frequent night clubs, dining, supping, dancing till all hours, forgetful or totally unaware of the thousands of gas masks that were being distributed daily throughout the United Kingdom; and of the air-raid shelters springing up like mushrooms not only beneath the offices in the City of London but in the gardens of suburban villas; and unheedful that the prolonged negotiations between Britain, France and the Soviet Union had come to no solution, while Russia was in two minds whether to become an ally of the two great opposing powers, or to sit on the fence between Hitler on one side and France and Britain on the other.

'And so you,' Archie told her, as Noel gives it, 'have joined the A.R.P. A wise decision, for, if Hitler invades Poland, we'll be dragged in to defend her, come what may. And as you are in or near your mid-thirties you are unlikely to be conscripted for service in the army.'

'Do you really think it will come to conscription for women? I mean – to fight?' she asked eagerly. 'I'd go like a shot. I could put my age back if there should be an age limit. But it isn't so serious as that, surely? Chamberlain wouldn't have gone to all those lengths with promise of peace for ever and signed that treaty or whatever it was, if it's to come to nothing.'

'In the words of Asquith during the last war, we must wait and see!' was all she could get out of Archie.

And now in that last week of August, Ribbentrop, the German Foreign Minister, was sent to Moscow.

'The fat's in the fire,' said Archie, who was in and out of the Harbords' flat in Marylebone these days. 'We must hope that we have sufficient extinguishers at our disposal to prevent a blaze.'

The Nazi–Soviet pact, signed as a result of Ribbentrop's visit to Moscow, that Russia should stay neutral in the event of war, was regarded as a deliberate affront to Britain, and an added thorn in her flesh, smarting from the nettle stings of doubt and the criticisms of Conservative and Labour back benchers who had taken a poor view of Chamberlain's policy. His 'Peace for our time' declaration was now regarded as so much hot air . . . 'And the air *is* hot,' said Archie, 'with the smouldering fumes that are wafted from Germany across Europe.'

'There never was such a Jeremiah as Archie,' remarks Noel in her journal dated 27 August 1939. 'One would think the Germans were invading us already. None in the A.R.P. thinks there will be war – yet, at any rate, or if so, *we* won't be in it.'

She, like many others, was blindfolded by the optimism of the Government that until the last minute appeared to be undismayed by the Nazi–Soviet pact. But on 25 August an Anglo–Polish treaty of mutual assistance was signed with a clause to cover Danzig and it was to be kept secret from Hitler.

'Danzig,' in Tarrant's view of it, 'is the spanner in the works.' He, who was acquainted with a number of members in the Commons and the Upper House, told how Kennedy, the American Ambassador whom he had met at dinner with Sir John Simon, Chancellor of the Exchequer, had said:

'The futility of the whole thing is frightful! After all, Britain can't save the Poles so why should *we* be dragged into it?' . . .

America had taken exception to Chamberlain's approach to Roosevelt imploring him to put pressure on the Poles. 'An admission that he can't do it himself,' as Tarrant asserted.

Chamberlain, who seemed to be running round in circles,

finding his approach to America had fallen flat, sought a Swede, a wealthy businessman, to offer Hitler a Lucullan feast if he would refrain from war.

'Going round with the hat!' wrathfully exploded Tarrant.

Hitler was jubilant since he had secured that Soviet pact, and with Britain still hopeful of a peaceful settlement between himself and Poland, his invasion of Poland, his ultimate prize, looked to be a certainty; but this he was keeping up his sleeve. He had fixed an attack on Poland for 25 August, but the Anglo–Polish alliance decided him to delay it. With a handful of dust thrown in Britain's eyes he demanded that a Polish intermediary be sent to Berlin and negotiate for a settlement, well aware that the Poles would refuse, but this was considered by Chamberlain to be a not unreasonable request.

'What!' demanded Tarrant, as reported by Noel when she, with Sinclair and Rhoda Penfold, was dining at Archie's flat. 'What in the name of all insanity can these old women in the Commons think they can gain by a settlement which will prove worth no more than the paper it is written on?'

Said Sinclair: 'They'll do anything to keep out of it, or rather Chamberlain will.'

'Not I!' Colin banged a fist on the table. 'Although thanks to the Huns in the last war I would *have* to keep out of it. As for you,' he turned to Sinclair, 'how comes it that your various visits to Munich and Frankfurt selling books or visiting your – relatives in Germany haven't managed to keep us out of it – or have they?'

'I have no relatives in Germany,' was the answer, 'or none that I am aware of. And no relations *with* Germany more than the selling of books. But as far as I can see,' he added cryptically, 'the sands of time are running down.'

'And so are we,' chimed in Rhoda Penfold. The years had dealt lightly with her. In her late seventies she could still express herself in no mean terms in an argument or for a cause, as she had spoken thirty-odd years before in many women's suffrage demonstrations. 'If we had the voice to speak,' she declared, 'we should have muzzled Hitler at Munich instead of handing him a bouquet wrapped in a scrap of paper. And even now' – she glared round at the four of them seated at the table – 'even *now* with an explosion imminent that could blow up the whole of Europe, as you,' to Sinclair, 'should know if you are in *our* Foreign Office and not Hitler's. Bah! I've no patience with Chamberlain, that ostrich-headed fool going begging Hitler for peace. Peace!' she snorted. 'If we had a voice in Parliament other than that Astor woman, who can't be heard above a squeak, we'd have muzzled Hitler long ago. And now at all costs, says Chamberlain, if we want to save our skins, we will keep out of it.'

But we couldn't keep out of it.

On 1 September news came that German troops had invaded Poland, and head-lines in the evening papers announced:

GERMAN AIRCRAFT BOMB WARSAW

Further details, relayed over the wireless and repeated in the morning press, gave it that the Poles had appealed to their ally, Britain, for help. This resulted in a warning to Hitler – not to be taken as an ultimatum – that if Germany would suspend hostilities a peaceable solution might yet be arranged.

Mussolini was reported to be considering negotiations since neither he, pledged to Germany, nor France, allied to Britain, was anxious to be dragged into war. Bonnet, the French Foreign Minister, on tenterhooks lest France be the next to suffer air attack with her army not sufficiently mobilized and dreading to be plunged into the conflict, was still hopeful that Mussolini's mediation might prevent what appeared to be inevitable.

'Not a hope!' went the opinion of the man in the street,

while the whole nation stood agog, and aghast at the news on 2 September, that the Prime Minister even now, at this eleventh hour, was holding out against an ultimatum.

'*We want war!*' went the cry in and out of Parliament; and the Commons, of whom the majority in Chamberlain's National Government echoed the man in the street, sat glumly silent when Chamberlain had inclined to negotiate with Germany that hostilities with Poland should cease.

But Arthur Greenwood, the Labour leader, was on his feet shouting at the House:

'Every minute's delay', he thundered, 'means loss of life to imperil our national interest and our honour!'

Amidst an uproar of cheers it was unanimously decided, despite Chamberlain's noncommittal silence, that war must be declared. Chamberlain, who could at last have realized how he had been tricked by Hitler, was forced to uphold the Commons' unanimity.

At nine o'clock the next morning on that fatal 3 September 1939 the British ultimatum was delivered to Germany. It received no reply. Two hours later, at eleven o'clock, came the Prime Minister's world-wide announcement:

BRITAIN IS AT WAR WITH GERMANY

SIX

September 3rd 1939

We were at breakfast this morning when Archie arrived just after we had heard the P.M. issue an ultimatum to Germany. Archie said he wanted to be in at the death with us! He has taken the keenest interest in everything that has been going on between Britain and Germany ever since Munich. He stayed here to listen to Chamberlain's announcement of war.

'And now,' said Archie, 'the curtain is rung up on the greatest conflict in the history of the world!'

Colin sat there silent and sulky, with 'Tim' stretched out stiffly in front of him. 'But for this,' he muttered, 'I'd have been in it.'

'But you *are* in it,' I told him. 'Even if we are the Cinderellas of the services, as the Post Warden calls us, we also serve.'

'And wait,' he said gloomily.

He has had no attacks, at least none to worry about, for months. Sir Jeremy said any interesting occupation would be of assistance in arresting occurrences, but he had found nothing to do since he left Paris and would have been at a loose end if he hadn't joined the A.R.P.

Then suddenly while we sat there after hearing the announcement, and I think the three of us were feeling a bit of a shock although we had been expecting it for the last week, the wailing banshee howl of the sirens came over the air.

'So this is it!' cried Colin, shaken out of his gloom.

'They're trying a Warsaw on us! Come on, let's get going.'

He started up and limped to the door. Tim has not been behaving too well of late; he needs adjusting. Colin went to fetch his tin hat and gas mask and brought me mine when Latimer appeared.

'May I take this opportunity, sir (always imperturbable), 'of giving in my notice from this day month?'

'Why – what!' exclaimed Colin. 'You can't!'

'Pardon me, sir, I can and I fear I must. You may remember I am on the reserve of my – of our regiment, sir.'

'But you are over age,' repeated Colin in a stare.

'No, sir, excuse me, sir, I am forty-five and when I joined the Rifle Brigade I was barely twenty, but owing to my flat feet, sir, I was posted as a batman.'

Colin rammed on his tin hat saying:

'Your flat feet wouldn't have mattered in the trenches.'

'No, sir, but this won't be trench warfare, mostly air force and tanks, sir, and I would still be wanted as mess servant or batman.'

'You'd better learn to fly and join the R.A.F. Hey! that's an idea! You don't need two legs to fly; I'll join the R.A.F. with you and Tim could do his stuff.'

He knew he couldn't and Latimer knew he couldn't, Tim or no Tim, because he wouldn't pass his medical, not since the legacy had materialized after he was invalided out.

But Latimer let him think so and saw us off to the post with: 'The R.A.F. would just suit you, sir.'

We were all assembled at the post – waiting. Our Deputy Post Warden had been in the Navy. It was his idea to have action stations for wardens to man at different sections of our area. Our Post Warden was busy marking on a rota pinned to the board where each one of us was to be posted at our nearest action station in an alert. He should have had that all fixed before today, but I suppose like a good many others he thought that Chamberlain's ultimatum would call it off.

So we waited . . . and we waited, expecting any minute to hear the raiders. Nothing happened; then one of the full-time wardens who had been a miner and applied to join the Army in 1938 before Munich but had failed to pass his medical called out: 'They're here, the sods!' And there they were overhead – or so we thought. We made a simultaneous dash for our respective action stations, wondering if we would have the first incident in our area. . . . Still nothing. It was our own aircraft, the R.A.F. reconnoitring. But at any rate it gingered up the evacuation of the school children for the supposed dangers of bombing, and of mothers with children under five. We were all fed up with this false alarm, but it wasn't only our regional alarm, the whole of London had heard the sirens.

'Just Hitler's bluff,' Colin said; and we thought that would be all it was and France would come to terms with Hitler when he had finished with Poland . . .

'The phoney war', as the Americans dubbed that interim peaceful few months since the declaration, continued without any German attack upon Britain, yet full precautions for civilian safety were enforced. Street lighting was extinguished, to result in as many deaths on the roads as any bombing would have caused. . . . Blackout in every household was demanded, besides the evacuation of school children of the poorer classes, while children of the wealthier were removed from cities to rural districts or sent to Canada or America, with nurses or their mothers. When, during the ensuing months, no bombs fell, most of the evacuated children returned, greatly to the relief of those who had to billet them. Many were the tales, doubtless exaggerated, of the verminous condition of some of the evacuees, badly brought up, lacking any parental authority, and of the damage done to the once 'stately' homes where, long sufferingly, many had been lodged.

Until May 1940 the 'phoney' war or, as the French called it, the '*drôle de guerre*', dragged on, after the tension following the fall of Poland had subsided. As Tarrant, according to Noel, said: 'It seems to be a storm in a tea cup, yet the storm could be transferred to a cauldron boiling over and then —'

Yes, and then?

Hitler, temporizing, was holding out an olive branch to Britain and France in the hope, if any such overture were accepted, that the western powers would be blamed for the continuance of hostilities. But as might have been expected and as Hitler cunningly foresaw, the olive branch withered when received and returned by the recipients with no comment.

Even when Hitler was still concentrating on devastated but courageously resistant Poland, with the British Expeditionary army garrisoned on the Maginot line, the British forces sustained only a few first casualties. But the Navy came in for more serious losses with the sinking of the aircraft carrier *Courageous* and the battleship *Royal Oak*. Yet still, to the less initiated, it looked as if the war would be over by Christmas or in the New Year.

'Do you really think it will be over soon?' Noel asked Sinclair during her time off duty for, as a part-time warden, she managed to go on with her work at Sinclair's flat.

'No, it won't be over soon,' was the reply. 'Chamberlain, ever optimistic, believes that Germany's military machine will break down, for if Hitler hasn't enough oil his industry will come to a halt. It won't. The U-boats are taking their toll of our merchandise but we have got our own back for the sinking of eight of our cargo ships by the *Graf Spee* in chasing her to Montevideo where Hitler ordered her to be scuttled. Don't you read or listen to the news?'

'I have not been following the news much of late,' she said apologetically, 'having to read that manuscript to do the jacket for this best-seller, as you all think it will be, about our Civil War. It's very well done, particularly as it's by an American who seems to know as much or more about our history – or at any rate about the Civil War – than many of us would know.'

'But,' he said, 'she isn't American. She is English, born, bred, and married here in London – to me.'

From the memoirs she tells us:

I was stunned. 'You – your wife!' I managed to articulate for my mouth was dry and tasted suddenly of lemons. 'The art department told me the manuscript had been sent from America and is to be published in New York and I understood the author is American. Her name – it's – is not your name.'

'She writes under her maiden name.'

I felt dizzy. The room was in a spin. He came to me, held me, and with his mouth to my ear whispering: 'My darling, she is here – in London and not New York. She rang me yesterday from Brown's Hotel.'

'But – the divorce!' I wrenched myself away from him. 'You told me she wanted a divorce.'

'I told you she came back to England because of pending war.'

'And to you?' I said weakly, 'has she come back to you?'

'No. She has another interest and he is also here. The one who came over with her on the boat.'

'On a U-boat?' I made a joke of it – with an effort, and then idiotically began to cry. Not aloud, silently, with trickling tears. He took his handkerchief and wiped them, saying:

'You haven't to mind this. She won't interfere with us. In any case even if there were a divorce you have always said you won't marry me.'

'I know, but I thought you had finished with her and now she is in daily touch and sight of you. She can see you all the time if she wants to see you and if you want to see her.'

'But I don't . . . Listen.' He sat down in the chair and

pulled me to him onto his knee. 'Let me tell you what I should have told you long ago and would have told you had you asked me.'

'What is it you ought to have told?' I was still feeling sore and apprehensive. She, his wife, here! And what about us? And as if he took that thought from me – we so often knew what the other was thinking, being so much at oneness together – he said:

'All I am, all there is of me is yours, now and for ever. And this I knew the moment I saw you when you first came into my life, a chance encounter on the Ponte Vecchio.'

'Yes.' I felt withdrawn from him. She, a shadowy third had come between us, no shadow now, but a substance . . . 'You were with Barton in Florence. You didn't matter to me then. You were just, as you say, a chance encounter. And I thought that you and Barton were —'

He interrupted quickly, 'We were not. Marcia, my wife, as she was —'

'And still is,' I reminded him.

'No, only that she bears my name as with you and Colin, less, in fact, than you and he because you live under the same roof.'

'Perhaps she will live under your roof too.'

'She will not!' he said fiercely and held me closer. I freed myself and got up and sat at his desk opposite him.

'You were going to tell me about – your wife.'

'I want you to understand —' he spoke with hesitating pauses, as the words were reluctantly dragged out of him. I gave him no encouragement.

'We, she and I – we were in Florence when I met you – at least she had been in Florence with me and with Sybil – whom you have always known as Barton since your art school days. She —' he paused again. I saw his hand clench on the arm of his chair – 'she was a – is a cousin of Sybil's. That is how I – how we got to know each other. She – Marcia was older than I. Older by a few years, and much older in experience. Then war broke out, and I joined up.

When I came back we met again. Sybil was married then to her porpoise of a husband – that tycoon. I was – yes, I suppose I was in love with her. I had seen no women in those hellish four years, except on leave and then they were only *pour passer le temps*. I got a Blighty one at Passchendaele, was in hospital over there, and sent back so soon as I was fit again. She was a V.A.D. . . . She nursed me some of the time, and we met again at Sybil's house and . . . I married her. We joined Sybil in Florence at the time you were there, and it was then – quite suddenly – she informed me it was all over between us and – she went off to Rome. She had found someone else. There were three more after him. Wonder it was she stayed so long with me.'

I found my voice to ask:

'Did you mind?'

'That she left me? Yes. Not that I was in love with her then. I know that I never loved her, not as I love you – being *in* love is not the same. There was nothing real in our marriage. No more than,' a bitter smile came upon his mouth, 'legalized copulation, and that had become,' he shrugged, 'just a habit. Does all this hurt you?'

'No. Not if she became just a habit. And suppose, if we married that *I* should become a habit . . .' And, getting up I took the sketch for her book jacket from the desk where I had put it, and had brought for him to see.

He came to me, saying:

'You think you'll become a habit with me? But you *are* a habit with me, and one that I can never do without. How do you suppose I could endure life, my life, without the habit of *you*? Your surprised eyebrows' – he ran a finger along them both – 'that are almost up to the fringe of your hair – and your blunt-cornered mouth that is even now twitching with that inner laugh of yours, as if you hid a chuckle deep down here.' He touched my breast over my heart and then caught me close to him. 'My darling, believe me, it isn't going to make a scrap of difference, unless —'

'Unless?'

'Unless you wish it and let her sue for a divorce. I think that is why she is here. Off with the third – or fourth – old love and on with the new.'

'I wouldn't wish it. If she wants to divorce you let her, but it must be always the same with us as we are now though there is one thing I *do* wish,' and taking the sketch I had made for her book jacket, I tore it across. 'I am not giving her this for her book. You can tell your art editor I don't like it. You must get someone else to do it. I am not indispensable.'

'You are indispensable,' he said huskily, 'to me.'

*   *   *

In November 1939 the first German bombs were dropped in Britain on a small island off the Shetlands, but while the U-boats continued their merciless attacks on our merchant ships and convoys, Britain suffered no serious threat from German aircraft.

Russia, who a few months earlier had been on the point of alliance with us, held back uncommitted and uncertain of a united strength between France and Britain in support of the balance against Germany. In August 1939 Ribbentrop had signed the Nazi–Soviet pact just before the invasion of Poland. And Russia, having successfully gained control of the Baltic states, Latvia, Esthonia, and Lithuania, invaded Finland. The Finns put up a valiant resistance at first and defeated the Russian troops, yet still the United Kingdom stayed free from German aggression except on the high seas.

In January 1940 Winston Churchill, First Lord of the Admiralty, announced in a world broadcast: 'Everyone is wondering what is happening about the war. For months past the Nazis have been uttering ferocious threats of what they are going to do to the British and French, but so far it is the neutral states that are bearing the brunt of German malice and cruelty.'

'I'm getting sick of waiting,' complained Noel, as were others in Civil Defence, and indeed throughout the country. In April 1940 Germany seized Denmark unopposed, and captured most of the airfields in Norway. And in May of that year, during the evacuation of Narvik, our Navy in defence of Norway suffered the loss of the aircraft carrier *Glorious* and two of our destroyers, but we got our own back when we sank three German cruisers and ten of their destroyers.

Yet June was a black month for the helpless victims of Hitler's aggression, although business went on as usual for Londoners. We hear from Noel that Birdie Amersham and other socialites, in cheerful defiance of gloomy news and the ever expectant fear of raids, gave cocktail parties, luncheons, dinners, despite that ration books had now been issued, but not until later did the combined distribution of ration books and identity cards cause any noticeable 'tightening of our belts', as was jocularly stated by the Ministry of Food.

It was at one of Birdie Amersham's cocktail parties after the invasion of Norway that Noel related how Barton, who was there and whom she had not seen for some time, had said:

'So you're doing your bit.' Noel had just been equipped with her A.R.P. uniform of navy blue laced with gold cords, peaked cap and trousers. 'Most attractive.' Barton screwed up her eyes, regarding her professionally. 'I expect Sinclair finds it so, and you'll have all the Lizzies after you. Do I hear he has given you a room in his flat for – a studio?'

'Yes, because there isn't room in our flat for a studio now. We have to keep Latimer's room ready for him when he is home on leave. His regiment has not gone out yet.' How, she wondered, did Barton know that J. L. S. was letting her use a room in his flat? And did she know more than that? . . . Just then Colin came up to them.

'Amersham says this Narvik disaster and the invasion

of Holland plus the bombing of Rotterdam mean that Chamberlain's had it and Churchill's in the running for P.M.'

'About time too,' as Noel notes in her journal. 'J. L. S. says we will lose the war if Churchill doesn't take over, but I wish he'd hurry up and not leave Chamberlain to dodder on with it. And now J. L. S. – (I can never think of him as James) – is off to Datchet to fetch his motor-boat. It is in the boathouse there. I didn't know he had a motor-boat as well. The people to whom he let the house furnished have gone to Canada with their three children, at least their mother has. The man joined up. He is in the Territorials. When I asked J. L. S. why he wanted the motor-boat, he said, "There will be many more motor-boats and every kind of boat required in a day or two." Which is all I could get out of him.'

And on the very morning that Sinclair went to Datchet we are told in Noel's memoirs:

Just after he had gone, saying he would be back again some time . . . (Some time! I couldn't get more out of him than that) I had a telephone call on the extension he had put in the room I use as a studio, and heard:

'May I speak to Mrs Harbord?'

'Mrs Harbord speaking.'

'This is Mrs Sinclair. I wonder if I may come and see you. I know all about you from my cousin, Sybil Farrell.'

'Oh . . . yes, I . . .'

I was completely lost. Had nothing to say. To come and see me . . . Why? And where? Not here. No. Not *here*! . . . But the telephone. The same number as his. How did she know I am here? From Barton who had said so bitchily about him lending me the studio? . . . And how does *she* know? I suppose Birdie told her. I met her at Birdie's only last week and I had told Birdie, like a fool, that J. L. S. has lent me a room at his flat because there was no room for one at home . . . All this flashed through me while I hung on to the receiver and found voice enough to say:

'Yes, do come and see me but I am on duty most days when I am not working here. Your husband' – I managed to get that out quite strongly, my voice at first having faded to nothing – 'he lets me a room in his flat as a studio.'

'Of course. You do his book jackets, don't you? And were going to do mine, as I was told, but they engaged another artist. I suppose you hadn't time with your A.R.P. duties especially as Marriott is rushing publication through to produce simultaneously with the American publishers. So please, can we meet? I want so much to know you, having heard all about you from Sybil. She knew your husband before you did. So will you have luncheon with me tomorrow?'

'Thank you, but – I am on duty tomorrow.'

'But surely you have time off for luncheon?'

'Not tomorrow I'm afraid.'

'Then shall we say the day after tomorrow?'

I couldn't go on refusing – making her suspicious if she wasn't already.

'Yes, I . . .'

'Then twelve forty-five at Claridges?'

'But I' – my voice was fading again, 'I – how shall I know you?'

'That's all right. I know you, I mean I've seen you – you were pointed out to me at — Well, at any rate I shall know you and I'll be waiting in the lounge at Claridges and I,' she gave a tinkling laugh, 'I will accost you.'

Of that meeting with Marcia Sinclair she gives a precise record, written while on night duty at the wardens' post.

J. L. S. phoned me from Datchet where he has gone to fetch his motor-boat. Doesn't say what he wants it for. I didn't tell him about her ringing me up and inviting me to lunch. I couldn't say what I wanted to say on the phone, nor to ask him how she knew I was using a room in his flat, and his phone number. I could, of course, have refused to see her, but out of curiosity I did meet her as arranged at Claridges. I was in uniform as I was on the rota for duty at 15.00 hours so there wouldn't have been time to go home and change had I gone in mufti.

Naturally I wanted to see what she looked like as a cousin of Barton. I wondered if there would be a family likeness. None. She is the complete antithesis of the pale Botticellian enchantment of Barton. She is tall, dark, has a good figure, might easily be a model except that she is a bit past it. If older than J. L. S., as he says, and they married years ago, she must be well in her later forties. Her skin is a clear white and has scarcely a line. I wonder how many facials she has had to keep it like that. (I'm being bitchy!) She was very well turned out in what I recognized as a Molyneux from his last show, which I went to – but couldn't, of course, buy anything. Her eyes are lovely, with long black lashes and hardly any make up.

'So glad you could make it,' she said having spotted me coming in. 'I recognized you at once.' . . . How? Where could she have seen me? Anyway I would find that out later.

'Come and have a drink,' she said, and led me to the table where she had been sitting. A man got up from there as we approached and I saw he was that Baron von Sveinshort – if that's how it's spelt which I'm sure it isn't – who had dined with us at J. L. S.'s flat more than two years ago before Munich, when I dropped that brick about him being a flying ace in the war. I wondered why, if he had been a German pilot in the last war, he is here in England now that we are in the second war. And also why he should be a friend of Marcia Sinclair and of J. L. S. . . . . I am thankful I knew about his marriage to her before she phoned me. How awful if she had announced to me that she was his wife if I *hadn't* known!

(While I write this old 'Mountie' is snoring his head off. We call him 'Mountie' because about fifty years ago he was in the Canadian Mounted Police. He insisted on joining Civil Defence as a full-timer, being too old for anything else, and is always on night duty hoping when they start bombing us he will be in the thick of it because most of the raids will be at night. He is lying on the truckle bed where we take turns for an every two hours break. Both of us are on the phone when I'm on night duty and in charge of the post but I never wake him, I let him sleep on.) Where was I? Oh, yes. This Baron Thingummy. He was saying:

'How wonderful to see you again, Mrs Harbord. It is too long since I had the pleasure of meeting you when we dined with Mr Sinclair at least two years ago. I have rarely seen your husband since then, although we are members of the same club. We used to play squash together!'

So he belongs to the R.A.C. too! – and a German flying ace or was . . . I said, 'My husband seldom goes to his club these days.'

He gave me a dazzling show of teeth. I remembered that when he smiled he had shown rows of teeth except when I dropped that 'almighty brick' and received a dirty look. 'None of us,' he was saying, 'has much time these days for relaxation. We have other more pressing commitments. But I miss my games of squash.'

He spoke perfect English with no trace of an accent. Then Marcia beckoned a waiter for drinks and asked us what we would have.

'No more for me,' he told her. 'I regret I must leave you now.' (I saw they had already had drinks. The waiter was removing the empty glasses.) 'I stayed just long enough to see this charming lady whom you told me was to be your guest. I hope', he showed more teeth, 'that we shall meet again. Goodbye,' to Marcia, 'thanks for the drink. I'll be seeing you.' And off he went, stopping on the way out to speak to a Brass Hat at a table with two women. Why, I asked myself, is he, an ex-German pilot, not interned and on friendly terms with our staff officers? No wonder the Americans call it a 'phoney war'!

She ordered a gin and tonic for me and she had a champagne cocktail.

She said: 'James and I knew Otto', (Otto. So that's his name thought I), 'when we were married – I mean before our marriage packed up. We met originally at Menton after the war, of course, and I believe he is naturalized.'

'Why isn't he interned?' I asked. 'Isn't it a bit unusual for a German who fought against us in the last war to come and live here as one of us?'

'Oh, no. We take them all in. We have German Jewish doctors as consultants here who escaped from the Nazis after Hitler came into power, and some of them are as good if not better than many of our own. Of course they have to take British medical degrees before they can practise here. He, the Baron, hates the Nazis and Hitler – they don't have to be Jews to hate them. Shall we go in?'

She had booked a table, by a strange coincidence the very table J. L. S. and I had when I lunched with him there that first time. The waiter passed us each a menu. She asked me what I would have and was told: 'Something light, please. I usually only have a snack for lunch.'

'So what about smoked salmon for a start?'

Smoked salmon for a start was agreed with chicken supreme for her, an omelette for me, and a bottle of Liebfraumilch. While attending to our smoked salmon, she remarked: 'I expect you were surprised when I rang you up.'

'I was rather, especially as you knew where to find me.'

'I knew you were at James's flat – if not living with him there, working there. And if you wished to sleep with him, you could, and nobody nor your husband the wiser. You don't have to sleep with a man only at night.'

All this was said as if it were the most jocular triviality.

123

But never before in my life have I experienced what romantic novelists describe as 'her heart stood still'. Well, mine did; or it may have missed a beat or two which I suppose is the same thing, but I momentarily lost my sense and speech. She was smiling at me, lifting her glass. 'Cheers! Drink your wine. You've gone quite pale. You don't have to panic, you know, because *I* know . . . Well? Have you nothing to say?'

I took my glass and drank; my heart that had slowed or stopped, began to race and emboldened me to tell her, evenly and cool:

'I have this to say – since you assume that I and your husband, or the man you married who is no longer your husband except in name, are lovers – Yes, we are. How you happened to know this does not concern me, nor do I care. My husband and I don't live together as man and wife any more than you live with the man you married.'

'Then you don't care nor do you mind if I cite you as co-respondent in a case for divorce?'

She was still smiling. None could have been a more cordial hostess to her guest. She might have been discussing the next course and if I would prefer sweet or savoury. In fact just then a waiter passed with a trolley of fruit and she stayed him saying to me: 'Will you have strawberries? I will – and cream,' to the waiter.

'Not for me, thanks.' I was still cool and smiling back at her. Strangely I quite liked her for the way she was bringing this off. To confront her husband's mistress with the knowledge she had gleaned and intended to use in so easy and nonchalant a manner, might have been contrived in a play by Noël Coward.

She, being served with strawberries, asked: 'But you will have coffee, won't you?'

'Yes, thanks,' and to another waiter hovering with coffee, 'White, please.' Then to her: 'I'm sorry but I'm on duty at three so I'll have to hurry. But may I hope that, if you intend to go ahead with this, there will be no publicity?

My husband is – well, he's not up to taking a shock, and it would be a shock if he read it in the papers.'

'I understand. Of course there won't be any press news about it. Yet I suggest, to save you any embarrassment, that James produces other evidence.'

'You mean hotel evidence with a woman provided by a solicitor. They do, I believe, provide women conveniently to play these parts.'

'Aren't you marvellous!' she exclaimed dipping strawberries in the cream. 'There's not a woman in a hundred who would take it as you are taking it without any fuss or hysterics.'

'I have been prepared for something of the sort,' I said, 'ever since J. L. S. – James – told me he had a wife. He wanted to be divorced so that we could marry, but I told him I loathe the idea of divorce. I could have divorced Colin if I wished to – but I wouldn't. I don't believe in divorce.'

'Are you a Catholic?'

'No, but if I were anything I would be a Catholic. It is the only true and living Church. Yet I do think that falsely to obtain a divorce by being discovered in flagrant delight is – flagrant hypocrisy.'

She looked across at me with a strawberry poised halfway to her mouth.

'My dear! I can understand why James finds you a *fragrant* – not flagrant – delight! You seem years younger than you are. I know you must be in your thirties because, as an art student, you were a contemporary of Sybil, but you look about thirteen with those wide-apart eyes and childishly naïve expression, and yet you can take it so matter-of-factly when I confront you with a possible service from the – what is it? – the High Court and Probate Division – or something of the sort. I had some such beastly thing served on me once by the wife of a friend of mine with whom she thought, incorrectly, I was having an affair. I managed to convince her that her husband and I were not guilty. But I can assure you I didn't take it as lightly and sensibly as you do. She rang me up in the middle of the night to tell me, "I know you have been sleeping with my husband." I said almost the same thing to you, didn't I – over the smoked salmon?'

'How did she know, and were you or had you – I mean,' I floundered, 'been enjoying, er, flagrant delight with him?'

'No. I was driving with him. He had given me a lift from Devonshire where I had been staying – oh, this was before I married James when I was about nineteen and as starry-eyed as you are or seem to be, and the car broke down, cars often did in those days, and we had to stay the night at a hotel on the way. I was recognized by someone who knew her and me – and told her. We had separate rooms and signed the register in our own names. Neither of us – he nor I – knew a thing about it till the papers were served on us. We both managed, with solicitors, to convince her that she hadn't a case. Not a cat's chance in hell, as my solicitor said, but I didn't take it so lightly as you do. Of course I was much younger than you are now, and quite unsophisticated but it gave me a jerk, I can tell you. When I married James – I was older than he and had been initiated long before then. I'd been to America, having made a smash hit with a first novel, came back here and met James who fell for me in a big way, but it didn't last. I'm not his type. You are. I see that. So why don't you marry him?'

'I am married, that's why. I am not going to divorce Colin and I don't wish him to divorce me. And I care too much for James to marry him.'

I glanced down at my wrist watch, and got up from the table. 'I must leave you now as I have to be on duty.' I held out my hand. 'Perhaps you will lunch with me next time and tell me how you found out about – us. Goodbye and thanks for the luncheon. I've liked meeting you.'

'No wonder,' she said, 'that James wants you. Yes, we

certainly must meet again if it won't interfere with the divorce. Ring me. I'll be at Brown's Hotel for the next month or so.'

*   *   *

Sinclair had not yet returned from Datchet. He had been gone almost a week after that luncheon and we can well believe Noel was 'in a state', as her journal records it, dated May 29th 1940.

. . . Not a word, not a line from him. Why hasn't he phoned? Has she confronted him as she did me with divorce? If so, why couldn't he have come straight to me? Is she trying to get him back with threats of divorce citing me, and sooner than I should be involved he disappears . . .? No. That isn't it. He would be only too delighted to be divorced, even if it did involve me, and any publicity could always be hushed up. . . . But why doesn't he get in touch with me? If she has told him what she intends to do he would surely have let me know. . . . Where *is* he? Has there been an accident with the motor-boat? Could he have been bringing it back to London by the river and been run down by . . . Impossible. He is far too good with boats, any sort of boat. How much longer must I wait to know where he is and why . . .

There is no more in the journal under this date but news came swiftly over the air and in the papers.

DUNKIRK EVACUATED

Churchill, who had now succeeded Chamberlain as Prime Minister, had warned the House of 'hard and heavy tidings'. How hard and heavy were those tidings was soon to be known with the destruction of the Belgian Army and the whole abandonment of Belgium.

What was known as 'Operation Dynamo' brought the French storming their way to the besieged town of Dunkirk to be swept back by the Germans 'like a sharp scythe', as Churchill put it in a memorable speech to the House of Commons on 4 June. It was a military disaster for both the French and British, but the British Expeditionary Force bore the brunt of it. While our Navy, helped by many merchantmen, strained every effort to embark the British and French troops assembled in their thousands on the beaches of France, Calais and Boulogne, the full weight of German bombing was centred on the beach at Dunkirk. If the evacuation of thousands of British and French troops could be regarded as a military disaster, it was also a triumphant victory. Every sort of voluntary seacraft from rowing-boats to fishing smacks, from river ferries to pleasure yachts, a fleet of boats both great and small joined our warships and hospital ships to embark the stranded armies in the sand dunes on Dunkirk's ravaged beach.

For four days and nights the ceaseless thunder of Hitler's *Luftwaffe* crashed down upon their victims, yet the casualties were few compared with the hundreds of thousands saved. Undaunted by the enemy's bombardment from sea and air and the deadly U-boats, the Navy's rescue ships and those fearless little ships plied back and forth across the perilous strip of sea that divided England from France.

In that fierce struggle for deliverance, the courage and devotion of rescuers and rescued alike never faltered. Many of those brought back returned to help in the transport of the British Expeditionary Force and the men of the French armies.

The Royal Air Force mustered all its strength, which was less than half that of Hitler's Air Force, to strike at the German bombers and miraculously succeeded in hurling them back.

'Out of the jaws of death and shame,' vociferated Churchill to the House of Commons, 4 June 1940, 'nearly a thousand ships of all kinds carried to safety 335,000 men, British and French . . . We shall go on to the end. We shall

128

fight on the beaches, we shall fight in the fields and in the streets and on the hills, we shall never surrender and in God's good time, the new world with all its power and might will step forth to the rescue and liberation of the old.'

Among those 'ships of all kinds' to whom those many thousands of armed forces owed their lives, was the motor-boat owned and manned by J. L. Sinclair. But not until his return to London did Noel learn of his part in the evacuation of Dunkirk when he telephoned her to say he was back again.

'Where have you been?' she wished to know and was told:

'I have been joy riding or more correctly surf riding. Are you on duty tonight?'

'No, but Colin is.'

'Then come to me here.'

'I'd rather not. I've never been to the flat at night, and especially now, because —'

'Because what? Have you something to tell me?'

'Yes, but not on the phone.'

'It's quite safe to talk on this line. I'm on to secrecy.'

'Oh, so! A secret service line. I began to guess as much when you are so often engaged — not on business at Marriott's but — elsewhere, at Whitehall, for instance?'

'I repeat, will you come to the flat this evening?'

'No, you can come here. I'll cook you a chop. . . . At seven then.'

At seven she saw him, and was shocked to see that though tanned by the sun his face bore weatherbeaten traces and had thinned, was hollow cheeked.

'What exactly have you been doing *surf*-riding!'

He told me, she relates, what he had been doing in the fewest possible words, making light of it.

'I took my motor-boat from Datchet when we had wind of —'

'We?' I interrupted. 'Who are "We"? And what wind blew you surf riding? And where?'

'Anyone who had any sort of seacraft ran for Dunkirk.'

'Dunkirk!' I rushed at him. 'So that's it! And you were one of them . . . No wonder you look washed out. Were you at it twenty-four hours day and night, as it said on the wireless? And here was I thinking you had backed out of – of me because she – or did she tell you?'

'She? Who's "she"?' He pulled me down beside him on the sofa. 'And what had she to tell?'

I told him of the luncheon and all she had said and he knew nothing about it! If she had intended telling him he was already on his way to France in his 'little ship'.

He heard me out.

'I see.' He was suddenly quiet; very still. His face – I had never seen his face closed like this. It became a mask. And then:

'I knew her capable of devious ways of getting *her* way, but I had not thought she would stoop to having me watched.'

'Watched!' I gasped. 'Do you mean she had a private detective watching your flat – and me?'

'Yes, since she wants to marry her latest, who is – I believe, my friend, the flying ace.'

'What are you saying? Not that Baron von Thingummy?'

'That very Baron Thingummy whom I have known for a good many years.'

'Before he became a flying ace in the last war?'

He nodded.

'Yes, I knew him at Bonn. I went to Bonn University to perfect my knowledge of German when I came down from Cambridge.'

'Marcia said she knew him years ago when you and she met him at Menton and that he afterwards became naturalized. Is he naturalized?'

'Possibly.'

'Is he married?'

'Not to my knowledge, although,' he gave me a twink-ling look, 'he may have avoided the legal tie of marriage – as we, or as you, will have it.'

'Never mind about me. What about Marcia and this German friend of hers and – yours? You say he is "possibly" naturalized.'

'He may or may not be naturalized but I do know that his sister married an American and took American nationality.'

'There seems to be,' I said pointedly, 'a lot of inter-marriage between English or Americans with Germans. What of your grandmother or grandfather, for instance? And what of *his* parents or grandparents? And why isn't he interned?'

He tweaked the tip of my nose, a trick of his when teasing.

'Do you think *I* ought to be interned?'

'How should I know? But what I do know is that as you are, or were, in the Foreign Office, I wonder you can be so friendly with a German, whether naturalized or not, who was a flying ace in the last war – for Germany. Besides our Post Warden is always warning us not to discuss in public places anything that might be overheard by enemy agents or fifth columnists.'

'A wise precaution. The fifth columnist bug is con-tagious, and careless talkers could drop a seed that might be reaped into a goodsome harvest if it fell on the ears of those who lie in wait to glean such droppings from some of your fellow wardens or – even from you!'

He was still chaffing me but I felt uneasy. How much or how little did he know of this baron or, come to that, how much did I know of him and his work other than his pub-lishing? Yes, I *had* caught the bug!

'How well', I persisted, 'does Marcia know this baron?'

'I understand she met him again in New York during the August of '39. He often goes to New York to see his sister or on his own business.'

'What is his own – business?'

'Which', J. L. S. said, suddenly cagey, 'is one of yours – or mine.'

I didn't like this.

'He was living here,' I reminded him, 'long before the outbreak, wasn't he? And he played squash with you at your club.'

'Yes, and he's a damn good player.'

'I hope he didn't beat you.'

'He did once and never again. But he had a Frenchman with him and he did beat me. The only time the French will beat me or any one of us, in spite of France letting us down.'

'France! Letting us down?'

'Just about. And I gather that our friend is off to Washington to tell Roosevelt that Marshal Pétain is asking Hitler for an armistice – a separate peace.'

'Off to Washington?' I repeated, parrot-like. 'Why should he tell Roosevelt that France is grovelling to Hitler for a separate peace? And how could he get to America with all these U-boats in the Atlantic? What's it got to do with America, anyway?'

'Quite something if America could be put off coming in with us.'

'But why should America be put off coming in with us if France backs out of it? They're bound to come in with us sooner or later.'

'Unless our friend – *my* friend – would wish it to be later or not at all.'

I was now properly steamed up.

'I don't understand you about this or about *him*. And why, if he's what you are making me think he is – why don't you intern him, unless —'

'Unless what?'

He was smiling, not at me, at something else – or to himself.

'Unless' – I had to come out with it – 'he, *your* friend, is no friend of ours!'

'I see.' The smile expanded. 'You think I'm a double?'

'You mean – a double agent?' I said, aghast.

I was greatly put about. I'd read some of the spy thrillers that Colin devoured when on night duty at the post.

'Yes,' he lighted a cigarette, cool as you please. 'A double agent or double crosser, working for and/or against us along with a dozen others.

'Why don't you intern your "possibly" naturalized or double agent or fifth columnist friend?'

'He may have that coming to him. . . . And now can't we talk about ourselves for a change? Or do you want to hand me over to the police as another suspected Fifth Columnist?' He stubbed his cigarette out in an ashtray, and crushed me in his arms. 'God! It's good to be doing this —' he kissed me long and close. 'There were times when I thought I'd never do this again, until we meet in Kingdom Come.'

I shuddered. 'All of you – all those little ships – under fire. Being bombed on that beach for four whole days and nights. How did any of you escape with your lives?'

'Some didn't. I was lucky considering that more than a hundred thousand German divisions had cut through Calais and Boulogne, and the French went down before them like mown hay – until Dunkirk. They had banked on wiping us out of Dunkirk as they wiped out Holland and Belgium, but we stalled them . . .'

It is evident these two, despite Noel's 'Fifth Columnist bug', were less concerned with the perilous situation that confronted Britain after the fall of France than with their own personal problems. While she admits she lived in daily expectation of divorce papers served upon her, she was relieved, she says, that J. L. S. had agreed, if Marcia really

133

intended to go along with her petition, that they would not defend.

'All I care about,' she told Sinclair, 'is that the press won't get hold of it. I daren't let Colin know.'

'The press will be far too cramped for space with the latest war news to report an undefended divorce case.'

But the confidence of the people remained unshaken, even by the cataclysmic events of the past few weeks when Churchill, in his world broadcasts, could offer nothing but 'toil, blood, tears, and sweat. . . . The whole fury and might of the enemy must be turned on us,' was his message. 'Let us therefore brace ourselves to our duties, and so bear ourselves that, if the British Empire and its Commonwealth last for a thousand years, men will say: "This was their finest hour." '

SEVEN

In August 1940 the people of Britain endured, with stoical fortitude, a series of devastating air raids on the eastern and southern counties when seventy-five daylight raiders were brought down by our R.A.F. and anti-aircraft guns.

When after those four days' attacks Hitler had failed to conquer our coastal air defences he sought to gain supreme mastery of England by a furious onslaught from his bombers upon London at night.

'We had ninety-seven non-stop raids over us,' Noel relates, 'because Jerry was after the stations to the north of our regional area, King's Cross, Euston, Paddington and, of course, the B.B.C. We were in the direct line of them as they came over. We part-timers didn't keep to our voluntary thirty-six hours, we went on voluntary full time as so many of our full-time men had left Civil Defence for the Army before they were called up. So we women, or most of us except the over-fifties, were filling in with Civil Defence before we thought to be conscripted in our age groups. I put my age back when it was certain that conscription for us would come in so that I could be called up with the twenties and not the thirties, for we all thought the war would be over before another year or two. How we were mistaken! We soon realized that we were in for it, 'until,' as Churchill told us in his broadcast of September 11, 'the last vestiges of Nazi tyranny have been burnt out of Europe. . . . This is a time for everyone to stand together and hold firm . . .'

They did hold firm while every day and night the thunder and crash of bombs hurled down upon them.

They stood together bound in one common cause to save and help as far as lay within their power and at risk to their lives, men, women and children. This barbarous bombing of civilians was Hitler's preliminary to his planned invasion.

And so we are told, in an excerpt from her memoirs, of Noel's reaction to her part in 'the Cinderella of the services':

It was the second alert that night but the All Clear went about half an hour later, and no incidents reported on my sector. And Marcia, who, surprisingly, had joined our A.R.P., came on duty for the first time while I was on telephone service. She lived in our area as her flat was just off Portland Place. She was then fully trained and gloried in her uniform. Not the one issued by our equipment officer, ex-Chief Petty Officer Chapman, R.N. (aged at least seventy but admitting to sixty, was torpedoed in the 1914 war). But Marcia wasn't going to wear a cast-off from one of our part-time girls who had joined the W.A.A.F. No, Marcia must have one made for her by a tailor and it was Savile Row cut so I guessed she had it made at the same place that Philpot had his. Philpot was my second favourite man there, passed medically unfit for active service, I mean the Army because we *were* active service actually only not recognized as that . . . Philpot (Potts) was very deaf and often drunk, but although a confirmed alcoholic he never lets up, is always on the spot and terribly generous with pheasants and things which he brings us from his father's place in Berkshire. He used to take Colin and me to dinner and a play whenever we were off duty which of late had been never. And he had his suit made for him at his Savile Row tailor and I'm sure Marcia had hers made there too, for I know he took her there one day.

My *first* favourite man was 'Buckie' – Habbabahkaba – that's what it sounded like (can't spell it). He was African and the Crown Prince of his father, the King or Chief of his tribe. He came over here before the war in 1936 and went to London University where he read economics. He could speak good English as he had been to school in England and he told me he wanted to teach his and neighbouring tribes phonetics so that they could make themselves understood to each other. He said that there would only be a short distance between two tribes. When war broke out he tried to join up but they wouldn't take him. 'Because,' he said, 'of my colour, I suppose, or my nationality.' He said it with no resentment. If they wouldn't have him in the Army they had missed a splendid soldier! So he joined A.R.P. and was one of our best. I used to talk to him more than any of them when I was on post duty and he warden in charge. He was extremely knowledgeable. And when the blitz was doing its damnedest and we were in an incident – we had two land-mines on our sector in one night – and heavy casualties – one child killed – he was in the thick of it. None of us had any fear when 'Buckie' was with us, and except for fires from incendiaries all one could see on a moonless night were his white teeth in his black face to let us know he was there! . . .

Excerpt from her journal dated September 17th 1940

We have just heard that 185 enemy aircraft were brought down and last week they made a daylight raid on Buckingham Palace! Luckily little damage. We are now in the thick of it. Colin in his element. He is on duty day and night. He sleeps – if he ever sleeps – in his uniform except when I insist he undresses and gets into his bed. I always have my uniform ready by my bed to pull over my pyjamas because all we part-timers are wanted now, and are taking voluntary full time. It's been a gruelling week . . .

September 19th

Marcia came into the post this pip emma looking very glamorous in a peaked cap and clever make-up. Colin was

there and Philpot (Potts). She had never been on duty before
when Colin was at the post but he happened to be there
and was just going off when she came in. As soon as she
saw him she recognized him having met him at Barton's
before I ever knew him, years ago.

'Why! It's Colin Harbord!' she exclaimed delightedly.
'I used to see you at my cousin's, Sybil Farrell. Don't say
you've forgotten me.'

'Forgotten *you*!' Colin was never at a loss when baited
with charm which she could turn on at will. 'How could
I forget anyone so lovely!'

I caught Potts' eye and he lowered a lid in the smallest
fraction of a wink.

'You are' – Colin obviously didn't remember her –
'Sybil's cousin, of course!'

'I'm Marcia Sinclair. You know my husband too and so
does Noel.'

'Your husband? Oh, so you are Sinclair's wife?'

'I was – I am – but I have been in America for some
years.'

I felt as if I were standing on the edge of a precipice.
Ever since she had joined the post I had been dreading
something of this sort, but was relieved that her times on
duty had so far never crossed with Colin's. But that they
were bound to meet eventually I knew, and could only
hope she wouldn't tell him about – us. But so far she
seemed to have not made up her mind whether she would
or would not go for divorce.

She was offering him a cigarette from her case, and they
sat together on the truckle bed in the corner where I would
be sleeping in turns with Mountie later tonight. And then,
to my relief, came the alert. We all made for the door,
including Colin, who, although off duty, was always on in
an alert with any others who had been off. From the large
inner room where the P.W. slept came Mrs Amery and
Polly. They had been playing ping-pong. Mrs Amery is one
of the oldest full-timers, in her fifties. Her husband, Major

138

Amery, also a full-timer, was killed in one of these ninety-seven non-stops. Polly (Pauline Dobson) joined up just before the outbreak. Potts calls her Polly The Pride of the Post which, if deliberate alliteration, is not unduly complimentary. She is twenty-four, a lovely natural blonde with primrose-coloured hair in a long bob to her shoulders, a pale primrose skin and large wide-apart grey eyes. She has already been married and divorced, but whether she divorced him or he her we would never know. She is always vague about it and about everything, never sure which of the men – they all queue up for her – is her latest. Potts says he and Colin are the last in the queue, and it's no use trying to jump it as they are both too old for her. 'She won't take on any one of us past forty,' he said.

Polly, leaving Mrs Amery, who is a senior warden with two stripes, crammed on her tin hat and grabbed my arm.

'Noel, stick by me,' she said in her pouting, drawling voice. 'It's going to be hell out there and two's better than one.'

She took out of her jacket pocket a lipstick and compact and in its little mirror she was making up her mouth. I laughed.

'You'll go down game, anyway. All right. Here we go.'

And there we went. It was hell out there, with a landmine on the block of flats in our sector. Wardens from the Westminster area had come to join us as we hadn't enough of our own to cope.

By the dimmed light of our torches and the flare of incendiaries and in the milling crowd of wardens and Heavy Rescue, we thankfully barged into Buckie. We saw he had blood on his face and was staunching it with his handkerchief. It was blood on the white handkerchief we saw and not his face – you can never see his face in the dark.

He told us: 'You two – get back to the post. You shouldn't be out in this.'

'But we are out,' drawled Polly, 'and it 'ud be worse

getting back. He's not likely to give us another one just here.'

I was digging my first-aid box out of my kit bag to plaster him.

'What's got you?' I asked him.

'Nothing. Only a splinter of glass.' And he disappeared in the crowd. We saw him again pushing aside what remained of the revolving doors of the entrance. We followed him – he was on his knees in the scattered glass and debris beside the fallen body of one of the night porters whom I had often seen when passing there on my way to our action station. I recognized him by his uniform. Buckie had his head on his arm and was bending to hear what he tried to say. We heard:

'My wife . . . She was with me . . . Find . . .'

Polly and I went pushing our way through the crowd of wardens, firemen and stretcher bearers. 'How are we to know her?' Polly asked.

I had seen her many times cleaning the steps of the entrance and the hall when I go to fit gas masks on the residents. We found her at last, or what was left of her. I got the ambulance men to take her away . . . Then we saw Colin and Potts. Colin was helping an old lady in a blood-stained nightdress. She was smiling, and saying in a fainting voice:

'I'm more frightened than hurt. Thank you so much,' to Colin, 'and you, too,' to us, 'you dear . . . good . . . brave . . .'

Then her voice stopped. Her head drooped on to Colin's arm . . . She was dead.

Colin laid her down gently. I often wonder how he stands up to it all, never a sign of the 'legacy'. He is at his best now in the Blitz. We were at it until six ack emma today. We got out all the dead, at least those we could find, but on the whole not so many casualties as might have been expected from the complete destruction of almost the whole block. The Heavy Rescue, firemen and ambulances are still at it searching for anyone buried in the shambles.

It is surprising how we get used to it and although Polly says she's scared stiff, she is in the thick of it always and doesn't bat an eyelid . . . Almost the whole block is in ruins. They were evidently after the B.B.C. That's why we get so much of it. There's a lot of signalling going on from the top floors in Harley Street, Portland Place, and all round our area. We spend hours during alerts getting lights out with Jerry overhead and it is usually German refugees who leave chinks in their curtains and no proper blackout.

I went to bed as soon as I got in and slept till eighteen hours when Colin brought me my breakfast. He went on duty again after the All Clear and has only just gone to bed but will get up for the next alert. He never seems to rest.

Throughout September and October the citizens of London suffered the most devastating raids the Germans could hurl at them. The destruction to property was heavy in the working-class areas of the East End, but the docks and the West End of London were also badly hit. The morning after the landmine on the block of flats in her area, Noel telephoned Archie to know if he was all right as there had also been a landmine on Grosvenor Square, and he would have been in the line of it. He said he had some blast and a window broken in his flat and some incendiaries on the roof. He, at over seventy, was fire fighting.

On 21 October Churchill broadcast an address in English and French to the people of France.

'Frenchmen! Tonight I speak to you at your firesides wherever you may be or whatever your fortunes are. . . . Here at home in England under fire of the Boche we do not forget the ties and links that unite us in France. . . . Here in London, which Hitler says he will reduce to ashes and which his aeroplanes are now bombarding, our people are bearing it unflinchingly. . . . Hitler with his tanks and other mechanical devices, and also by Fifth Column intrigues with traitors, has managed to subjugate, for the time being, most of the finest races in Europe . . . And his little Italian accomplice [Mussolini] is trotting along hopefully and hungrily and very timidly at his side . . . What we British ask of you in this present hard and bitter struggle to win the victory is that, if you cannot help us, you will at least not hinder us. . . . Remember we shall never stop, never weary, and never give in! Never will I believe the soul of France is dead . . .'

As Noel related, she heard this broadcast when on telephone duty at the post. There had been two alerts during the evening but only one incident reported in their area. 'Mountie' remained in charge of the post and she, who had already been on duty for twelve hours, was told by him to go home.

'What did you think of Churchill's broadcast to the French?' she asked him.

'Too easy on them,' he answered. 'The French have deserted us and left us to carry on alone.'

'Some of them haven't deserted us,' she reminded him. 'Those French we brought back from Dunkirk are with us, and there is the Resistance in France working underground.'

'You get along home,' Mountie repeated, not to be drawn into a discussion concerning the fall of France which he, an Englishman who had lived most of his life in Canada, could only regard as a treacherous and cowardly desertion of an ally.

Polly then came in to take over the telephone and Noel went off.

On the way to her flat came another alert and she turned back to her action station for, although off duty, she knew that all available part-timers were now needed in the shortage of full-time men wardens, who had been called up for the fighting forces.

142

'Not that we weren't also the fighting forces,' as she recalls it. 'We had as much active service as many of the men out there.' And she told how on one night shortly after Churchill's address to the French she had been in full charge of the post. Mountie was on sick leave, much against his will. He had bronchitis and nothing short of death would keep him from the post unless threatened by doctor's orders. It was, she relates, 'one of our worst nights. Ten houses down in Harley Street and two landmines, one in Portland Place by the B.B.C., and one in Weymouth Street. I was calling the services non-stop when an officer came down into the post which he had no right to do. He was shaking with shock, could hardly speak. I told him he must not be here and he said, 'I can't stay out there. It's worse, far worse than anything – even Dunkirk – with houses falling all round you – and no cover.'

He staggered to a chair and passed out. At first I thought he was drunk but he wasn't. I got him a glass of water, he came to and tried to get up. I told him he could stay put for a while as I saw he was not in a fit state to go out in it. I couldn't tick him off properly for coming to the post when there is a shelter a few yards along the street, for I realized that those who had experienced the hell of Dunkirk and other fronts in active service would have been in open spaces and not hemmed round with houses toppling down on them and no escape unless they could get to a shelter. Almost as many casualties were caused to people in the streets as in the houses during a blitz . . . Then the All Clear sounded and those wardens who had been out in it came back. Three did not come back. Two dead and one taken to hospital . . .

I went off duty and on my way home came the fourth alert. I thought to hell with that! I've had enough and I'm not going out again, but as I crossed over Portland Place I ran into Marcia. She had been off duty that week with 'flu.

'So you're better now,' I said.

'Only just. This is my first time out.' She had a flat round the corner in Hallam Street. 'I shall have to give up the post. My doctor tells me I should not be in London during the winter. He advises Switzerland. I had T.B. as a girl and there's a suggestion, he says, of a recurrence.'

I knew she would never stick it. Then, as she went on her way, I saw a light in a top floor of one of those expensive flats in Portland Place. I turned back and told the porter, 'There's a light on the fourth floor.'

He said, 'I know. It's one of those German refugees. I've been at them night after night. You'd better go up to them. They won't take it from me.'

I got into the lift, it was self-working and shot up to the door of the fourth. I pressed the bell and waited.

After I had rung again the door was opened by a shirt-sleeved Israelite.

'You have a light showing,' I said.

'There is no light,' he protested in a guttural German accent.

'I insist you put out that light. You must have heard the alert.'

He spread his hands. 'No light anyvere in ze flat.'

'I must examine all the windows in the flat,' I said firmly.

At that with a shrug and a resigned 'Ach! So!' he drew back and I passed through ornate wrought iron gates into a large luxuriously furnished drawing-room. Seated at a card table in the centre were three other men playing poker. Two in their shirt sleeves all dark and noticeably Semitic, except one not so typically Jewish. He had a shock of reddish hair, and small gingery side whiskers. They all stared at me aggressively as I walked over to a window heavily curtained, yet a width of at least eight or ten inches was undrawn. I pulled it together and turned to the four of them.

'I understand from the porter that you continuously show a light from this window whether there is an alert or not. If you do not observe the blackout I will inform the

144

police. I cannot arrest you but the police can. So I warn you.'

'No needt,' said the one who had let me in. 'We haf blacks outs at all ze windows. Siz one he stick. We haf to pull hardt.'

I took no notice of this and walked into a communicating room, evidently the dining-room. The window looked out at the back and the curtains at the window were closely drawn. I went systematically into all four other rooms, two double, two single bedrooms and two bathrooms. In one of these there were no curtains and the light was full on. A blonde in black satin pyjama trousers, a bra, and nothing else was making up her face at a mirror over the basin. She rounded on me flourishing a lipstick and demanding 'Who's she?'

'She iss ze warden.'

'I can see that. What she want?'

She was an English cockney and possibly the girl-friend of one or all of them.

He who had let me in and accompanied me in my inspection answered her:

'You did not pull ziss curtain. I haf tell you alvays not to usse zis badt room. It has no curtain.'

I switched off the light by the door as I went out, leaving her in the dark.

' 'Ere! Don'chew do that!' she called after me. 'Gimme a torch someone.'

As I returned to the drawing-room, the redhead rose from the table and said with not so pronounced an accent as the other one:

'A t'ousand apologies, Madame, if we have caused you any concern in the execution of your duty. We can assure you it vill not occur again zat dese windows are not all blacked out.'

And as he said that we heard the anti-aircraft guns deafeningly near, and the screeching whistle of a falling bomb followed by the inevitable thunder of its blast.

The blonde came screaming: 'For Gawd's sake!'

There was a sound of crashing glass. 'I'm goin' down,' she cried hysterically. ' 'E's over'ead.'

'He has passed now,' the redhead soothed her. 'An' de British Raaf – they get 'im. Madame,' to me. 'You will not go out in it?' For I was making for the door.

'Of course I'm going out in it – and mind you keep those curtains drawn. It's because you showed that light from here that you've had a near hit. They're after the B.B.C.' And as I darted in through the wrought-iron gates I shouted over my shoulder, 'Serve you right if they get you!'

I went down in the lift and found the entrance hall crowded with residents, mostly women all on their way below stairs to the cellars. Among them a few men who were going up in the lift either to their flats or on to the roof to watch for and tackle incendiaries. The porter who wore the ribbon of the 1914 war on his uniform and another order that might have been a decoration, asked me:

'Did you get out their light, miss?' I am often called 'miss' which is encouraging at thirty-four.

'Yes, I got it out and another one too at the back. If you see them come on again any time give the post a ring. You have the number?'

'Yes, miss, one of the other wardens give it me.'

'What I can't understand,' I said, 'is how they – if they are refugees – can afford to live here or anywhere in this area which is so expensive.'

'They claim to be refugees and can tell 'orrifyin' tales of what they've been through at Belsen and places – roasted alive in gas ovens or wherever they've supposed to have escaped from. But I 'ave me doubts of that. 'Course some of them did escape – those who are genuwin – but 'ow they can afford to live 'ere beats me. These flats are a thousan' or more a year an' will be double that after the war. I wonder 'ow much 'Itler pays 'em to give 'em 'omes 'ere an' jobs, to do a spot o' 'spionage for 'im. I tell you, miss, that the

Kaiser's Germans of the last war were a cut above this lot. Murderers of civilians, men, women an' children. In trench warfare as we 'ad it, the Jerries didn't fight civilians . . . I'll keep a look out for those lights, miss.'

It had been quite a night and although off duty I went on to my action station in case we had an incident on us, and not until five ack emma hours did we get the Raiders Passed.

Colin was not at the flat. I rang the post and spoke to the P.W.

He told me he had run into a lot of flak, put his foot in a crater and fallen. Jenkins (an ex-miner who was about to be called up, as were so many of the full-timers) was with him, said he thought he had passed out or been concussed, but he was up in a minute or two and didn't know he had fallen. 'Jenkins brought him back to the post and I kept him here until Raiders Passed and he's on his way home now. Perfectly O.K.'

I waited until I heard him come in. I felt a bit worried that he hadn't known about the fall, although since he had been in A.R.P. there had been very few symptoms, as I reported to Archie, who agreed that the best possible occupation, as Sir Jeremy had suggested, was his full-time in Civil Defence.

I went into his room. He was lying on his bed still in his uniform.

'Are you all right? The P.W. said you fell in a crater!'

'It was nothing – just wrenched my back a bit.'

I felt reassured, for although he looked pale and utterly worn out – no wonder as he had been doing more than his full time this last month, something like seventy or eighty hours a week – if his fall had only been caused by his foot in a crater, I need not worry.

I went to my room, threw off my uniform, too tired even to wash or brush my teeth, and was asleep as soon as I had my head on the pillow. And as I was falling into nothingness I heard the ringing of a bell, ringing, ringing . . .

ringing! It was the extension from Colin's room by my bed.

'Yes?'

'Thank God! Darling, I've just heard there had been a direct hit on your post.'

'Not on us. I was in Portland Place putting out lights. He dropped it just by the B.B.C. but he didn't get it this time. Are you at the flat?'

'I've been at – I was at the club.'

'The R.A.C.?'

'No . . . yes, he wasn't near us. When can I see you? I *must* see you. It's three whole days since we – and I'm in a tizz whenever there's an alert knowing how you're in his direct line. You are having the worst of any of the West End areas.'

'We're all right so far – touch wood. We've had a rough time but considering the non-stops, we've had far less casualties than might have been expected.'

'Well – tomorrow? Will you come tomorrow?'

'If I can.'

'You must. I can't wait.'

'I will come – about 16.00 hours. I'm on night duty to-morrow so I'll be finishing the last of the Janes and will bring you what I've done. I've only three more headpieces to the chapters to do. Goodnight or – good morning.'

'Were you asleep?'

'Just, but I was glad you rang. I am always bothered about you, too. Jerry has been in Bond Street and he'll be after St James's Palace for sure and the club is next door to it.'

'Darling, I love you.'

'And I love you . . . Tomorrow.'

Extract from her journal

I'm writing this when I came off duty today. After J. L. S. phoned, I hung up and prepared to sleep again, and heard

Colin's door open. He was coming in. Panic seized me. I had forgotten to switch on to secrecy. Had he been listening in? He came into the room. He had taken off his tunic, his hair was tousled, his face feverishly working. He held on to the bedrail to steady himself. He had been drinking, I could see that and his voice was slurred. Leaving the foot of the bed he leaned over me and I could smell drink in his breath.

'Was it Sinclair on the . . . the phone?' he asked.

'Yes, he had been told we had a direct hit on the post.'

'He sounded very – bothered about you.'

He leaned closer and put his hand round my throat. 'You – you and he – I guessed what has been going – on between you for mon'ss – no, years, which is why', his grip on my throat tightened, 'why you didn't mind about me and – and Viola. You bitch! . . . You bloody bitch!' He was squeezing my throat, his fingers digging into the flesh. I struggled, clawing at his hands. 'Don't! You'll throttle me!'

'I would too, you and that – that – swine – he's a Hun! I always knew him for a Hun!' He had loosened his tightening grip. I scrambled out of bed and rushed to the door. He shouted after me: 'I know what he is – he spoke of his friend – a – a fine friend – of Hitler's! Yes, you and he – and that German he was so *friendly* with . . .'

'You're tight,' I managed to say, while fear for him mounted. 'Go to bed. You're exhausted.' I could see he was on the verge of an attack. His eyes were wild, his face flushed, and even as I spoke he was still shouting at me: 'You won't get away with it – you and he and his Hun friend – back again! Make no mis-mistake! I'll have him. I'll get him! . . . I'll kill him and all of them . . . those Huns . . . I've killed before and I'll kill . . . kill . . . kill the sods!' He was gabbling confusedly, his fists shot out beating the air as if it were a face, and then he fell writhing on the floor with foam on his lips and his eyes glazed. It was one of his worst attacks.

I knelt by him and raised his head, he did not seem to see

me. I noticed the pupils of his eyes were dilated and then, suddenly, he hoisted himself on to his feet, saying drunkenly:

'What the – bloody hell d'you think you're . . . doing? I heard Sinclair and you on the phone – I know what's going on between you —'

And now it was beginning all over again but without any physical assault. I think he had forgotten everything except what he had overheard on the telephone. I had read in the medical book about the effect of *petit mal* and that when recovered after a few minutes the patient would be unaware of the attack. . . . I said, 'What if Sinclair and I *had* been having an affair, don't forget our agreement to live our own lives.'

'Your agreement – not mine.'

'Whatever you wish, but I stick to my arrangement. And now you had better go to bed. You've been doing far too much full time. I'm going to ask sick leave for you on a doctor's certificate.'

'I'll have no bloody doctor cert–tificating me. I want a drink.'

'No, you've had enough. Get to bed.'

I took hold of his arm and urged him to his room. He stumbled to the bed, fell on it and was instantly asleep. I stayed with him until I could be sure it was a healthy, normal sleep, and then, as the rose light of a fine October dawning filtered through the curtains, I made myself a cup of strong black coffee and finished off the last of the Jane headpieces.

Yes, it had been quite a night!

* * *

In an address to the House of Commons on 8 October 1940 Churchill said that 256 tons of bombs had been dropped on London in one night resulting in a hundred and eighty killed, apart from the wounded.

'We have been lucky so far,' Noel told Sinclair when, as

she related, the day after he had telephoned her, she came to his Piccadilly flat. 'But the flats and houses around our area had the worst of it last night.'

She then went on to report about the lights in Portland Place.

'They are refugees, I suppose, and German if not Jews. But if they are Jews and have escaped from those appalling internment camps and God knows what awful tortures, then we can only be thankful they did escape. Yet if they *are* refugees, how can they afford to live in those flats or anywhere around there, unless they have friends or relations here who subsidize them? They had a girl-friend with them too, living there, or perhaps she's the wife of one of them, and she is English, at least I think so.'

'No reason why the poor devils shouldn't have an English wife or girl-friend, but they can't disregard the blackout, especially in so vulnerable an area as yours. There is also a training corps – a barracks within your area. Anyway we are checking everywhere. It isn't only the West End that is getting it. The docks have had it just as hot, if not hotter than you.'

While he talked he was examining the sketches she had brought him.

'These are good, very delicate pen work. I thought you weren't keen on black and white.'

'I'm not. I'm doing them because one needs must when Lucifer drives. But I'm almost level with him now.'

'Come here.' He pulled her to him; she was sitting on the arm of a chair. 'I've not done this,' he said, cupping her chin in his hands to kiss her mouth, 'for three whole days and nights, and I've been living on air ever since I phoned you. Do you remember what you told me?'

'I didn't tell you much – what did I tell you?' She drew away from him, alarmed. 'I know that Colin overheard us – he was listening in. I forgot to switch on to secrecy as I usually do in case you ring me when he is at home.'

She was not going to tell him how he had attacked her.

'You told me, as you rang off, that you love me and that's the first time you have ever said it. Did you realize that?'

'I didn't – because I have never thought it necessary to say the obvious. But if you want me to say it – I'll love you, for ever and a day.'

There followed an interlude which is not recorded, and when, in the aftermath of their union, she came down from a seventh heaven to a sixth, 'What I want to know,' she said, 'did your "friend" go to America, to get in touch with Roosevelt – or didn't he?'

'Search me! I'm not my brother's – or my "friend's" keeper.'

'I don't understand. You told me you thought he was off to Washington to tell Roosevelt what he must already have heard about France letting us down, and now you say you don't know. You're so contradictory.'

'And if you look at me with those eyebrows surprisingly raised and that young lost "where am I" expression of a fourteen-year-old, do you wonder I'm contradictory when I can think of nothing else but you? Though if he didn't go to the States – since you are so interested in him, it doesn't say he didn't make the voyage even if he didn't disembark.'

'How do you know?'

'We have our ways of knowing,' he told her with a twinkle.

'Oh!' She turned from him impatiently. 'If you of the F.O. don't want to tell me anything you think would be giving away your secrets, whatever your secrets may be, then I'll tell you something. I wasn't going to tell you, but Colin, who listened in to us last night, or rather yesterday morning, when you phoned me in the early hours, he had one of his worst attacks and was telling me you are German and that he was going to kill you.'

'That,' he said slowly, 'is my greatest fear. No!' as she drew from him startled, 'not for myself but for you. I cannot and I will not' – he spoke with fierce intensity –'let you go on living with him in his condition. If, in one of his fits, he should harm you —'

'He won't. It's for *you*, I fear. He has this thing against Germans and because he dined with you that first time we met the Baron at your place and then he found out your second name is German and that you are half – he thought, half – German, but I told him only a quarter – Oh, I know it is all part of his illness and what he went through in the first war and killed a German face to face, but has never forgotten it. He dreams of it, he used to talk in sleep of it – when we slept together . . . No,' as she saw his mouth tighten – 'we don't now – I mean we have never been husband and wife for – ever since the Barton affair. And when he came to my room having listened in to us, I realized he had this hate in him – for you, just because of what he thinks you are. It's *you* I'm afraid for.'

'For me you need not fear. Come to me,' he said strongly. 'Let us be together openly and be done with this backstair, hole-and-corner intrigue. It is sacrilege to our love – or,' he added, low-voiced – 'my love.' He held her away from him, reading what lay in her eyes. 'Is it any use my telling you what I have told and told, and begged you to divorce him? You could. You have evidence enough if you would follow up his association with that Gibbon woman in Paris.'

'No! I can't! I won't. How could I do that to him? Divorce! You know how I feel about divorce, and to leave him alone!' Her voice broke. 'He is ill. You would not want me to leave him in his condition! You *can't* want that!'

'It's not what I want that matters. You want it too, don't you – don't you?' he repeated drawing her to him. 'Whatever you may say against marriage, I think – I dare hope you would come to me as you said just now for ever and a day.'

'I didn't say that meaning marriage. How many marriages do you know or I, for that matter, that have lasted for ever – and a day. Many don't last more than the day after the honeymoon is over. I mean a real marriage. Look at us. Well, we, Colin and I, did last for a few years, and as for *your* marriage – that reminds me.' She released herself from his arms. 'I meant to tell you this before. I met Marcia going out as I went into that Portland Place flat to put out the lights. She has been off duty with 'flu. She can leave when she likes as she is voluntary and she said she isn't coming back. Her doctor has told her she must not be in London in the winter because she had T.B. as a girl.'

'First I've heard of her having T.B. So you were putting out lights in a flat full of Germans?'

'What's that got to do with meeting Marcia in Portland Place?'

'I am overturning many stones and I take care to leave none unturned. She said she is leaving London?'

'Yes, I expect she has had enough of the Blitz here. She didn't think when it began it would be as bad as this. She never goes out in a raid and is always on the phone in an alert. She's evidently joining the bomb dodgers. When you married her' – she paused – 'you mustn't mind my asking this, but had she any money?'

'She had enough to marry on.' He quizzed her, pulling a lock of her hair. 'Do you think I married her for her money?'

'Don't be silly. I only wondered —'

'You are always wondering, in wonderland. What now?'

'She seems to have such a lot of money. She spends so much and even though we're rationed she always brings food to the post for us, black market, I suppose, and special things like cakes and sweets. She brought a jar of caviare when she was last on duty, none of them liked it. Nor did I. And she has that flat in Hallam Street and always has marvellous clothes.'

'I make her an allowance – the same third of my income which she would have under a legal separation or divorce.'

'I only wondered because she was so – friendly, as you were, with the Baron. And, if he is here in England and didn't go to the States, whether he is subsidizing her apart from what you give her.'

'That', he nodded, 'is not unlikely. And he may also be leaving London if not for the States for some other where. Switzerland perhaps.'

'Why Switzerland? She wouldn't surely be in with him if he is what you believe him to be. And could either of them get to Switzerland now, although it's neutral?'

'I told you there are no stones left unturned in the F.O. Do you ever see Barton – or Sybil as I knew her – these days?'

'No. She isn't in Grosvenor Square now – not after the landmine. She has gone to Cornwall. Marcia is Barton's cousin, isn't she?'

'Second, not first cousin. Well . . .' He held out his arms. 'What are we going to do? Continue to live in sin or —'

'Sin!' She laughed, evading his arms. 'I prefer it to unsinful marriage. I have to go now. Colin will be home and I don't want to answer questions. He heard me say I would be here tonight.'

'I'll drive you back.'

'Better not. He mustn't see us together and he may have come off duty by now, although he has probably forgotten all he said about you, and having heard us on the phone he would know I'm with you. But Sir Jeremy says they can forget after attacks anything they have said or done.'

Let us hope, she prayed inly, that he has forgotten . . .

* * *

Extract from Noel Harbord's journal, November 1940

Since Colin listened in to that phone call from J. L. S. three weeks ago and his reaction to it he has not mentioned it again. He and all of us in Civil Defence have been in action day and night. I say 'in action' deservedly, because the raids on London have been worse than ever. The Germans have now launched a new form of air frightfulness, thinking we will give in and give up, unable to take any more, but we *are* taking it and will go on taking it until *they* give in. And with redoubled fury seeing that our R.A.F. are giving back as good – or as bad – as they are given. They have sent a great fleet of Jerries over Coventry and killed two hundred and fifty civilians, to say nothing of the hundreds wounded. And that same night our bombers revenged us by raiding Berlin. So now we are in for it again. As J. L. S. said when he rang me up – he rings every day and night with these incessant alerts and no time for us to meet as I am doing full time as we all are now – he said, 'If we get through the next three months we'll get through the next three years.'

Which means we'll win in the end, but three years! And as things are going it may be longer . . .

Later:

Last night we had five incidents, not all on our area. It was one of the hottest nights so far and – I can hardly bear to go on with this. But I must get it down and get it out of me – somehow.

We went to help Westminster as they were having it even worse than us and so short of men wardens with many being called up, so the women have to do it if not yet called up. . . . Polly has been called up and is – was – waiting to be gazetted to the W.A.A.F. The P.W. told us, when we had dealt with our incidents, to go over to Westminster. They were after the Houses of Parliament. Colin had gone off already with Potts and one or two of the others who are medically unfit for active service – as if we were *not* active service! I was with Polly . . . I can't think straight, can't believe it . . . but I must. I'm writing this because if anyone should read this that I am telling about what we Londoners and other cities in Britain went through in the Second World War, and if they could read my scrawl it might be of interest to them who would have been too young to know about it . . . Where was I? . . . Yes, Polly. She and I went off together. She had been in all our five alerts and as always, even as night was waning and Jerry had been beaten off, or had done his stuff, and Raiders Passed had gone, Polly was looking as she always looked, lovely as ever, with her dazed wide eyes, her hair in a long golden bob, and the same drawling lazy voice with a pout in it saying: 'Funny how one gets used to all this. I'm scared stiff when there isn't an alert in case I have to go out in it and when I do – I like it! I shan't like the W.A.A.F. nearly so much,' she linked her arm in mine, 'because you won't be there, only some bossy officer bitch and you have to call her Marm like the Queen.'

She smelt of Chanel Five. I sniffed appreciatively.

'How do you get it? There's not a drop of perfume – French perfume – in all England.'

'Potts gave it me. He has a sister in New York. She sent it to him. If I marry again it will have to be an American. And if they come in with us they will be over here in shoals. I've always liked Americans. So nice and broad in the shoulder. I had an American boy-friend last year – no, two years ago – he's gone back now and he used to give me orchids whenever we went out anywhere. He wanted to marry me but I hadn't got rid of my Ex then. I've not heard from him since he went back to the States . . . I don't think he meant it, anyway, only for the night . . . Ooh!' she clutched my arm. 'Here he is again.' She threw back her head apostrophizing our search lights that were guiding our fighter-bombers.

'Piss off, you sods!' Her red pouting lips drawled the words flung around the post which she would pick up from the wardens and say them as if they were endearments. 'We shan't get to the Houses of Parliament if he drops it on the way.'

And he did . . . as we turned into Piccadilly.

It was a terrific one, not a landmine but the next worst thing. There was a tremendous blast and a falling of bricks, slates, roof tops, glass, and a sort of haze drifting about in our torch lights. Flak was coming down thick and fast, and suddenly something thumped me bang on my head and I went down into blackness ... I don't know for how long, it might have been a minute or it might have been an hour. It was actually only about fifty seconds and I heard someone call my name.

It was Potts, leaning over me. 'Here, take a swig of this.' He put a flask to my mouth. Brandy. It pulled me together. There was the usual inferno of confusion, wardens, firemen, ambulances, and – 'Polly! Where's Polly?' I screamed above the crash of falling bricks and hurricanes of glass.

I felt something trickling down my face, it fell on my hand and by the light of my torch I saw drops of blood. I dabbed at it with my handkerchief. Potts, holding my arm, was leading me through the crowd of wardens, firemen, people from the hotels. It didn't fall on the hotels in Piccadilly or any houses, only shops and thank goodness nowhere near the flat of J. L. S. Potts was saying: 'I'll get one of the ambulance chaps to plaster you. You've stopped a pane of glass.' Trying to make light of it – I must have been bleeding pretty much.

'Only a scratch. Did I pass out?'

He didn't hear, of course, in that din although he was wearing his hearing aid. He wore it all the time to be sure he wouldn't miss an alert.

I said, 'I lost my tin hat in the blast. Something fell on me.'

He heard the word 'blast' that I shouted into his ear.

'Yes, the hell of a blast,' he said. 'I say,' to one of the ambulance men. 'Can you give me a plaster? She's cut.'

'No.' I wrenched myself free of him. 'I'm all right,' but I was still dripping blood from my forehead – it didn't hurt. 'Where's *Polly*?'

'Best get in the van,' an ambulance girl driver was saying. 'We'll be taking this lot to hospital,' she gestured to one of the stretcher bearers. 'Casualty will see to you.'

'I'm not going to hospital for a ... for a scratch.'

'Better have the doctor look at it.' Potts had got hold of me again. 'You did pass out, you know. May have been concussed.'

'I'm not! – if so you shouldn't have given me brandy – and I'm not concussed. I must find Polly. She was with me – beside me. She must have gone to help someone. I must *find* her!'

Incendiaries had started a blaze. Firemen were there shooting up fountains of water from their hoses. I dashed away from Potts and barged into Colin. He grabbed my arm. 'Get into that ambulance. You're all over blood.'

'Get out!' I yelled at him. 'I'm looking for Polly. I must find her.' I fought my way through the shambles of debris, broken slates, bricks, glass, churned paving stones, and bodies, wounded, dead, where the ambulance men and doctors, nurses, were busy with deputy and chief wardens from our area and Westminster. We could know them by their white tin hats – directing, guiding, helping the wounded, or identifying the dead . . . 'Polly! Polly!' I kept yelling it but of course couldn't be heard if she *could* hear above the noise of hoses, the awful crackling of flames, the shouting of directions from wardens, and then by a miracle . . . I found her.

She lay among three or four others, all quiet, save for an occasional moan, quickly suppressed, and a weak voice trying to ask me – 'If you could just get this . . . this beam or whatever it is – off my leg . . .' He was a uniformed soldier, his khaki battle-dress red-dyed down the front.

'I will . . . in a minute.' I knelt there in the debris: 'Polly! Are you all right?'

She was lying with her face upturned, her eyes, those wide, grey long-lashed eyes, staring at me – or what? . . . Her lips, just parted, brightly red with lipstick, her hair framing the whiteness of her face like an aureole of gold. The fire flares of burning buildings lighted the scene like a madman's inferno and we, the damned . . . I felt her pulse, so still.

'Darling,' I whispered, 'wake up. I'm here. You're only concussed.' I bent close to her mouth. Not a breath, only a lingering smell of Chanel Five above the stench of smoke, and filth – and 'blood and sweat' – as Churchill had promised us.

'Polly!' I cried. 'Oh, no! You ... not *you*!'

A tall figure rose up beside me as if sprung from the earth.

He said gently, 'Just move aside, my dear.' He had a stethoscope slung round his neck, unfastened her tunic, listened, and straightened up.

'Is she ...?' My throat closed.

I heard him say:

'You go along to the ambulance, and have that cut seen to.'

'But she? Is she ...?'

So young, so lovely and in an instant ... struck down.

EIGHT

Further extracts from Noel Harbord's journal

The P.W. has put up a Roll of Honour on the board listing the casualties from the post during these ninety-seven non-stop raids. There have been half a dozen wounded and three killed from our area alone.

Major Amery was the first at the beginning of the Blitz. Jenkins died in hospital from wounds on the night of November 21, and Polly ...

Of her he gave this brief obituary:

Mrs Pauline Dobson, aged twenty-four, was killed in a devastation attack from enemy bombers on November 20th. Death, we understand from the medical report, was instantaneous. 'Polly', as the post affectionately called her, will be remembered by us all for her courage and devotion to duty. Any warden who wishes to attend her funeral at St Saviour's Church on November 24th at 11.00 hours please to notify me.

Most of us did attend but were interrupted in the middle of it by an alert and a bomb dropped almost on the church. Jerry is doing his stuff not only at night but by day. Jenkins had requested to be buried in his native village in Wales.

I did not go to Polly's funeral because of my back. When the blast flung me down. I thought it was lumbago as all last week Potts was complaining of lumbago but when I asked the doctor who saw to the cut on my forehead, and asked him to give me something for the pain in my back, he examined me and said it wasn't lumbago. He said, 'You are dislocated. A referred pain.'

So here am I, according to the orthopaedic surgeon's orders, laid out on my back for at least eight weeks. A damn nuisance when we are so short of wardens.

And this from her memoirs:

Although the Blitz continued with a toll as reported in November of four thousand and fifty-eight civilians killed and over six thousand wounded, there was a slight falling off in December from bomber attacks on London so that Colin did not have to give up all his days and nights to more than his full-time hours' duty.

On one occasion when he returned in the evening he intercepted another conversation – listened with his ear to the door of my room and heard something that brought matters to a head . . .

She gives but sparse details of Sinclair's revelations concerning Marcia and themselves but we may gather from the gist of it enough to reconstruct the scene that followed.

'I don't suppose,' Sinclair was saying, 'that you have heard Marcia is in Cornwall with her cousin Sybil, or Barton as you know her.'

'Marcia has been back and forth to Barton in Cornwall ever since that landmine on Grosvenor Square. But what of your friend, the Baron? Is he in Cornwall too? You say he didn't go to America, so where did he go?'

'He didn't go anywhere as far as I know, at least not now for he isn't a hundred yards from your action station.'

'How? What do you mean?'

'That he is in company with other flat dwellers in that neighbourhood where you so zealously watch for lights, among those who have escaped the horrors of Hitler's concentration camps. He, and some – I do not say all – a specialized few who have been given safe harbourage in Britain, have been aiding their war efforts and, indirectly, ours.'

'I can't understand you. How can they – if they are fifth columnists or German agents, aid *our* war efforts?'

He hesitated a moment, his eyes sliding from mine.

'By insufficient cover of their whereabouts, although our own particular friend has covered his activities for several years.'

'But how does Marcia come into this? She isn't in with him, is she? I know she has plenty of money and used to bring us, as I told you, things which I'm sure were black market saved from her rations as she used to say...'

It may have been that Colin, as Noel recalls it, came in from the post, having heard much of this, and then:

'Let us not', said Sinclair, 'talk of them who do not concern us – at this moment. What does concern us is that I love you to distraction and beyond all sense and reason. For is there ever reason in love? And to see you lying here, and I able to have of you only these snatched minutes, is more than I can stand. Listen. You require complete rest —'

'As if', she broke in, 'I hadn't rest enough – weeks of it and only allowed to get up and go to the bathroom. But I can walk very soon – on sticks – the doctor says.'

'What I intend to do with you,' Sinclair resumed, 'is to take you in the car to Cornwall where I can do my surveillance of whatever – or whoever – I may find to survey.'

Disengaging from his arms, 'How right you are,' she laughed up at him. 'There is no reason in love, such as yours, at any rate! How do you suppose I can account to Colin for going to Cornwall with you?'

'Grierson is now engaged on *Rambles in Devon and Cornwall* and Marriott wants you to do the illustrations. Owing to paper shortage there won't be so many as in the Tuscany book, nor will it be so long a book, but you will have to go through Devon and Cornwall to see the places of which he writes.'

'So I am to do the illustrations. Why was I not told of this before?'

'Because I have only just thought of it. And, in fact, we have not yet contracted Grierson for his latest *Rambles*. We have only discussed his terms, which are pretty steep, but now I will accept them and commission you for the illustrations. So you see – how within reason, love's reason or not – you can account to Colin for going to Cornwall with your publisher.'

There was a scuffling sound and steps in the communicating room, Colin's dressing-room.

'Go down by the other door,' she whispered. 'He has come in. I don't want you to meet. He is already asking why you come so often.'

'Well, now he will know. I am not sneaking down back stairs. Think over my offer. It is a commission. I'll have the contract drawn up and bring it to you tomorrow.'

He took himself reluctantly away, and met Colin in the narrow hall as he went down.

A cool 'Hullo. You here again?' was Colin's greeting and Sinclair's reply: 'Yes again and – again. I have work for Noel to do and a contract for her to sign.'

And no other word was passed between those two.

It seems that so soon as Sinclair had left, Colin came to her room. He looked, she related, pale, haggard, his lips quivering, a finger pointed threateningly at her and his voice harsh to question:

'You! Are you – you and he? . . . I knew it! Do you think he's in love with you. In *love*!' Clenching his fists he brought them down on the table by her couch. A decanter and glasses stood there; Sinclair had taken sherry. The glasses bounced, the decanter toppled and fell, its stopper rolled off and sherry was spilt. She said calmly:

'That decanter is Georgian. You had better see if it's cracked or broken.'

He remained standing, took a step nearer, his fists still clenched as if prepared for fresh assault with repeated accusation of that which he had overheard when Sinclair had telephoned to her a few weeks before.

'Sinclair! He's a bloody Nazi! So's his "friend" – that German ex-flying ace. He's in with him. Foreign Office be damned! Our security's riddled with them. And you – and he —' His face was distorted, his eyes glazing, his voice rose to a scream. He staggered and fell forward on the couch where she lay.

Painfully, for her back was not sufficiently recovered for her to lift him, she endured his weight across her body. He was pinning her down until within a few minutes he stirred, and got up, as usual unaware of his attack.

'I've been doing too much,' he said, 'falling about on top of you. Came over faint. *Trop de zèle*, I suppose. Twenty-four hours non-stop and Tim playing me up.' And then, 'Is there anything to eat?'

'There's some spam,' she told him, 'and Archie sent his man round this morning with half a dozen eggs from someone he knows who has hens at his place in Surrey. I'll make you a spam omelette.' She was getting off the couch but he told her, 'No, don't. You're not to use that back more than you must. I'll boil an egg.'

He returned presently with sandwiches and an egg. He said:

'I've done you a spam sandwich,' and he stooped to the fallen decanter. 'What's happened here? . . . Only a little gone and nothing broken I see. The stopper's all right too. Lucky it's a thick carpet. I'll get another glass. Did you push it over in your love transports with Sinclair?'

He was treating it as a joke, deliberately forgetting the cause of his seizure – if he had forgotten.

'Sorry I flew out at you like that.' So he had not forgotten. 'But it's getting a bit much, you know.'

'What is?'

'You and Sinclair. I've blinked an eye to it so far but there's more now than *meets* the eye. I couldn't help hearing about you going to Cornwall with him ostensibly to see his friend – that Nazi ex-flying ace. I've spoken to the P.W. of those lights in Portland Place that you put out, and I've put them out twice since then. It's a hot bed of German refugees, pseudo-refugees, and one of them is – or was – the "friend" of Sinclair. Yes?'

'No. You're on the wrong track. At least three of those four I saw are German Jews and not one of them could have possibly been that Baron. He's red-haired and nothing like him.'

'They can dye their hair and have surgery done to their faces. And I've always had my suspicions of Sinclair. Ludwig!' He offered her the dish of sandwiches. 'Have one before I eat the lot.'

'No. You have them. What did the P.W. say?'

'Nothing much. Said he had checked up on them after our reports – yours and mine. He questioned the porter of those flats about them and he told him that three of them were residents but one of them doesn't live there – that's the red-haired one – he visits them from time to time. He's a Swiss, a German Swiss, and may or may not be a Jew nor a refugee, having lived here long before the war.'

'Doesn't that satisfy you?'

'No, it does not. Anyone can say they are of any nationality and produce a passport. Hitler's agents are up to every trick – could have lived here for years. I don't suppose you remember, but I do, that just before or during the General Strike of 1926 there was a terrific outcry that Soviet or Communist agents had engineered the strikes with a few White Russians, so-called, living here and received by everyone, having escaped the revolution and passing themselves off as Prince something or other or Count or Countess or what have you. And then there was that Zinoviev letter, the "Red Letter".'

'Of course I remember that. It was after we were married.'

'Yes, but you didn't take any interest in what was

166

making a great stir with Zinoviev as president of the British
Communist Party commanding his lot to revolution and
down with the Government.'

'It was proved to be a forgery.'

'Not by all of the Government nor the Foreign Office.
They were properly taken in and to this day I believe they
are divided as to whether it was a put-up job or not, to get
Labour out – and they did get out.'

'You're obsessed with Fifth Columnists and enemy
agents. You read too many of Gavin Johns' spy thrillers
when on night duty!' She turned to take a copy of bound
proofs from the table beside her. 'Go away now. I want to
finish this because I have to do its jacket for Kell and
Wrotham.'

Nevertheless, we are told, she had suffered a shock.
There was no knowing, in his condition, to what ends his
'*trop de zèle*' might lead. He had evidence enough from
what he had overheard to suspect the worst between herself and Sinclair. As for his obsession concerning J. L. S.
either as *agent provocateur* acting for the Germans, or a
double agent for Germany and Britain using his publishing
firm and the Foreign Office as a blind, any such suspicion
was preposterous and symptomatic of his state of mind.
Yet, as she dwelled upon it with increasing anxiety, it
struck her that if Colin could sufficiently convince those in
authority – the Chief Warden who could get in touch with
the Regional Controller and he would know whom to
approach at the Home Office – there was a likelihood that
Colin could have started something that might involve
J. L. S. in an awkward situation. She threw aside the proofs
and cried: 'I'm sick, sick, *sick* of this hole and corner business.' Since Colin now suspected that she and J. L. S. were
lovers he could pursue his hostility against Sinclair with
heaven knew what disastrous result. . . . Well then, let him
go ahead with it and divorce me! Her thoughts whirled
about her like a swarm of wasps . . . No! I'm mad. After all
I've sworn that never would I agree to a divorce, whatever

he might wish to do or that J. L. S. might *want* to do and let Marcia divorce him, I could never leave Colin. He needs me. He's ill and getting worse with each attack. It is only when on duty in the thick of a Blitz that he reverts to normal . . . Then, hearing a sound in the next room, she got off the couch and with a walking stick to aid her she limped to the door.

Colin had opened his compactum wardrobe. It held his suits on one side of it and, on the other, drawers for his underclothes. Unseen, she watched and saw that he had taken out something wrapped in brown paper and in the shape of a pistol. . . . Yes, she remembered he had shown one to her years ago and had said he should have handed it in when he was invalided out, but for sentiment's sake had kept it.

'Colin, what are you doing with that pistol?'

He swung round.

'Damn you! You made me jump. I had my finger on the trigger and if it had been loaded it could have gone off. Why do you creep in on me like that when you ought to be resting your back?'

'I'm not "creeping in" on you, but I wanted to see how you are. You fainted just now.'

'Fainted? I didn't faint. I'm tired. Done too much – more than my full-time hours. We, whom the P.W. calls the Cinderella of the Services, the disabled or too old for the Army have to replace the called-up, and no recognition for it or a pension if we're wounded.'

'I don't think you ought to have kept that pistol.'

'Why not? It might be useful. I kept it for old times' sake, but of course I didn't know we would have another war and Huns swarming all over us and into our private lives – and into the Foreign Office and publishing the enemy's books.'

She went up to him, looked at him closely. Her face had paled but her tone was sharp and clear.

'Listen to me. You must rid yourself of this insane

obsession against Sinclair. You've nursed it – fondled it as if it were a viper – a pet viper in your bosom.'

He gave a snorting laugh.

'You abound in clichés. A viper in my bosom. Is that the sort of tripe you illustrate?'

'Cliché or not, I warn you. You'll get yourself in trouble if you keep that thing. You should hand it over to the police.'

'I'll do nothing of the sort. And don't you tell me what to do or what not to do. I know what I *can* do, which is that this affair between you and your J. L. S. *Ludwig* – hah! – has gone on long enough, and I've all the evidence I need to divorce you.'

Shaking her head she smiled admonishingly, speaking as to the boy he so often looked despite his forty-odd years.

'Don't be silly. And, don't forget, two can play at that game and that I could divorce you if I had wished to follow all the evidence I could have raked up. What about you and Barton and your gibbon and the monkey tricks you played with her – in Paris?'

Then as his eyes, startled, moved searchingly over her smiling face she told him:

'You know neither of us would ever sink to that. We've had it out together in the non-Pharaoh-like brotherly–sisterly marriage we've agreed upon. So don't let's tease each other.'

He stood sulkily silent, then suddenly took hold of her and pulled her to him, saying in a choking voice, 'I do love you – you know that. I always have, but I won't be told what to do and how to do and what *not* to do.'

And she saw his eyes bright with tears; they fell, and turning from her he sank into a chair and laid his head on his arm; his body shook with soundless sobs.

That broke her.

'Darling. Please – you're overtired. We'll forget all this. Go and rest. You've been doing too much.'

He raised his head.

'I know – I know . . .' And he lifted the weapon, held it out to her. 'Here it is. Give it to the police.'

'No. You keep it. I trust you not to do anything you shouldn't do.'

And she left him.

Had she done wrong? Ought she to have taken it and hidden it? She went back to her room and telephoned Archie Tarrant.

She told him everything, asked his advice.

'You did right. Let him think you trust him but watch him. I'll speak to Jeremy and hear what he has to say.'

What Sir Jeremy had to say was delivered to Sinclair with some doubt as to how he would take it.

He took it ill-graciously.

'Sir Jeremy thinks that the visit to Cornwall – this is what he wrote to Archie who showed it to me.' And taking a letter from her pocket she read – ' "would cause Mr Harbord a hazardous effect should his wife accompany Mr Sinclair to Cornwall in view of his suspicions, doubtless unfounded",' she looked up. 'That is tactful of him – "concerning Mrs Harbord's relationship with the publisher of her illustrations".'

Sinclair, listening with growing impatience to the doctor's opinion, came out with:

'You have been discussing our relationship, both professional and . . . amoral . . . with Tarrant, who passes it on to his doctor friend?'

'To the neurologist attending Colin,' she corrected, her face clouded. 'You surely can understand that Sir Jeremy has to be told how Colin reacts to you and to his suspicions concerning not you alone but all men and women who he imagines are enemy agents. It is all part of his illness. I'm sorry but it has to be. I can't ignore medical opinion. Colin is sick and it is my duty to follow Sir Jeremy's instructions. I am responsible to Colin as my husband – which he is and ever must be, in sickness or in health.'

170

'To whom you have never sworn responsibility before God's altar.' Then seeing her face close he was instantly contrite.

'Darling, I know I'm unreasonably bloody-minded, but I'd banked on this trip to Cornwall – you and I together, which we never have been yet on' – he slipped her a grin – 'on purely professional business.'

'*Purely* professional?'

And he felt her lips against his.

*   *   *

That Noel did not go with Sinclair to Cornwall on 'purely professional' business is certain; also when Sinclair arrived, in pursuit of a possible capture, he found that his quarry had flown.

'Literally flown,' on his return he reported to Noel. 'In either his own or a confederate's aircraft; or by any other means of transport by which Hitler's protégés can come and go, here, there – or anywhere.'

'So what will you do, and where has he flown?'

For answer he handed her a cutting from one of the daily newspapers, which in a brief paragraph gave it:

'Baron von Schweinvort is now in Switzerland, where he has joined M. Laval.'

'Laval!' she exclaimed. 'Isn't he the French quisling who stabbed France in the back?'

'Yes, and in league with Mussolini, described by Churchill as "crafty, cold-blooded, blackhearted", who had thought to gain an empire on the cheap.'

Noel, who had partially recovered from her injury to her back, was still on sick leave when she received a telephone call from Lady Amersham. 'Birdie' had frequently inquired after her and sent fruit and flowers with sympathetic messages; and now came an invitation to go with her to Cornwall, where her son had taken a cottage for his children to be out of London's raids.

She was more than ever inconsequential when she rang
Noel to tell her, as she recalled it:

'My dear! A little bird, tee-hee, not myself but one of
my kind who was in Holloway with me on hunger strike
. . . No! I wasn't striking as I couldn't face those tubes
stuck down my throat and into my tum but she did . . .
Yes, your aunt, the Amnesian – I mean Amazon is it or
Lesbian? The ancient Greek women who made love to
each other and behaved like men and went to the wars like
they do today. And Johnnie who has been pestering me to
leave London and says he is worried to death that I remain
here although we in the Wood – St John's – haven't had so
much of it as you have perhaps because of being *Saint*
John's Wood if he ever lived here which isn't likely if he
was in Palestine or Jerusalem and anyway it might have
belonged to the Ancient Britons in B.C. or something or
would it have been A.D. when he wrote his Gospel? But his
wife – Johnnie's wife, she has joined the W.R.N.S. as an
officer and thoroughly enjoying it being able to boss them
all which she can't do at home as all her staff men and
women except Nannie have joined up. I'd have joined your
A.R.P. if I were a bit younger and without my varicose
veins but I could turn somersaults at your age as we used to
at the Gaiety in one of our turns in the chorus. We wore
skin pink tights and of course the whole front row stalls
was booked full every night with the boys and that's when
Amersham first saw me and fell – plonk! His people kicked
up a fuss as he was the heir and I did try to hold him off but
nothing doing and I'm glad because I wouldn't have had
Johnnie but I'm afraid his boy – the heir, you know – is
taking after his grandfather and all of the Amershams
except Johnnie even to no chin and no brains. But Johnnie
has more brains than any in the Lords unless created from
Labour, and so many being sons of us at the Gaiety and
Daly's. So you will come with me, won't you, dear? Just
to get over your back and away from the Jerries if only for
a month or a week or two?'

After some difficulty interpreting this monologue Noel said:

'Yes, I would love to go with you to Cornwall as I am actually entitled to convalescent sick leave, although as a part-timer unpaid I can take what leave I want but I don't really want to, or didn't.' And she thought: 'I'm getting as scatty as herself, it's catching! And to Birdie: 'It's sweet of you to think of me. As a matter of fact I was supposed to be going to Cornwall with my pub – with the author of a book Marriott are publishing and which I have to illustrate. It is by Grierson on his travels in Devon and Cornwall, but then I got this back and so I couldn't go. But now, thanks to you, I can.'

Extract from Noel Harbord's memoirs

Colin surprisingly had raised no objection to my coming to Polperro with Birdie. It made a welcome break after those eight or nine weeks on my back. I could now hobble on a stick and the doctor said I could soon do without it. The cottage, as Johnnie Amersham called it, was scarcely a cottage. Possibly Tudor, with eight rooms, thatched roof, low ceilings, beamed, and perched on a hill with a view of the sea so deep a blue it might have been the Mediterranean.

The Amersham children, two girls and a boy, were not as their grandmother called them 'her cup of tea', nor were they mine. The girls, respectively eight and nine, were dumpy, plain, their teeth in a brace, their hair in a plait and again to quote Birdie, were 'dumplings'. The boy Freddie Marchbanks was, according to Birdie, an Amersham down to his chin or the lack of it.

'Pity', their grandmother said, 'that none of them takes after me. Of course the girls may turn out to be beauties – the hopelessly plain often do. Although what chance with those teeth and no chins? But I can remember, you wouldn't, I won't mention names – the first of us to marry into the peerage and I knew her when she was what you call a teenager or barely that at thirteen. We used to play hopscotch in our street. Her father was a greengrocer and my father a grocer without the green, tee-hee, I mean he served in a grocer's shop and we lived over it. And *she* was quite hideous then – such a nose, and a face like a pie and she grew up to be lovely and married a duke, well he wasn't one then only a younger son but the heir got himself killed in the Boer War so that dates *me* to have known *her* – so don't you let on. A woman's age after thirty should be her own secret. And she left the chorus, was snapped up by Tree – just imagine! And is now a great star and her own actress manager but is also a beauty – you wouldn't get far without it, at least not in my day although Marie Tempest was nothing to look at and look at her now! . . . Is that the car come for you?'

I had to hire the village taxi as I couldn't walk far. I was not sorry to leave her and go on my way with my paints and my portable easel, because in her usual indirect fashion she is almost impossible to follow.

So off I went and was driven to a delightful little fishing village which Grierson particularly marked for me to sketch and had put up my easel and board and was working away when I heard my name called.

It was Barton.

'What on earth!' she began, 'are you doing here?'

'What I am doing,' I answered, 'is, I should think pretty obvious.'

'Is Sinclair with you – or Colin?'

'No. I'm staying a few days with Birdie to do sketches for Grierson's next Marriott book.'

And I shaded my eyes from the sun, leaning back on my stool to get the perspective and to by-pass her questioning stare.

She was wearing brown corduroy slacks and a khaki-coloured shirt open at the throat, no hat, and she looked more than ever like a depraved Botticellian Virgin with her transparent skin slightly sun-tanned and that vapid, rather dazed expression enhanced by her absence of eyelashes and those pale eyes set flat in her face. And always, as when at the Yew Tree I felt her indefinable charm, or as Aunt Rhoda would call it, the spell of the mantis ready to pounce on her prey.

She lowered herself to the soft springy turf of the cliff top and sat clasping her knees.

'So you're staying with Birdie.'

As that required no answer I waited for what would come next.

Colin came next.

'I knew you were here because Colin telephoned me the day you arrived. He wants to come too and asked could I put him up.'

'Oh?'

I carefully mixed cobalt and chrome yellow. I was working in oils for the first of these sketches and, if Grierson insisted, I would do them in water colour from these, but they would not be so good as in oils.

'Colin', she said, 'is in quite a taking.'

'A what?'

'A fuss, if you like, about you.'

'About me?' Mixing my colours, I still didn't look at her.

'Yes, about you and Sinclair. He knows you are staying with Birdie but he thinks she's a blind for Sinclair, and that James will be somewhere near here.'

I asked: 'How did you know where to find me?'

'My dear, everyone here within miles knows where everyone is and what everyone does. I was told you have hired a car for your sketches, and that you were off to this view, and on this day at this time.'

'Quite a sleuth, aren't you?'

'Not in the sense that James is or may be. I've never been sure about James.'

That one-toned voice of hers changed not a note. I, still

intent on my palette, made no remark to this which I knew was a challenge; nor did I look up but I guessed she was smiling with her lips closed.

From her pocket she took a gold case, lit a cigarette, inhaled and said:

'Colin asked my advice as to what he should do. He doesn't want a divorce any more than would I to be dragged through the Courts for defence.'

The smoke from her cigarette blew in my face from the slight breeze drifting from the sea.

I looked round at her then. Her small even teeth became visible.

'If I had wished to divorce Colin,' I said, 'I would have done it long ago. You knew – he must have told you – my views on divorce and that he and I were free to go our ways with whomever we chose, unmolested.'

And I returned to my palette.

'Of course,' she went on as if I had not spoken, 'Marcia could cite *you*. I understand she made herself clear on that point when she met you. She told me she discussed it when you lunched with her at Claridges. But after that she seemed to have called it off. She was down here with me until recently. She couldn't stand the Blitz. And now she is gone or is going to Switzerland if she can get there.'

She got up and stood over me.

'We haven't got very far with all this, have we?' she remarked.

'Did we have to go far?'

She stamped out her cigarette on the grass, and laughed softly.

'You were always a dark little horse. One never knows if you mean what you say or are what you seem to be.'

I said: 'Never a horse. A mare if you like, since you look to be seeking a mare's nest.'

'To find perhaps a hornet's nest?'

'If you say so.'

176

She came nearer to examine my sketch, with eyes narrowed.

'That's good.' She defined with her thumb the line of the cliff. 'But you've too much chrome with your cobalt and the white is too white. Not that I know what you know about paint, nor about anything other than clay.'

'A modest understatement,' I told her politely and watched her stroll off.

That night I wrote to J. L. S.

. . . I didn't want to phone you because I have no extension in my room here, and Birdie would be all ears. Barton came upon me today when I was out sketching. She tells me Marcia is going to Switzerland, but how can she get to Switzerland? I thought you ought to know as our 'friend', you say, is also there and she is well – too well? – acquainted with him. Barton was very communicative about Colin, you, me, Marcia and – divorce! I can't be more explicit in a letter but please believe that what she was trying to put across me didn't cut any ice, in fact it froze into a glacier! Colin is coming to stay with her. I wish – how I wish you were here. But I will be back again soon and then . . .

*   *   *

The Old Year roared to its end with the thunder of bombs, not only on London but on the provincial cities in Hitler's attempt to subjugate Britain by the ferocious massacre of vast numbers of civilians. He hoped to terrorize the inhabitants of these islands and so to distract the Government's anxiety from the menace of the invasion that he was now preparing. But far from his intent to overrun the whole of Britain as he, the yellow dwarf with a giant's stride had trampled down half Europe, he had mistaken the resistance of that indomitable barrier beyond the cliffs of Dover.

Although in the New Year there had been a slight easing

off of air raids during the winter months, the Royal Air Force had grown in strength and numbers and was becoming master of the daylight raids with which Hitler's *Luftwaffe* pounded London as the short days lengthened.

Noel's brief visit to Cornwall had not been without significance. When Colin, as Barton informed her, had duly arrived, he phoned her at Birdie's to ask if he could see her – 'and meet you somewhere. I must talk to you alone. I can't stand that Birdie woman's gabble which is for the most part unintelligible.'

'I have to finish the sketches I am doing for Grierson's book before I go back,' she told him. 'If you would like to see me this afternoon you had better be here at two o'clock.'

Of that meeting she gives this account.

He came with me in the car that was taking me to my location where I had begun another sketch. I dismissed the car and told the driver to fetch me in three hours, set up my easel and started to paint.

I could see that Colin was, as Barton had said, in a 'taking'. His mouth twitched as always when he had something on the tip of his tongue that he could not bring himself to say; but he did, with an effort, come out with it, jerkily:

'Barton tells me she has – spoken to you – about me – about us – and our – this impossible marriage. It has gone on too long. I'm fed up with – sick to the teeth – of being cuckolded.'

The sun was casting lovely shadows from the cottages at the foot of the hill that led from the cliff road down to the sea. And although spring had not quite broken through, yet here in the west the air seemed filled with an indefinable scent as of unseen primroses starring the hedges.

The sea was a sheet of gold shot with the blue of the sky, and in cottage gardens below, daffodils blew their yellow trumpets among the crocuses, a colourful mosaic. For

178

winter dies so quickly in the west that it is almost summer before the frosts in the east have gone . . . 'I can't paint it!' I said. 'It is too good for me. Only a Corot could do it . . .'

He, who had sat on the grass studded with small yellow flowers shyly opening to the sun, got up and grabbed at my hand which held a brush poised over the canvas.

'Did you hear what I'm trying to tell you?'

'Yes, I heard, but it's nothing new. You've been telling me this ever since we decided we would live together and – apart.'

He said pettishly: 'Yes, but I've never told you I know you are if not wedded – bedded with Sinclair.'

'You have said so scores of times without describing yourself in that old English word as a cuckold.'

He let go my hand and sat down again, plucked a blade of grass, nibbled it and asked: 'Well, what are you going to do?'

'What should I do? If you want to divorce me you may – I won't defend it. But of course you don't mean to divorce me,' I said, selecting another brush. 'You'd hate it as much as I would do, so what is the use of discussing it with me or with Barton, who is your *alter ego*, unless you want to marry her, which you can't. Her husband is agreeably complaisant. Or do you want to marry someone else? Your gibbon for instance?'

'Don't be a fool. But,' he said angrily, 'I'd be the *blood*iest fool if I let Sinclair have what you refuse to give me. I won't stand for another man having you. I've stood it too long!'

'You began it,' I reminded him. 'When Barton was taking her fill of you, it was I who stood by and let her take you. I knew it wouldn't last but it gave me a *tu quoque* chance to do likewise.'

'You admit that you are Sinclair's mistress?'

'It's a horrid word – savours of Victorian novels.'

'His whore then, if you like it better.'

'I don't like it better.' I smiled round at him. 'Is that what you wanted? To make me admit I'm Sinclair's whore?'

For answer he got up again and seized hold of me. 'What is it about you,' he muttered, 'that makes one want to wring your neck or – tumble you?'

He fastened his mouth on mine. I pushed his face away. 'I think you had better forget all this. It gets us nowhere. We stay as we are or you go ahead and divorce me. But for goodness' sake don't beat about the bush in this meandering damn silly way . . . And now you have Chinese white all over your sleeve. Do go – will you? I want to get on with my work while the light lasts.'

In spite of Noel's decision that nothing would induce her to give Colin grounds for divorce unless he wished to marry again, when she might then agree, none the less she was anxious to have Sinclair's opinion as to her rejection of Colin's demand – if it were a demand.

She was now back at the post but according to the surgeon's advice she must not risk further injury to her back while on Civil Defence; her duty must be confined to sedentary work, such as the telephone service.

'If he thinks there's less risk of injury to my back on the telephone during a Blitz he'll have to think again,' she told Sinclair. 'It is safer outside in the street where you do get a chance of survival than underground in the basement of a six-storey building which if hit will come toppling down to crush you like a beetle. The only time I get the wind up in an alert is when I'm on telephone duty deep down in a cellar.'

On her return from her visit to Cornwall she discussed with Sinclair her meeting with Colin. 'And why,' she asked, 'should he speak to Barton about a divorce from me? It's nothing to do with her – or is it? But I did remind him that I could have divorced *him* ages ago had I wished to be dragged through all that grubby business. I have an idea she is encouraging him to break with me – I mean legally to break with me, but why she should I can't imagine. She doesn't want him. She has irons enough in her fire without him, not that Colin is iron, more like putty in her hands – or clay. And in any case she would never wish to be divorced from a millionaire husband. She is quite happy to know he is always aloof and complaisant. So many marriages today seem to run on those lines. Aunt Rhoda says that ninety-nine per cent of marriages made in a church are already foresworn to the devil. So what should I do?'

He gave her a twinkling look.

'No use to ask me. You know what you should do and what I want you to do.'

'And that I can't do unless he wishes to marry again, and there's no one I could trust to look after him except the gibbon. She did take care of him in Paris. She got him into a nursing home for psychiatric treatment, but that did him no good so we remain at a deadlock. I can't let him loose on his own. Besides he needs me.'

'So do I need you.'

'Divorce,' Noel said, 'although accepted today as a matter of course is, to my thinking, degrading.'

'Far less degrading than legalized marriage devoid of love and the merging of two beings in one with mutual interests and desire.'

'You had all that, or thought you had, with Marcia.'

'No. Desire, yes; but that fades like a mirage to leave a desert waste. The merging of one with the other increases as the years mould them to a complete unified entity.'

She turned her head away.

'You make it very hard for me. I too need you – but I can't leave Colin in his condition and he doesn't *want* to be left. He has never outgrown his thwarted childhood and the lack of mother love. He is always looking for her, and he never found her in me. I have not told you – have I? – what he told me the first time we met all about himself, which accounts for so much that is unaccountable in him, apart from his – what he inherited.'

Taking her hand he turned it over, dropped a kiss in her palm and said:

'So we go on as we are, you and I, until he finds a permanent substitute for a mother, or until the destiny that shapes our ends decides for us?'

'Which might happen any day or night. How many thousands – or maybe one of us – will be struck down in a minute if destiny has shaped *our* ends?'

'Which is probably the means by which Divine Intelligence seeks to depopulate an over-populated world. It happened in 1914 and is happening now.'

'Or perhaps it's the end of this world. I often think' she took the cigarette he offered and he lighted it for her, 'that the life we live here on earth is the purgatory that Catholics believe in, a sort of cleansing station before they go on to that other life which is promised us in the Resurrection – a life where there are no wars nor frightful hates and tortures, no marriage nor giving in marriage, only love.'

'And no maniacal subhuman devils. No Hitlers – or would you think that even Hitler may be working out his own salvation in *his* purgatory along with Caligula who sat feasting while he watched his victims tortured, burnt to death, until the smoke of the human torches faded and in the Colosseum the roar of the lions savaging their prey was silenced.'

Then, just at that moment while, as she relates, they exchanged their thoughts, 'For we shared always the same interests and all else which made us one complete entity – even as I had spoken of what came into my mind and he took my thought from me, we heard the howl of the sirens in the fall of the night . . .'

'Here he is again!' she cried. 'I must go.'

He seized and held her feet.

'You shall not go. You will stay here. I won't have you out in this.' Already the anti-aircraft guns were firing at the approaching bombers of the *Luftwaffe*. 'Your duty,' he told her, 'is voluntary and you have done all and more than you were entitled to do in the worst of the Blitz, so you'll stay here with me until Jerry has done his stuff, although he won't do all he is out for. Our Fighter Command is on his tail and the Poles are with us. They are almost as good in the air as our boys. Sit down. I want to talk to you of what you told me in your letter.'

'What,' she said wearily, 'did I tell you?'

Her defences were weakened. She longed – how she longed to surrender to his want of her. To be his wife, his love for ever, 'till death us do part' – and afterwards.

His arms held her closer.

'You said that Marcia was advised to go or is going to Switzerland, but of course she can't go there, not with a war on. It is likely, however' – he lifted her chin and looked down into her eyes – 'that I must go to Switzerland.'

'You? Why? If Marcia is not permitted to go, how can you?'

'Because I have my work, which I am under orders to obey and for whatever purpose I am voluntarily committed.'

'Oh, no! Not — Is it dangerous?'

'Far less dangerous than that to which *you* are voluntarily committed.'

A whistling hissing sound preceded a terrific explosion to rock that block of flats as in a seismic convulsion; then a bomb came hurtling down. The ceiling heaved, plaster fell, the door of the room swung off its hinges. The black-out curtains were blown apart, and glass from the windows poured through them in a silvery fountain of splinters.

He held her close and closer.

In a gap of the curtains could be seen a red flare that lit up the darkening sky.

'The lions,' he said, 'still roar while they savage their prey, and the torches or, as we call them today, the incendiaries, devour their victims – despite the Cruci-fixion.'

She released herself from his arms and gathered up her equipment. 'I should be at the post. I'll be wanted on the phone . . . Oh, you're bleeding!'

'Only a glass splinter.'

In the door still swinging on its hinges his manservant appeared.

'The kitchen window has fallen in, sir, and half the crockery has had it.'

'Are you all right?'

'Yes, sir. The blast knocked me down but I'm only a bit bruised. They've had it bad on the top floor.'

'I'll go up and see.'

'I'll go with you,' Noel said. 'But first let me see to this cut. Come to the bathroom.'

She washed and plastered the cut on his face 'which has luckily just missed your eye', she told him.

The top floor above Sinclair's flat was a shambles but no casualties as all three flats had been vacated by the tenants and the daily helps that attended them had already gone home.

Sinclair drove her back to the post since she insisted she must go on duty. It was a heavy blitz, but the worst of it had been on dockland.

* * *

And now, since all Civil Defence men were being conscripted, Noel was put on full time for Civil Defence.

She was given two weeks' leave for, as a part time voluntary warden, she had taken no leave more than sick leave since the outbreak.

Aunt Rhoda, she relates, had been very concerned that I had been injured while on duty and insisted that I go to her house in Kent 'for recuperation', she said, 'and respite from your work in Civil Defence'. When, as a child, I used to live there and went to a school at Dover as a boarder, it was, as I recall it, unobtrusively early Victorian, mellow-bricked, with windows either side of the door, six rooms excluding the attics, and a garden cared for, not by my aunt who cared nothing for gardens, but by one Hogg, whose chief joy was his vegetables. I remember I spent most of my summer holidays in the orchard making sketches and dabbling in the box of paints my aunt had given me for one of my birthdays.

Since my marriage I had not been to the Chantrey, as my aunt's house was named, more than half a dozen times. Aunt Rhoda had never approved of my marrying Colin and he disliked her and all that she stood for, which was the antithesis of what he subconsciously desired in a woman. Some years before the outbreak of war, during the early 'thirties, the country surrounding the village, Boulton St Paul, on the outskirts of which my aunt's house was situated, had been partially ruined by the building of awful bungalows that had sprung up like a rash on the innocently rural beauty of meadow and pasture land. The Government had not then brought in the Green Belt Act to preserve the English countryside from vandalism.

When obeying Aunt Rhoda's command to take what she called a 'respite' from the 'murderous onslaughts of Hitler', I was driven down to the Chantrey by J. L. S. He had booked a room at a hotel in Canterbury. Aunt Rhoda's invitation to visit her had not been extended to him even for a meal, although I had told her he would give me a lift down because, he said, he had business to conduct in the neighbourhood.

We drove into Kent past the devastation caused by German bombers in the vulnerable centres of Chatham, Rochester and also wherever our aircraft factories were turning out more and more of our fighters as directed by Lord Beaverbrook, Minister of Aircraft Production, who was producing machines as fast as he had produced newspapers. I noticed as we came into what used to be lovely unspoiled country that the tall factory chimneys were vomiting smoke from their machine-driven bowels.

'Beaverbrook,' J. L. S. told me, 'is moving the position

185

of many factories in the eastern counties, and although it has temporarily caused a halt in production, it will add to greater security because the German air force won't find it so easy to get their targets. They will be sending their scouts – their refugees, such as you have spotted signalling to incoming raiders – to guide them to replaced factories that "the Beaver" is using to turn out more Spitfires. So you had better watch for lights, or any suspicious "down-and-outs" here.'

He spoke jokingly, but I guessed he had reason to warn me and that his 'business' in this neighbourhood was not unconnected with his own particular service, whatever it might be.

I had not looked forward to this visit, but after these hints that I could be of use here, either in or out of a raid, I felt less reluctant to face Aunt Rhoda, for she was sure to be there with me some of the time.

J. L. S. dropped me at the gates of the drive, and, refusing to come in and have tea or a drink, drove on to the hotel in Canterbury where he would be staying for a few days. He would telephone me to know where or how we could meet – 'somewhere away from the Aunt,' he said.

I found on arrival that I was not the only guest. I had heard that during the evacuation of children, of mothers with babies, or pregnant women, or of the blind and disabled, that Aunt Rhoda had taken in evacuees, but the several she had housed at The Chantrey had gone back when the first few months showed no sign of a raid in the then 'phoney' war.

But there were a new lot now; four of them, three boys and a girl. 'They go to the village school, thank God,' Aunt Rhoda said, 'but when they first came here,' her nose wrinkled, 'the district nurse and I spent two days delousing their heads.'

'Are they all from the same family?'

'No, two of the boys are twins, the mother brought them here. Their father was killed in a submarine, torpedoed by

186

a U-boat, and she works in a munitions factory, had no time to keep them clean so parked them out and they were sent to me in a filthy condition. The other boy is a Jewish child, the orphan of parents murdered in Hitler's gas ovens. How he escaped we do not know. I gather a grandmother had him before she and her husband were victimized. The Red Cross may have saved him, we have no details as to how he, aged six, arrived here. The fourth of my wards,' she grimaced, 'is a girl, a little minx. Her mother is what, in the Napoleonic wars, would have been a camp follower. She is still following them in the N.A.A.F.I. and makes more than her pay on the side.'

It was during this visit to her aunt that Noel was involved in what she describes as 'a most exciting and extraordinary adventure'.

Her journal records it under the date April 1st, 1941.

. . . A not inappropriate date for the one who was the perpetrator – or should I make a doleful pun and say the perpet-*traitor* of this unexpected encounter.

I was in the orchard with the Jewish evacuee boy, Freddie, short for Frederic Herman Stein, a handsome child, dark haired with a nose like a delicately carved scimitar and the long-lashed lovely eyes of his race, so eminently paintable that I inveigled him to sit for me.

It was a morning of young spring sunlight with a mist of early April green in the orchard where tall daffodils speared their gold from the grass.

I had given him a box of watercolours for he showed a great aptitude for drawing and had a remarkably good colour sense.* I spoke to Aunt Rhoda about him and said that I considered he should ultimately be sent to an art school. He was an excellent model. I placed him with a background of an apple tree; the foliage not yet in leaf gave an almost Japanese effect of filigree branches to throw

* F. H. Stein, A.R.A., 1974.

off a dappled pattern of sun and shadow. With us, an interested spectator, was Bob, the old gardener's dog, a cross between a collie and a labrador with a touch of the Alsatian.

I, intent on my work, suddenly heard Bob utter a growl followed by a short sharp bark, and he was off like a rocket into the wood that bordered the orchard. This did not belong to The Chantrey grounds, it was part of the estate of a retired colonel, an octogenarian who seldom lived there. Until recently his house had been requisitioned by the Army. There was no one there now and I understood from Aunt Rhoda that the house had been left in a deplorable state by the Army and would have to be redecorated and reconditioned before another lot came in. The grounds were also entirely neglected and overgrown with nettles. Tanks had lumbered through when the boys were in training.

'Freddie,' I told him, 'go and see what Bob is after. He may have scented a fox and you are due for a rest. You have stood too long,' for I had placed him standing against a tree trunk. 'You need to stretch your legs. But look out for rabbit-traps. Some brute has laid traps there; Hogg's cat got caught in one the other day.'

He flashed me a wide white grin and ran after Bob, who had plunged into the thicket. 'And don't you get your foot in a trap,' I called out to him.

I went on painting the background with a glimpse of the lichen-slated roof of Hogg's cottage at the gates which merged pleasantly into the distance under the blue-tinted sky. So engrossed was I that I did not at first heed a shout from Freddie and a bark from Bob, a loud baying rather than a bark as if he were trying to call my attention to something. I got up from my stool and hastened away to the wood. There was a fence topped by a tangle of barbed wire. Freddie had scrambled through a hole in the fence where the wire was half broken down and Bob could have forced his way in. I did not much care to get caught on the

188

wire for I was wearing a skirt, not my uniform trousers, and had on a pair of new stockings, not nylon; we didn't have nylon during the war but ersatz silk. However I managed to get over and into the wood following Bob's bark and I heard what sounded as if Freddie were speaking, or rather shouting at someone who answered him in – German!

I ran on, my heart was banging away at my ribs for I had also heard Freddie answering in German which I translated as:

'What do you here – I will call the police,' and a savage barking and snarling from Bob.

And then, as I came into a clearing, I saw a crumpled heap of what could only have been a parachute, and a man standing over it or in the midst of it, entangled among thistles and undergrowth. He was wearing a distinctively British tweed suit, his hair rumpled, and his face, I could see, was bleeding from scratches. He must have fallen as he came down.

And Freddie was speaking to him in German!

Then the man spotted me and as I neared them – Bob still frantically snapping and snarling at him – I saw, unless I was hallucinated, that this man who had parachuted, baled out I presumed, from an aircraft – whose aircraft, his – or – whose? – was, or I thought he was – our "friend", the Baron!

Then he spoke. He had also recognized me, and stepping out of the clutter of his parachute came forward saying in his well-remembered, pleasant English voice:

'Do I dream – are you part of my dream or is it Mrs Noel Harbord in the flesh?'

I captured what little breath was left to me to ask:

'If you are Baron von Steinvort how do you come to be here and – in that?' I pointed to the fallen parachute.

'I realize you require an explanation but if you could call off your excellent dog —'

Bob had ceased to snarl and was exhibiting an apologetic

attitude to the man whom he evidently believed to be no longer an intruder but an acquaintance.

'It's all right, Bob,' I told him, 'stand by.' He did not stand by for he had seen something that needed further investigation. He made a dash for it, his great tawny body was flung into the bushes, and from the tangled parachute he dragged out – a red wig!

NINE

According to Noel's report of that 'unexpected encounter' in her journal on that not inappropriate date of April the First ('April Fool's day', she commented, 'and who's the fool?'), she invited him into the house and introduced him to her aunt, Rhoda Penfold.

'Baron von Steinvort,' she told Miss Penfold, 'baled out from his plane while reconnoitring, so he said, and dropped into the wood.'

'Indeed?' Summoning a militant, aggressive look, Miss Penfold pinioned the baron with a frozen eye and the glacial inquiry:

'For whom were you reconnoitring and from where do you come?'

'Madam,' he bowed low, 'I come from Switzerland. My father, a Swiss, was a naturalized British subject, my mother was English. I have lived in America and Britain for a number of years and I am employed by the British Intelligence Department. I have endeavoured to explain to Mrs Harbord my unconventional and admittedly suspicious arrival, for which I can, I hope, satisfactorily account if required.'

He finished with another bow and a dazzling show of teeth. Noel remembered those teeth; and she said, exhaling a held-in breath: 'Any information that may be forthcoming I have reason to doubt. What about this?' She produced the red wig that Bob had salvaged from the parachute. 'You must have dropped it when you came down.'

Bob, who had followed her in, uttered a low growl at sight of the wig into which he was evidently panting to get his teeth, having been done out of the satisfaction of using them upon the baron.

'This,' she said, watching that smile which diminished not at all, and evoked rising indignation – the brazen devil! – 'this,' she repeated, 'or one very like it was on the head of a certain German gentleman in a flat in Portland Place and in company with three other German *gentlemen*,' she emphasized the word, 'who were showing lights in a window of their flat, and those lights I insisted must be put out.'

'I admit the wig was mine,' the teeth were slightly less in evidence, 'I was wearing it as a disguise when you so gallantly fulfilled your duties as an air raid warden.'

'And why,' demanded Miss Penfold, 'should you have disguised yourself in order to fraternize with your compatriots?'

'Not *my* compatriots, madam,' turning the smile upon her. 'May I suggest that they, to whom Mrs Harbord alludes, are German, and I – am not.'

'You may suggest what you like, but *I* suggest,' Miss Penfold's voice had a razor-sharp edge to it as if intended to cut through that smile, 'that you verify your statement.'

'I most certainly can ... Mrs Harbord,' he addressed her in a tone that defied contradiction, 'you must know that there are many refugees who have entered these hospitable shores from Germany and are here to conduct their investigations into our defences of these islands and any other matters that might be of interest to the enemy in the conduct of the war. I am well aware,' he said, holding Noel with his eyes in a look that was reminiscent of the look he had given her when she dropped that 'brick' at dinner with Sinclair the first time they met, 'that you and your fellow wardens in Civil Defence suspect the lights which appear at windows in the vulnerable areas of the West End of London, to be of use in the guiding of bombers to their selected targets.'

'Yes,' she returned, with an unconscionable desire to tear that smile from his face or knock his teeth into it, 'and you were excusing your *non*-compatriots for showing lights.'

'It is necessary, as your friend and publisher who is also my publisher knows, that since we are both employed in the same service, and in order to pursue my inquiries it is sometimes necessary to assume to be what I am not.'

'Your ambiguity,' rasped Miss Penfold, 'does you credit in the assumption – as the saying goes – of one who can assume a virtue if he has it not. Your descent on this land adjoining mine and in an aircraft, which I am to believe came from Switzerland or from wherever your employers have sent you, and which must have returned to its base with a co-pilot in it, since there is no sign of nor as far as we know any report or sighting of an aircraft from our Air Ministry, is suspiciously evident of your intent to conduct your inquiries in this area.'

'You judge rightly, madam, in that I baled out in this convenient locality in order to contact a fellow officer who is located a few miles from this village and unfortunately my parachute packed up as I landed.'

'A likely story,' was all he got from her. 'Don't waste your breath in implausible invention – on *me*! I went through the First World War when we had your Kaiser's locusts here striving to devour us – but *we* devoured *them* as we will devour you! I know all about you and your familiars who came here when your Führer was planning to dominate Europe with the same ambitious desire as Napoleon had – for power. But neither Hitler nor your Kaiser had the genius – the military genius, nor the brilliant intelligence of a Napoleon who, had he not been defeated, as we British have always and will always defeat all those who attempt to invade and conquer us —'

'All, madam?' he interrupted with that smile. 'You have forgotten Julius Caesar who conquered Britain, and William of Normandy.'

'Well, what of Hitler, that sadistic maniac, should he succeed in conquering us? Don't talk to me!' as he attempted to speak. 'I know all about you and your minions. How you come here, live here, marry here if you find it to your purpose, are received by some of us who wear blinkers and can't see sideways, but I do! I was not one of Pankhurst's militant army for nothing. And I learned a damn sight more how to run our country and govern our people than the anti's could teach us –the women who have won our rights. Your number's up, Herr Baron.' She made a swift move to a bureau under the window, opened a drawer and took something from it.

Noel, struck dumb with amaze, saw him give a shrug, and still smiling, said:

'This is all very melodramatic but none the less I am in complete accordance with what you have told me.'

'Put up your hands.'

And Miss Penfold pointed a revolver at him, saying: 'Make one move and I'll shoot.'

Bob, having stayed on guard beside Noel, now and to her increasing astonishment came to the baron, who had snapped his fingers at him and the dog was wagging his tail in friendly welcome.

'Good dog!' he said. 'You know a right 'un from a wrong 'un, don't you? One of your grandsires was probably trained as a police dog.'

Miss Penfold turned to Noel.

'Take the dog. Go out of here and lock the door behind you. Telephone the police and stand with the dog under the window should he attempt to escape that way. Hands up, Baron.'

'You may search me, if you will,' he told her pleasantly. 'I am armed but have no intention of using the weapon I am entitled to carry on my exploits. Continue to point your revolver at me, while Mrs Harbord obeys your instructions, and allow me further to explain who and what – I am!'

Extract from Noel's journal dated April 1st

I did not call the police as Aunt Rhoda, in supreme command of this incredible situation, had ordered me to do.
But I did take Bob with me, hanging on to his collar while I
telephoned J. L. S. at his hotel.

Luckily he was in his room. He is back there this week-
end.

'I was just going to phone you,' he said, 'to arrange
where we could meet as I am not the most welcome of
guests at The Chantrey. I believe there is already one visitor
whom Miss Penfold has reason to find an embarrassment.'

'I don't know what you mean – or how you know about
him. Something awful has happened – is happening. He is
here and Aunt Rhoda has got him under her eye with a
gun . . . He came down in the woods in a parachute. I found
him, no, Bob did actually. And he tells us – at least he is
trying to tell us that he is in with *you*! I can't make it out
except that he says he is not what we think he is . . .
What? Oh, yes, your "friend", the baron. Who else should
it be if he *is* your friend and I am beginning to think he
must be . . . What? . . . No. I'm not in a flap. Well, who
wouldn't be? You'll come over at once? Yes . . . You must
come *here*! Aunt told me to call the police but I thought
I'd better call you first . . . Are you laughing? . . . What did
you say? . . . What? He's *made* it? Who's made it? . . .
Whoopee? What do you mean *whoopee*? Are you mad or
am I or is he? . . . *Not* to call the police? Why not? Of
course I'm a one for questions. Who wouldn't be and Aunt
Rhoda with a gun.'

'I'll be over,' he said, 'in fifteen minutes. And don't you
call the police. I'll deal with him.'

He rang off.

I don't know if he could have made head or tail of my
information which must have been as inconsequential as
anything Birdie could have told him. What on earth is

going on and why that note of jubilation? 'Whoopee!' . . .
I suppose because we've caught him . . . And why not call
the police?

The seeds of suspicion within me were sprouting, to
wonder if J. L. S. was what *he* purported to be. I know he is
a publisher, managing director *and* chairman of one of the
world-renowned British publishing firms, a friend of Archie
Tarrant who introduced me to him, and a friend of this
baron, flying ace in the first war, German born, or not?
Naturalized? . . . And what did that porter of the flats
tell the P.W. who checked up on them – that he or one of
them who didn't live there is a Swiss. What am I to
believe?

My mind ran round in circles . . . What with all our C.D.
warnings and Churchill's broadcasts of Fifth Columnists in
our midst who were enemy agents, and the *least* to be
suspected . . . I can't wait for J. L. S. to come. I *will* call the
police. Why not? . . . James Ludwig Sinclair. Ludwig! And
he was back and forth to Frankfurt and Munich before
'39 . . . Why should I *not* call the police? They are the ones
to deal with a spy if he is a spy . . . baling out from a parachute and even now being held at pistol point by Aunt
Rhoda! . . .

But, as her memoirs relate, even as she was hunting
through the telephone directory for the number of the
nearest police station, the telephone rang. She lifted the
receiver and heard:

'Is that The Chantrey, Boulton St Paul?'

'Yes.'

'Police Superintendent, Canterbury, speaking. Is a Mr
Sinclair with you?'

'No, he . . .' her voice dwindled . . . 'I expect him here
presently.'

'Thank you.'

'Why do you . . .' she was about to ask, 'why do you
want to know if he is here?' but was cut off.

196

The day following that 'incredible situation' Noel returned to London a week sooner than she had intended. She explained to her aunt that the Post Warden had telephoned to say she must return for duty as three more full-time wardens had been called up and they were now greatly short staffed.

That invention may or may not have satisfied Miss Penfold, but for Noel it served its purpose since she could not, under the circumstances, bring herself to face another meeting with Sinclair. He, still in Canterbury engaged on what business she dared not guess, had been utterly non-committal in answering her questions concerning himself and his 'friend', the baron, and why he did not wish her to call the police.

The events of these twenty-four hours, as related to Archie Tarrant, to whom, immediately on her arrival in London, she had gone with her account of what she called her 'ghastly experience', 'had completely shattered me,' she said.

And in the train that was taking her back to London in a first class compartment occupied by one other passenger, an elderly gentleman reading *The Times* with an occasional myopic eye on her, she wrote this in pencil regardless of punctuation and partly illegible.

How can you expect me to believe in you after the long decep [*sic*] you have kept up to make me [your?] fool I know what you say you are supposed to be but how could you tell me all those lies about your friend being a flying ace in the last war flying ace he may be but not for us employed in the F.O. as you say *you* are a secret [agent?] and he says so too because he is bilingual with an English mother if that's to be believed born in German Switzerland and not Germany and his father Swiss whatever his mother was. No wonder Colin is suspiciouos [*sic*] and that he was naturalized. I don't believe a word of it. I hate to say this but I can't trust you and as for him why that wig so he can go back and forth from Switzerland or Germany disguised. Is that why? And unless the newspaper you showed me is a blind with him in Switzerland with Laval and we know he is a traitor – Laval I mean if not your friend. How do you expect me to trust you or anything you say you are. You admit your grandfather was or had been a publisher. A German one? And you have a German Christian name. I know this sounds muddled but I *am* muddled after all this and finding von Thingummy is actually secret [service?] for us. Aunt Rhoda didn't believe him any more than I did and Colin isn't so far wrong either. So if you have read this far and have understood what I am trying to tell you with my pencil jogging about in the train at sixty and we are almost in now and I want you to know that I never want to *see* or *hear* from you again and by the way why was the baron one of those four showing lights in Portland Place because he I'm sure *was* one of them and putting on a German accent when he speaks perfect English and a side whiskers and a red wig for his hair is dark and not a streak of ginger in . . .

It is here that the point of her pencil broke. She uttered a loud 'Damn!' and then came a rush of tears. She mopped at them with her handkerchief, and the old gentleman looked up from *The Times* and removing his reading spectacles put on another pair the better to observe her, saying: 'Pardon me, madam. Have you a cold?'

'No, I . . . I have something in my eye.'

'You must excuse my asking you but I am peculiarly susceptible to colds having been a victim of the influenza epidemic of 1918–19 which,' he added gallantly, 'was before your time.'

'It wasn't. I was at boarding school when that awful 'flu, a sort of plague, was killing people off.'

'Pray forgive me for asking you if you have a cold, but owing to my susceptibility to infection, I shun all crowded places and endeavour to travel in a train where, if possible, there are no other passengers in my compartment, or any crowded places. I see,' he continued, reverting to *The Times* and again changing his spectacles for his previous pair, 'that the Lease–Lend Bill, when it was signed by the President of the United States, has declared that America will devote the whole of their industrial financial strength in securing – hem —' he coughed and produced a handkerchief – 'you must forgive me, but I hope you are not sickening for a cold? I feel a tickle in my throat.'

'I have no cold,' Noel assured him, wondering if she could ask him if he had a penknife for her to sharpen her pencil and thinking: He is either hypochondriacal or barmy.

'Which means,' her fellow passenger proceeded, scrutinizing her from behind the horn-rimmed spectacles he had again exchanged from his reading glasses, 'that America will come in with us eventually as they should have done a year ago. Did you hear Churchill's recent world broadcast? . . . No? You should, if you have a wireless. He said that Hitler's invasion plan has failed so far, thanks to the splendid exploits of the Royal Air Force. But will – achew!' he sneezed – 'excuse me, the east wind on the coast at Deal – I have property near Deal but my house there is vacated being in the danger zone in the event of invasion, yet I have to inspect it at intervals – and naturally Hitler being foiled in his plan to invade Britain by the courage of the civil population, whom he hoped to terrorize into surrender by his ruthless bombing — Is that' – he cocked an ear – 'the siren?'

'No, only the train bellowing. We are almost in now.'

'My London flat,' she was told, 'has been bombed twice, but only some valuable furniture damaged and my cat – a great loss to me. Killed instantly. But I escaped with only cuts from glass splinters. I am thankful my son is in Australia and past military age.'

The train was slowing down as it neared the terminus. Noel got up to take her suitcase from the rack.

'Allow me to assist you,' he offered, making no effort to assist.

'Please don't trouble. I can manage.'

At which he raised himself with some difficulty from his seat. 'I am somewhat hampered in my movements for I suffer the result of a wound sustained in the Boer War. Yes, I have lived through two wars and this is the third – if I live through it.'

'Here we are.' Noel opened the door of the compartment. 'There is an alert but this is not what you heard. Can I take you to a shelter? There should be one on the station.'

'Thank you so much, but I would prefer to stay here for a while. Shelters are always overcrowded and teeming with infection.'

'Goodbye, then.'

'Goodbye. A pleasure to have met you . . . Was that a bomb?'

'Yes, but not near here. Are you sure you won't go to a shelter?'

'No, I won't do that though I think I will go out and find a taxi.'

'That is what I am going to do.'

'Then shall we go together?'

He had no luggage with him and in the confusion of the station, lack of porters to carry her bag, and her concern for the old gentleman who she believed, if not barmy, was evidently in need of someone to take charge of him, they walked to the exit.

The anti-aircraft guns were firing at oncoming bombers.

'Can I get you a taxi?' she asked him, offering her arm.

'Thank you, but I quite forgot – I have my car meeting me. May I give you a lift in it when' – he peered around – 'he comes. He should have been here.'

As they came out of the station no one appeared to be in the least concerned by the bombers and the anti-aircraft guns but nothing was dropped in that vicinity. People were

200

going about their business as usual; city clerks, girl typists, women with shopping baskets, uniformed officers, boys home on leave, a sailor or two, a few wardens on duty, and a chauffeur who accosted Noel's charge.

'I am sorry I am late, my lord. I've been held up.'

'There's a raid on, isn't there?'

'Yes, my lord, but nothing much.'

'Where are you going?' Noel was asked.

'To Grosvenor Street.'

'I am in Grosvenor Square so I can drive you there. Take the lady's suitcase,' to his chauffeur.

As they drove through the West End, the shoppers, mostly women, evinced not the least concern for the boom of guns which Noel thought must be firing from the docks. The distant fall of bombs could be heard.

'May I ask,' her companion turned his horn-rimmed spectacles upon her, 'what you do with yourself as you seem completely unaffected by the sirens and this raid, as do most of the women' – he peered through the window – 'who are so busily engaged on their lawful occasions.'

'I don't do anything much more than in Civil Defence.'

'Are you married?'

'Yes.'

'Any children?'

'No.'

Further interrogation elicited the fact that she illustrated books and book jackets for publishers.

'Who publishes your work?' he inquired coughing into his handkerchief and clearing his throat. 'Excuse me – so troublesome – I happen to have an interest in publishing.'

'I work for Marriott and also for Kell and Wrotham.'

'A long-established firm, but it is Marriott with whom I am connected. I hope,' he told her, suppressing a sneeze – 'that I am not getting a cold – these east winds on the coast — Yes, I am one of the directors of Marriott, and

James Sinclair, the chairman and managing director, is my nephew.'

'Oh,' she uttered blankly, 'is he?'

'My brother's son. My brother died of that influenza – or plague, as you call it – epidemic of 1918. I also caught it, but I escaped with my life.'

'I see.' . . . So this brother of his, father of J. L. S. who had married a German girl, or half German, makes him quarter German as he had told her.

The car pulled up at Archie Tarrant's flat in Upper Grosvenor Street. The chauffeur opened the door of the car.

'Thank you so much for the lift.' She held out her hand to receive a firm clasp of hers.

'A pleasure. May I ask your name? I must have seen your work many times in or on Marriott's book covers.'

She gave him her maiden name which she used for illustrations.

'I shall look out for your next – achew! – Excuse me – I hope we shall meet again.'

She pondered while she waited for Archie's return, his man having told her he was expected back in about half an hour . . . So J. L. S. *must* be what he says he is unless his uncle is also in with them . . . His uncle. I didn't know he had anyone belonging to him . . . Yes, there was an uncle. That time, she remembered, fhen she and Sinclair had gone to the ballet. He said he was going to take an uncle but he was in bed with a cold. So this must be the uncle with a cold . . . Lord Somebody.

She took from her handbag the unfinished letter. She must rewrite it. Too much of a muddle . . . But first to hear what Archie had to say.

What Archie had to say did not much allay her doubts of him to whom she had given, she told herself, her faith, her hope, and all of her . . . 'I must know,' she demanded of Archie, having poured out to him a similar incoherent

202

account to that which she had scrawled in the train to Sinclair, 'is he in the Intelligence Department of our Foreign Office or our Secret Service or is he not? If not, then who is he working for and who or what is that so-called baron who he is supposed to have known for years, and publishes his books translated from the German, and has also written books in English published by Marriott under a pseudonym – probably his mother's name who the baron now says was an English woman. I don't understand it. And why should he have been in that flat with those German refugee Jews if they *were* refugees and not of Hitler's lot, showing lights and he in a red wig! I'm positive it was he with an assumed German accent for he speaks perfect English and his hair is dark. He looks more French than German, but the porter at those flats says he is Swiss. So what do you make of it?'

Archie cocked an eyebrow.

'As much, or as little, as you – so lucidly – make of it. As for Sinclair, I know him as a member of my club and that he is chairman of Marriott, a highly reputable publishing company. Of this baron, I know no more of him than you know or than he has told you.'

'A lot of help that is! But if Sinclair belongs to your club, do you know anything of his family?'

'Only that he has an uncle and that his father died and left him the chairmanship of the Marriott publishing company. This uncle is a widower, and as far as I know, is Sinclair's sole surviving relative other than a cousin, his uncle's only son who is in Australia sheep farming, I believe. That is about all I can tell you of Sinclair except that he took an honours degree in modern languages at Cambridge.'

'Languages . . . Yes, very useful for an international – whatever he is. And how did he come to be in the Foreign Office after the 1914 war in which he is supposed to have served in our Army?'

'He went into the F.O., as I understand, before the death

of his father. And when he took over Marriott's he continued voluntarily in the Intelligence Department of the Foreign Office. His proficiency in languages, especially German,' Archie examined the tip of his cigar, 'must have been a considerable asset.'

'What of the baron?' she persisted. 'You have told me nothing of Sinclair that I didn't know, and that doesn't prove what I believe he is, only what he tells me, and as for the baron —'

'Your incredulity,' he interrupted dryly, 'does you credit, yet I have no doubt our security and the Foreign Office have all who are suspect well marked.'

'He, the baron, said that the Foreign Office know all about him.'

'As it is their business to know, but the English law maintains a man to be innocent until he is proved guilty.'

'Which should not apply to suspected spies, especially during a war and daily expectation of invasion. Oh, I meant to tell you – about Sinclair's uncle – this is quite a coincidence. I travelled up with him on the train. We got talking and he gave me a lift here. The chauffeur called him his "lord", but he didn't tell me his name, only that Sinclair is his nephew and that he is a director of Marriott. Do you know who he is?'

Archie smiled. 'I gather he must be Lord Aviemore, late of the Grenadiers and on Haig's staff in the last war. Aviemore had inherited the barony in his twenties. His brother, Sinclair, a younger son, had the money as chairman of Marriott and he married a girl whose father was senior attaché at the German Embassy over here and her mother, Sinclair's grandmother, was English.'

'Which, I suppose, accounts for his being, as he says, a quarter German if his grandmother was English and his grandfather German.'

'Exactly. So your Sinclair —'

'He's not *my* Sinclair,' she interrupted flushing. 'He is the publisher of my illustrations and book jackets – at least he *was*. I don't know if I will do any more work for him unless I can get to the truth as to what he is and for whom he works – he and that baron, an ex-German flying ace as Sinclair led me to believe and who is still flying, purporting to have come from Switzerland and parachuted in our woods! Why?'

Removing the inevitable cigar from his lips, 'Admittedly,' Archie said with pacific calm, 'there is reason for your doubt of this baron, but what I know of the Foreign Office and our security is that they must be fully aware of those agents who work for or against us and run the gauntlet of suspicion as to their rights – or wrongs.'

'Most helpful!' she tartly replied. 'Either you don't wish to tell me what you may or may not know about those two or you know more than they or you would want me to know.'

The lines around his blue unfaded eyes wrinkled with inward laughter.

'I admit that your pertinent and somewhat equivocal quiddity does not immunize *me* from suspicion. But as you are a conscientious member of our Civil Defence, it is part of your duty to be on the alert for any untoward event that might indicate Fifth Column or enemy agents' activities. And Hitler's main objective is invasion of these islands.'

'We all know that.'

'Precisely, although for the present he is holding his horses, or rather his Messerschmitts, until he considers the time ripe to descend on us. But I understand that every inch of the coast and particularly in Kent and the rural districts of the eastern counties are closely defended. So it is possible your baron in his parachute was taking the lie of the land.'

'For Hitler or for *us*?'

'You may be sure that those in authority will ascertain if any German agents are not yet rounded up, and that

Hitler's hesitation in making the decisive move has served to tighten our defences. But the Nazis have not been idle. Perhaps you did not read or hear the latest news that one Rudolf Hess, Hitler's close friend and confidant —'

'The baron,' she broke in, 'is supposed to be Sinclair's close friend if not his confidant!'

Waving away that remark with his cigar, 'I repeat,' he said, 'that this Hess is Hitler's close friend and he arrived in Scotland by parachute in an aeroplane piloted by himself.'

'I didn't know that, but if he did the baron did the same and may also have been snooping around on our defences. When did this Hess arrive?'

'Yesterday, but you were so busily engaged in "snooping around", as you put it, on the baron and Sinclair, that you have obviously missed this more intriguing incident which is evidently intended by Hitler to engage us in another offer of peace.'

'Not a hope! He can't think that. Sending this Hess to negotiate for peace with us would mean our surrender if we agreed to it.'

'Since Hitler believes himself to be invincible and that we are so battered by his bombs and the indiscriminate massacre of civilians that we are ready to give in, he sees us all but conquered now.'

'As if we would ever give in!' she cried hotly, 'and we haven't been conquered for almost a thousand years.'

'Hitler does not believe that and Napoleon didn't believe it although we today are fighting a far more merciless assailant, one who matches his monstrous arrogance with barbarous excesses surpassing the worst abominations and heathen cruelty of savages.'

She shuddered. 'It doesn't seem possible that any *sane* men can tolerate such a leader – their Führer and his Gestapo to whom they say their prayers!'

'Hypnotic mass hysteria. There will be,' Archie said grimly, 'a rude awakening for some of them!'

'Well,' she got up, 'I must go back to Colin. He will be home from duty' – she glanced at the clock – 'unless he is on nights this week. Oh, and there's something else I have just thought of. If the baron or his father is or was Swiss, how does he come to have a German title? The Swiss don't have titles, do they? He is von something, meaning "from" wherever in Germany his ancestors derived.'

'Or Austria. The Swiss, especially those of German Switzerland bordering on Germany, can claim German ancestry without necessarily being German.'

'As Sinclair can claim to be descended from the French – Normans, so he says.'

'As many of us are if we take the trouble to trace our antecedence. Must you go? Won't you stay and dine?'

'No, I can't. I want to see Colin and whether he is in a state about me and – Sinclair. He knows Sinclair has gone to Canterbury and that I am coming back earlier than I had expected. I phoned him. I haven't got very far with my inquiries of you, have I?'

'Which, as I said, makes me,' his thin smile expanded, 'also under suspicion.' He bowed her out with his usual courtesy. *Arrivederci*.'

She found Colin, as expected, so she tells us, in 'a state'. He accosted her with:

'Why didn't you stay till Friday as you said you would? Did Sinclair come back with you?'

'No. As far as I know he is still in Canterbury – minding his own business.'

She went into her bedroom, took off her hat and coat and began to unpack her suitcase.

He followed her.

'Marcia Sinclair has been here today. She wanted to see you.'

'Marcia? To see me – why? I thought she was still in Cornwall with Barton.'

He sat on the edge of the bed fidgeting with his hands, pulling at the bedcover.

'She,' he blurted, 'had something to tell me – something that I already knew, except that she has now definitely decided to take proceedings against you – and Sinclair.'

Noel drew in a breath.

'Proceedings – for what?'

'Divorce, of course.' He did not look at her. He was examining his finger nails.

'She has no grounds, no evidence for divorce.'

'Hasn't she?' He lifted his head, staring at her, saying with ominous quiet that she felt preceded a storm, 'I know she has and you know it – you and Sinclair – that German! He *is* a German whatever he may pass himself off as – I know!' The storm was about to break. 'He and you – all this time you and he – you have been his woman. He has had you, *all* of you in his flat where you were supposed to have been lent a studio. Did you think to cod me and everyone by that? Everyone knew – Barton knew.' He started up from the bed, raising his fisted hands and beating the air as if at a face. Then he flung himself at her, caught her by the throat. His eyes were bolting, bloodshot. She felt his fingers tighten in a vicious grip on her bare neck. 'You whore!' he screamed. 'You bloody whore! I'll kill you – I'll kill *him* . . .' He was digging his nails into her flesh. She tried to pull his hands away, saying calmly although her heart was pounding at her ribs, not in fear for herself but for him: 'Don't do that, you're hurting me.'

'Wha' . . . Wha' you . . .' His voice was thick, his lips sagged, his hands loosened and he fell back on the bed in a writhing convulsion . . .

In her journal she records the end of that day.

It is terrible to see him in these fits. They are getting worse, more frequent but thank God they last only a few minutes and he never knows they have happened. I phoned Archie after making Colin lie down, he said he had a headache and was still harping on Marcia's visit, but he had taken a more temperate view of it . . . He said: 'I have known a long time about you and Sinclair – I've given up minding because you have known about *my* little – affairs, and we did agree to be brotherly and sisterly. But I'd hate to have you mixed up in a divorce case, cited as the woman taken in adultery – is that how they would call you in a court of law?'

I hoped he was being sensible about it and not bluffing me into thinking he could actually accept this beastly thing if she really intended to do it . . . Archie was out when I phoned. I left word for him to call me and was relieved when Colin went on duty at nineteen hours for, even with the secrecy switch on, he might listen in.

When I had finished telling Archie all about it – and Marcia, he said:

'I think it were better you persuade him to come to me for a while. I had spoken to him when you were at The Chantrey about taking a holiday. Jeremy Gore suggested it for I told him his attacks, as reported by you, are lately more frequent. I think I could get him to agree to go away with me, somewhere away from the coast while this invasion scare is keeping our Home Guard and defences on the *qui vive*. He would want to be in on anything that might be pending but there is a lull in the raids at present . . .'

Colin, surprisingly, did fall in with Archie's offer to go away with him. He admitted he felt 'all in' of late, too much night duty; and a medical certificate from Sir Jeremy gave him three weeks' sick leave. He was due for leave in any case as he had not taken any time off since he became a full-timer . . .

* * *

Since that episode with Colin when she returned from The Chantrey she had not seen Sinclair, but she had heard from him. He had telephoned her continuously; she refused to speak to him merely to repeat: 'You have had my letter. You know that I mean what I said. All is finished between us. I will send you the two more illustrations I still owe Marriott for Grierson's book.'

In vain did he appeal to her and wrote at last in desperation.

'I deserve everything you think of me, but how could I give away top secrets even to you? I had to put you off the scent about him. He is one of our Inner Circle as we call them, who have to play what looks to be a double game. My darling love, believe me I had to keep it up. Can't say any more in a letter, but you who are in Civil Defence must realize that we have to be on our guard even with our closest and dearest...'

She did not answer his letter for she felt he had deliberately deceived her all this time and could not believe, despite his protestations, that he and his 'friend' of the so-called 'Inner Circle' were not playing a double game ... For whom? For us, or for ...? She was torn between her love of Sinclair and her mistrust of him, more deadly than the gnawing uncertainty of doubt. The 'Inner Circle'. Was that what they called the people who worked in secret for ... us? She remembered how during the Cromwellian era, those loyalists called the Sealed Knot went in all manner of disguises dedicated to securing the restoration of the exiled King Charles. Perhaps this 'Inner Circle' has the same sort of dedicated service. She would want to think so.

It relieved her of immediate anxiety to know that Colin had so readily agreed to take the prescribed sick leave and go with Archie Tarrant to a hotel in Malvern well away from the coast that bristled with defence precautions against pending invasion.

On a morning about two weeks after Colin had left for Malvern, following a temporary lull, the Blitz had been renewed with increased savagery. There had been three landmines and heavy casualties centred on the North

London termini and the B.B.C. Noel, returning to the flat having been on night duty, was greeted by the daily help with:

'What a night of it, ma'am! We had a bomb at the end of our road in Kentish Town – two 'ouses down and the blast! Somethink awful. The glass of my bed-sitter window blown right out, splinters all over the floor and gas pipes burst in the street – no gas nothink to cook by and the electricity gone too.'

'Anyone injured?'

'Not s'far as I know. The wardens were ever so good an' 'elpful but we 'ad it nothink like so bad as you've 'ad it 'ere. But larss week they got the school next street to us – luckily after the kids was gone 'ome but there was some of 'em playin' in the road when they ought to 'ave been indoors – 'e was a bit earlier than usual that night, and he killed two of 'em.'

'I know – I know. God! When will it cease?'

'Not till we can 'ang that 'Itler and all of 'is murderin' gang. What can I get you for your breakfast, ma'am? There's spam and Mr 'Arbord's butter ration. 'E didn't take 'is ration book with 'im but I expect the hotel will 'ave enough.'

'I had better send it on to him in case. I only want toast and a cup of tea, thank you, Mrs Hodson. While you are getting it I'll take his ration book to the post.'

As she went down the stairs the door bell rang.

'I'll see to it, Mrs Hodson,' she called.

A short squat man stood at the door. Raising his bowler hat:

'Mrs Harbord?'

'Yes.'

Alarm seized her. Had he come with bad news of Colin? She had told Archie to tell her if anything went wrong but he would have telephoned, surely?

'Pardon me, madam.' He held out a long envelope. 'I have to give you this.'

She took it, wondering. A bill? A writ? Colin in debt again? But he hadn't bought anything – or had he? She had paid off almost all his overdraft, and he never dined out unless Potts took him. Yes, he had bought some whisky, and gin, not on account...

'Good day, madam.'

His hat raised again politely.

She watched him cross the road and hail a passing taxi. She then posted the ration book with a note in it to Colin: 'Hope you will soon be back. We all miss you at the post. The P.W. was only saying yesterday how conscientious you are . . .' That would please him. He had recently got his second stripe.

Mrs Hodson had a tray ready for her with toast, a jar of hoarded marmalade, a pot of tea.

She felt deathly tired. It had been a long and dreadful night with three houses down. No casualties among the wardens more than glass cuts and bruises from falling beams, but the Heavy Rescue had reported five killed in the houses, and nine injured taken to hospital . . .

She ate a slice of toast, sipped the tea, then opened the envelope, took out its enclosure and read:

In the High Court of Justice
     Probate, Admiralty and Divorce Division . . .

So Marcia had meant it!

Her head swam, she had a feeling as if all the blood in her veins had been drained. She gulped hot tea, set down the cup with a hand that shook, and continued to read:

The humble petition of Mrs Marcia Sinclair . . .

A sudden laugh, unmirthful, broke from her. Humble! To whom was Marcia *humbling* herself? And what had the Admiralty got to do with it and Probate? Couldn't a Divorce petition stand on its own? . . . And then: It's not what I wanted, but J. L. S. did, and now he has it. I suppose the same beast of a thing has been sent to or given to him

. . . Damn! What a hellish . . . But it won't make any difference. He wanted to marry me and now he could if I would but I won't . . . Why does she start it all up again? Does she want to marry – who? The baron! Came over in the same boat with her . . . What am I to *do*?

She got up from the table, called to Mrs Hodson: 'I'm going to lie down, Mrs Hodson. You can clear these things away and then go home. You don't have to stay. You must be tired out after being up all night in the Blitz.'

Mrs Hodson, pippin-faced, rotund, came to the door.

'Thank you, ma'am, I'd be glad to get back and clean up the mess in my room. I meant to tell you – a gentleman called just as I come in this mornin' and asked for you. I said you'd be off duty about nine.'

'Yes, Mrs Hodson, he did come, that same – gentleman. He had a message to give me from my – from my bank.'

She went to her room, took off her uniform, and lay down on the bed. She would *have* to ring J. L. S. She must know if he had one too. Would he be at his office? She dared not ring there to be overheard. She waited for Mrs Hodson to leave, having washed up the breakfast things. It was now only ten o'clock. He might not be at his office yet. She would try his flat.

He answered promptly, giving his telephone number.

'James – J. L. S.?'

'Darling! Are you all right? I was just about to ring you knowing you must have had a hell of a night.'

'I've had a hell of a morning – with a – a thing served on me. Have you had one too?'

'I have. Are you alone?'

'Yes, Colin has gone away with Archie on sick leave.'

'I'm coming to you now.'

What passed at that meeting between these two she recalls as:

He didn't seem to mind about that beast of a thing dropped on us. 'So we've both had it,' I said when, hearing

213

his car outside, I opened the door to him and as we went upstairs to my room: 'It's worse than a bomb.'

'Oh no, only a dummy bomb, and as far as *I've* had it – a blessing.'

We were in the sitting-room; he took hold of me, lifting me off my feet, saying: 'I've been waiting two – no, three weeks for this. I got your letter written in the train and you didn't finish it when your pencil broke. I loved it. I hadn't done laughing all that day.'

'I'm glad,' I said coldly, extricating myself, 'that it amused you. I meant to rewrite it but found Colin in a state and gave it in a hurry for Mrs Hodson to post.'

'You absurd baby! Did you really think I am a spy?'

'Why not? When you led me to believe – as good as told me the baron is one and then he turns out *not* to be – unless you are as bad as he is.'

'I wish I were half as good. I'm just an amateur and given all the easy jobs, unpaid. He is one of the high ups.' He stepped back. 'Let me look at you . . . You are more lovely, my Caro, than ever, in spite of being on duty all night. I rang you here – was all het up knowing you had it so heavily in your area, but there was no answer. Colin was on duty too, I suppose.'

'No, I told you, he's gone away with Archie on sick leave. He'll be back next week.'

'I can explain everything if you'll let me.'

'You can explain another time if there is an explanation but I've more to have explained to me than that. I want to know about us and *that*.' I pointed to where I had flung it on the floor.

'The main thing about *us*,' he said, 'is that I am seeing you again after telling me in that adorably incoherent letter you would never see or speak to me again.'

'I meant it and would have kept to it if it were not for *this*.' I picked up and smoothed out the crumpled document. 'I had to see you to know what you – what we are going to do.'

214

'I'll tell you what I'm going to do.' He pulled me on to the sofa and kissed me long and hard. 'That's for a start,' he said, out of breath. 'And now down to earth from heaven. You will have to marry me whether you like it or not.'

I drew away from him.

'Oh no! It makes no difference from what I've always said. I'll not be divorced from Colin even if he wanted to, which he doesn't and never did. He doesn't love me, not as he loved or thought he loved Barton and his gibbon as a kind of Oedipus mother image. He is all mixed up and then his awful childhood and killing that German. As for his love for me it's as an article of furniture, one of his possessions, as is his love for these.' I indicated a Ming vase and a set of Chinese rice bowls he had salvaged from the liquidation of his antique business. 'These are insured and I am not, and that makes it all the more necessary for him to hold on to me. He would never part with these any more than he would part with me. He is jealous – dangerously jealous – of anyone who would take these or anything else belonging to him. And I belong to him. I had to sell some of his things because of his overdraft and one of them was his favourite Chinese piece. I thought it hideous – supposed to be the god of literature dressed in green and red and sitting on what looked like the pot in gilt. I've forgotten his name – Wen Cheng something, but it fetched a lot at Sotheby's.'

'You are always so full of surprises. Is there any other woman served with a divorce petition whose first consideration would be for her husband – in sickness or in health – and with whom she has not co-habited for how long is it? Living *for* him but not *with* him, although under the same roof. And you take it all so calmly.'

'How do you expect me to take it? To fall into hysterics or attempt suicide or something? Shall we have to defend?'

'Defend? Good God, no! Would you want me to defend against your freedom to marry me?'

'I don't want to and will not,' I said determinedly, 'marry you. I've told you this a hundred times.'

'And now it's a hundred and one times. In any case there is no defence. We are the guilty parties. She has had us watched to give evidence enough to convince a judge.'

'But she hasn't actually seen us in flagrant delight?'

He caught me to him again.

'Darling! You're wonderful.'

'I think I am rather,' I said, modestly. 'But how, if we haven't been caught in the act – I mean not seen by a chambermaid or somebody in bed together in a hotel or by your manservant at your flat, is there evidence enough?'

'There is evidence enough if opportunity is coupled with desire.'

'There has been opportunity,' I said, 'but what about desire?'

'Since she has had her Private Eye watching us and I have frequently taken you back to your flat and kissed you goodnight on your doorstep with obvious desire, then if we don't defend it's in the bag.'

'It's all too horrible,' I exclaimed. 'You don't *mind* about the beastliness of it. And what of the publicity? I can't have that. Not for my sake but for Colin although she did tell him she was going for divorce. He went for me over it at first, and afterwards seemed to accept it, even to welcome it. He doesn't know *his* own mind from day to day or hour to hour.'

'There need not be any publicity. I'll see to that – and my solicitor will stop the press.'

I hadn't thought of a solicitor. This was awful. 'How could we keep it quiet from Colin?' I asked. 'And I haven't a solicitor anyway.'

'I have – a friend of mine.'

'Like the baron?' I said nastily.

'Not quite like the baron and nothing like so good at his job as he is, but he'll do what I tell him. He is the solicitor for Marriott Limited, and limited to me. And now that you know we are in for it, come back to the flat and live with me there to be seen in flagrant delight by whoever wants to see us. And I'll take you to and from the post when you're on duty.'

'I'm on duty tonight.'

'But there is always ... tomorrow.'

'Only tomorrow,' I said, 'never comes.'

As at all anxious times Noel, as she recounted, took that 'beast of a thing' to Archie Tarrant. Colin, back again on duty at the post, appeared both mentally and physically improved; nor did he seem to have heard of Marcia's petition.

Archie received the news of it with reassuring cool and the offer to consult his solicitor on her behalf.

'Sinclair,' she told him, 'is seeing to it all.'

'And you are both agreed not to defend?'

'There is no defence. I – we – are guilty. It's all here.'

Archie screwed a monocle into his eye and examined the document she held out to him.

'Brief and to the point,' he said. 'The petitioner claims that you and James Ludwig Sinclair committed adultery on several occasions at the said – m – m's – flat in – where? Ah, yes, Piccadilly.' He looked up. 'You were seen in the act?'

She flushed indignantly.

'Like cats on the roof? Of course not. We had the opportunity and the – the desire which is all they want.'

Archie's lips twitched in the ghost of a smile.

'Which could be sufficient evidence if undefended, but why not defend?'

She got up and went to him.

'Archie, don't you hate me for it?'

'Hate you? My dear girl, considering what you have given Colin, helped him, borne with him all these years, could I have wished him a better wife? And I applaud your decision as more proof of your selflessness, in that if you do not defend you would be free to marry the man you love and who loves you. Colin could then go for *his* divorce.'

'How could I leave Colin? Who else would care for him?'

'He knows that you and Sinclair are lovers,' Archie said quietly.

'He has spoken to you about – us?'

He nodded. The monocle dropped and hung on a thin black cord against his waistcoat.

She said: 'He minded dreadfully when Marcia – there's a bitch, she is – told him, but he already guessed that we —' she bit her lip. 'I didn't deny it. We agreed long ago to go our own ways. He and Barton were having an affair – and then he went off to Paris with the gibbon, but all the time he wouldn't let me go. He wanted everything his way and he *gets* everything his way, he always will. I dread to think how he'll take this if she goes on with it. It is bound to be in the papers.'

'She may not go on with it,' Archie said, 'although I have reason to believe she is wanting a divorce so that she can marry again.'

'Has she someone in mind to marry?'

'Yes. I happen to know that she has had this particular man in mind for some time, ever since she came over in the same boat with him from New York.'

'Oh!' She clapped a hand to her mouth. 'Not von Steinvort?'

'Yes, Sinclair's friend, von Steinvort, whom I also have known for a number of years.'

'You too!'

She looked at him searchingly. 'How well do you know him and what do you know of him?'

'Only that he is attached to our Intelligence Department.'

She admits she was staggered; and to this reconstruction from her verbal reminiscences she adds a self-condemnatory rider in her journal.

How could I have been such a fool as to be taken in by both of them! I consider it inexcusable of J. L. S. They must have found my incredulity side-splitting that I should fall for his – the baron's – mountebank 'activities'! That red wig and the whiskers, for I know it must have been him I saw with those refugees when I put out the lights in their flat. But how can he explain why he came to be with those three and their blonde, and assuming a German accent to pass himself off as one of them? And then why come down in a parachute if he was surveying our defences – why could he not have done whatever he was supposed to be doing as *himself*? To go to such lengths to deceive not only me but everyone else? I can hardly think his German opposite numbers over here can be impressed with *our* 'agents' secret manoeuvres'! I had it out with J. L. S. and made him explain it for it doesn't make sense to me . . .

The explanation offered by Sinclair did, she allows, make 'sense'; but none the less it does seem, she told him, 'that your operative agents, or this particular "highly valued" one as you say, has gone to unnecessary extremes.'

'He was taking an aerial survey to ascertain how much an enemy aircraft could observe, not only of our defences but where our factories have been removed from their original sites. Beaverbrook has had them transferred because of heavy concentration on them of late. They won't be so easy to locate now. But we've had our whack at their factories too, particularly on the opposite side of Lake Constance, across the border where German factories have been belching smoke day and night for some years before the war, as our friend, back and forth from Switzerland, has verified and reported to the Air Ministry.'

'But why,' she persisted, 'did he come down in those woods in a parachute?'

'That was a bit of bad luck. He had to bale out for lack of juice. He has been over twice since you,' he chuckled, 'fell foul of him.'

'He was a flying ace for Germany in the last war,' she reminded him accusingly. 'How does he come to be with us and *for* us now?'

'He has never been anything else but for us.'

'But you said he was a German pilot in the last war.'

'I never said so. You assumed it because of what you thought was his German name. It is Austrian actually, and he was *our* flying ace!'

'He told us – Aunt Rhoda and I – that he was a British subject, and when I saw him with Marcia at Claridges she said she had known him before the war and that he is a naturalized German.'

'He was never naturalized nor German. His father was British – a naturalized Swiss, his mother was English and he was born here.'

'Marcia seems to know a lot about him.'

'Yes, but nothing of what or who he actually is. I do know. He was educated in England and at Bonn University, where I first met him. He has proved himself to be an invaluable asset to our Intelligence Department.'

She was still dubious.

'But what of that paragraph you showed me in the paper about him meeting Laval in Switzerland? And Laval is a traitor to France.'

'It's his job to hunt traitors.'

'And *your* job to throw dust in my eyes! What am I to believe?'

He took two cigarettes from his case, lighted both and handed one to her. 'Believe this. Even to you, who are so zealous and dutiful a member of the Civil Defence, we cannot give away our top secret agents or their works.'

'You think I would talk!' she said indignantly. 'You don't trust me.'

He slipped her a smile.

'More than you trust me?'

'How can I trust you? It all sounds so cock and bull . . . Pass me an ashtray.'

The ashtray was passed. She flicked ash from her cigarette into it, a querulous frown between her eyebrows.

'What do they do with traitors?' she asked, not looking at him.

'They shoot them.'

'Then your friend the baron, if he is one or whatever he is' – her eyes met his straightly – 'runs the risk of being shot for a traitor?'

"He, as do all Number One operatives, carries his life in his hands.'

'Do you,' she drew a sharp intake of breath, 'run that risk?'

'I am only a cypher in the game, a stand-by if I'm wanted – to take orders.'

But she was off upon another tack.

'Those refugees whose lights I put out – our area is stiff with refugee Jews. Why did he have to disguise himself with a red wig and a German accent when he speaks perfect English?'

'Because they are not all refugee Jews. Yes, Jews they may be, as are others in this country working for Hitler. They are extremely useful in vulnerable areas such as yours and dockland and the larger cities bristling with factories, where they have been given compassionate harbourage by us. And you should know how useful they are in guiding enemy aircraft to their targets by signalling with lights and – other activities. For the treacherous few which our friend and his colleagues have rounded up, there are millions of Hitler's innocent victims being massacred in Germany and tortured in Belsen and similar horror camps for whom we are fighting this war, and

222.

against Nazi totalitarianism. But those who are here and in the pay of their Führer to save their skins, we are all out to catch *them*. And they *will* be caught, make no mistake.' He was watching the fleeting expressions on her face that alternated between mistrust, doubt and dismay. 'As to our friend, he is known to a good many of Hitler's agents, some of whom are doubles. We have them taped. But he is not likely to go among them to be recognized. He is a man of many parts, and has been to Hollywood acting in some of his own spy thrillers that have been filmed. He is also expert in the art of make-up and moreover,' he laughed softly, 'he thoroughly enjoys playing in fact what he has played in fiction.'

'You said you publish his books – I understood from you,' she determindly pursued, 'that he is a well-known German author.'

'I did not say he is a *German* author, and I do publish his books, his translations from the German, but chiefly his detective and spy thrillers in English under a pseudonym. Anything else you want to know?'

'What name does he write under?'

'Gavin Johns. His mother's name was Johns and Gavin is his second name.'

'Gavin Johns!' she exclaimed. 'Colin reads them on nights at the post and I've read some of them. Is *that* who he is, or are you putting me off the scent because I fell foul – you've said it! – of him?'

'Which would make me as bad or as good as he. All right, doubting Thomasina, I'll give it you. We, he and I, are two of Hitler's top agents – have been for years working over here to smash Great Britain and *all* of you. *Heil Hitler!*'

'Oh!' She turned angrily away to stub her cigarette in the ashtray. 'I'm beginning to hate you! I'm not the moron you think I am. You can't pull that stuff on me. But if what you have told me is true about him, how can you explain why he looked at me in that suspicious way when we dined with you before the war and I said how strange it was that we four should be sitting there together when he fought in the last war as a pilot for Germany?'

'He is a champion leg-puller and if he thought you believed him to be a German acting for Germany, he kept it up rather than that you and Colin or anyone else should guess what he is or what he does. But you may have imagined that look.'

Yet she still had her doubts.

'As for leg-pulling, I'd say *you* are probably the supreme champion leg-puller. What about Hess? Was it coincidence that Hess should have baled out on almost the same day as your Gavin Johns von Steinvort – or whoever he is – came down?'

'Not so coincidental. Our fellow was on his track as well as engaged on his own job. And now can we talk about ourselves?' . . .

But their personal problems looked likely to take second place, when, a week or two after Noel was served with 'that beast of a thing', Hitler's fury against the indomitable defence of Great Britain increased fourfold. His latest threat hurled at us was to get rid of Winston Churchill, the one obstacle to his complete conquest of these 'miserable islands' with only a narrow slip of water between him and invasion. This first attempt had been thwarted at Dunkirk by a gallant fleet of 'little ships' which evacuated all the survivors of the British Expeditionary Force. Hitler's boast that he would utterly destroy Great Britain by dropping one hundred bombs on us for every one bomb our Air Force dropped on Germany or, alternatively, the riddance of Churchill, resulted only in Britain's confidence renewed as expressed in a speech to the Commons by the Prime Minister whose political extinction Hitler craved.

'Hitler's Empire has nothing to sustain it beyond espionage, pillage, corruption and the Prussian boot . . .' But the British 'boot' was heavily applied in the grim battle

224

of Crete that would affect the whole course of the Mediterranean campaign which our Navy in the Battle of the Atlantic suffered, with the severe loss of the *Hood* and all her men and officers; yet reprisal followed swiftly in a series of attacks by the Fleet Air Arm to sink *Bismarck*, the most powerful battleship in the world.

Meanwhile Britain bore the brunt of enemy raids, more devastation of property, murder of civilians and the exigeant demands on those in Civil Defence of our cities and in especial of London. Night and day Noel was on duty, calling the services and, despite medical advice, was out during incidents on her and other action stations, as more and more full-time wardens were called up to man our depleted armies in the unceasing fight for survival.

'Let the tempest roar,' vociferated Churchill, 'let it rage. We shall come through ...'

And three days after he made that speech, on 7 May 1941, the House of Commons chamber was destroyed by enemy action.

Extract from Noel's journal May 1941

It has been a hectic time for all of us but now with a momentary cessation of continuous Blitz after they got the House of Commons, I went with J. L. S. to see his solicitor. His lawyer apparently thought we could go for a defence as there was no actual evidence of what he called 'intimacy'.

'Meaning,' I prompted him, 'adultery?'

He was square-shouldered, bull-necked, with a pugnacious chin, looking more like a farmer than a man of law. He said little. I did most of the talking and impressed upon him that I had admitted to Marcia when she invited me to lunch and said she knew about us – that we were lovers.

'Hearsay is not evidence,' he said. 'Opportunity —'

'And desire,' I interrupted, 'and there has been desire

if being kissed goodnight at my door – she had us watched – is proof of desire.'

The main thing, and I insisted on this, is that I am determined not to defend, and that it must be kept out of the papers.

The lawyer's name incredibly, or that of his firm, is Faith – Hope, and Charity? I wondered, but it isn't. It is Faith, Faith, Good, and Son. I didn't see any Good nor any son nor any other Faith, but solicitors always seem to have several members of their firm and most of them trade under a century-old name, the original bearers of that name being long since dead. In this case J. L. S. told me, when we left the office in King's Bench Walk, the lawyer's name was Tripp.

I said, a trifle hysterically, 'I hope he doesn't trip us up!'

His car was parked with a dozen others, and as we drove off, he said:

'I believe you're enjoying all this.'

'I know,' I told him, 'I ought to be sad and sorry, but you must admit that your solicitor s name and the name of his firm, are both rather funny.'

'Not so funny, or funnily apposite, as the name of Marcia's solicitor, which is Truelove, Sharp, and Cutter.'

'I can't believe it! Do they give themselves those names on purpose as an advertisement?'

'The firm of Truelove, Sharp and Cutter, of whom Sir Frederick Sharp is the head, requires no advertisement, and Sharp can cut deep. As Tripp suggested, she will demand heavy costs in this undefended suit.'

'Do you think,' I asked, 'as Archie implied, that she wants to be married again and to him – your friend the baron?'

'Yes, she lives in hope – if he'll have her, which is unlikely. He is a confirmed bachelor and prefers the society of men to women.'

'Is he one of those?'

He took a hand off the steering wheel to tweak a lock of my hair. I had taken off my hat and my hair was blowing in the wind through the open window.

'He has quite a lot of money. His father was a director of one of the great banking firms of Switzerland. He also has a title and she is very keen on titles.'

'But she was keen enough on you and you haven't a title.'

'I wasn't altogether impecunious and I inherited a flourishing business concern, a still more favourable asset than a title, for she enjoys the fleshpots that money can buy.'

'You are rather hard on her, aren't you?'

'I was too soft once.'

She recalls that when Sinclair left her at the post Colin was just going off duty as she went in. Since Marcia's visit to him and the result of it he had shown little interest in the proceedings that ensued, whether defended or not.

'He is too indifferent about it,' she told Archie. 'It worries me. Can it be the calm before another storm?'

'I shouldn't worry,' he advised her. 'He has talked it over with me quite sensibly, and so long as he is certain that you will not leave him he will accept the conditions under which you live together as they have been and will continue, God and you willing.'

'I am willing,' she said, 'but God may not be willing. Man – or woman – proposes and God disposes.'

Meanwhile the law took its time to begin legislation in the case of Sinclair v. Sinclair with a formidable list of undefended suits in priority.

During the drama of the Atlantic that, despite the loss of the *Hood* and the revenge of our Fleet Air Arm attacking the German Navy with torpedo-carrying seaplanes, the raids on London that had again held off in a momentary lull, were now savagely renewed.

It was after a night of heavy bombardment that Noel, who had been on duty for eight hours, and Colin, who had been out in the thick of it, returned to the flat together. Mrs Hodson prepared breakfast which Colin took and Noel did not. 'Only tea, thank you, Mrs Hodson,' she told her, and went straight to bed. But before she closed her eyes, Mrs Hodson had fetched the tray and with it gave her the morning paper. 'Came late and the post too,' she said, 'after last night. Wonder it is the postman was here to bring the letters and the papers as well. They go on printing 'em just the same even with Fleet Street bombed.'

Noel read the headlines.

GERMANY DEMANDS BASES IN SYRIA FROM THE VICHY GOVERNMENT

'Huh!' she snorted, 'and Germany'll get them. Vichy will hand it them on a plate.'

GROWING STRENGTH OF BRITAIN'S AIR DEFENCES

And in smaller print:

THIRTY-THREE RAIDERS SHOT DOWN

How many of our lives were lost in those thirty-three down, she wondered, as she turned to the Roll of Honour, scanned the list and went on to Births, Marriages and Deaths. She always read the Deaths to see if anyone she knew had been killed in a raid, and she saw:

On October 10th at Perth, Western Australia, the Hon Alban Sinclair, son and heir of Lord Aviemore, beloved husband of Marion and father of Janet and Anne.

She dropped the paper . . . Lord Aviemore's son and heir, which means that his nephew, J. L. S., must be the next one, if his son only had daughters. Or perhaps there's another heir somewhere . . .

She yawned, turned over on her side and was instantly asleep.

228

Colin came to call her in the afternoon.

'I'm on again now, but the P.W. says I've done more than my full time and can take this night off.' He waited a moment before saying quietly:

'I had a dream. I've had this same dream before – it repeats itself. You – and Sinclair.' He came to the bed leaning over her. His eyes were bright, his cheeks flushed as if with fever. 'He's had a good innings and now it's my turn. I've seen it going on – all – all! You and he!' He clutched her shoulder shaking it, pulling at the open shirt of her pyjama jacket, 'More than a dream. I've seen it – he – *having* you! Marcia can divorce him and he'll be free but *you* won't be free for *him*. No! Not if I know it! You and he to go on as before and I – the cuckold! You thought I didn't mind. Did you think I'd take it lying down while you and he – and letting you suppose I'll condone it, dragging me and my name through the divorce courts for everyone to know. They *all* know already – known for a long time. Everyone! You can't keep it out of this!'

He loosened his hold of her and snatched at the paper she had thrown on the bed, pressing it down on her face. And then he laughed on a high cracked note. 'You think he'll get away with it and that I'll divorce *you*. Not on your life! Not on his life – for what it's worth!'

She tore the paper from her face.

'Don't!' she gasped. 'You're not well. You must get back to bed. Go . . .'

'Blast and damn you!' he shouted. 'It's you who'll go. Get up! Go to the post and do your stuff and then go to him. You can have the night off with *him*!'

His lips were drawn back from his teeth in a snarling grin.

'I'm sick to death of you!' again that awful laugh. 'Sick of waiting and watching and – dreaming! In Paris there are places where you can go and see it done –they perform for you – tarts and their men as you and he perform for me to – dream.'

229

'Colin,' she said out of a dry mouth. 'You're not well. I'll tell the P.W. . . . . You must stay off duty.'

'You can't kid me!' He went on as if she had not spoken. 'I know what he is – and what that other one is – the pair of them. Do you believe all that balls he told you of his friend – Yes! And Goering's friend and the friend of Hess – your *Ludwig* Sinclair! He was there, wasn't he? At The Chantrey or Canterbury. I've known it all along and you – you my wife, you *are* my wife – in name, and it's my name you've dirtied. *You*, to be dragged through the divorce court for bedding with a German spy. A spy! And you know what we do to spies when they're caught!'

With that he turned and staggered from the room slamming the door after him.

She lay there trembling. God help him! she cried within her. Is he mad or – it's not one of his fits – or is it?

She got out of bed and went to his room. He was standing in front of his shaving glass attached to the wall. He had an electric razor in his hand; he turned to her.

'You'd better go if you're going. You'll be late.' As if nothing had happened. Quite normal.

'Shall I get you something? Don't you want coffee or a sandwich? You have had nothing since breakfast.'

'I'm all right. I took one of those tablets they gave me in Paris in that loony bin – they called it a psychiatric nursing home. They make you sleep – and dream.'

Extract from Noel's journal

. . . What a night! And that awful scene with him. Four alerts and I having to go through all our anti-aircraft with Jerry overhead. I saw him in the searchlights. Everyone at their action stations not even a cat to be seen in the rubble of houses down. A grey misty sky above, the ruins below, and the Heavy Rescue and ambulances still hard at it as I went home off duty. . . .

'How many casualties?' I asked one of the Heavies.

230

'Six so far. Not so many as might have been expected. One dead.'

No sign of Colin when I got back. Where was he? A flash of horror went through me as I remembered how he had spoken and threatened and looked when I left him before going to the post . . . J. L. S.! Could he have gone to him? But he seemed to have calmed down when I left him. He had been searching through a drawer of his desk. I asked him what he was looking for. He said the P.W. told him to make a revised version of our area after the last month's incidents. I told him, 'You did one the other day.'

'Did I? I didn't know . . .' He put a hand to his head. 'I'm all in.'

I asked him: 'Did you take another pill?'

'No, I can sleep without it. I'll go to bed again and dream some more.'

He looked at me with that grin on his face – that snarling grin. There was a bottle of whisky on the table, half full. I didn't like to leave him but the sirens were howling again and I must go back to the post to relieve Mountie on the phone.

'Bit early,' Colin said. 'Daylight now, but Jerry doesn't mind that. I'll go to bed and if it gets worse I'll go although I'm supposed to be off.'

I knew he had been drinking, but even if loaded he seldom showed it. I left him lying on his bed. He hadn't undressed, was still in his uniform ready to go if it got much worse.

It was an all-out strafing with flak as big as drums from our anti-aircraft fore and aft – but better fore than aft because you could see what was coming. No one in sight, all at their action stations. No sign of Colin at the post. Not like him to stay off when it was as bad as this, even if he were told to be off having done much more than his full time.

I asked the P.W. if he had been in before I got here because he might have gone to another incident out of our area as we are so short of wardens. No, he hadn't been in. Then where was he? . . . My opposite number on the phone came to relieve Mountie. The P.W. said I had done enough in four alerts. The All Clear came after a terrific bang and Control reported landmine in Regent's Park.

I rang J. L. S. thinking Colin might have gone there, remembering the way he had looked and spoken. I must know. . . . Got the out-of-order signal. Called operator. Told me the cables were down. Was ticked off by the P.W. for using the phone for a private call . . . Went back to where our wardens, ambulances and Heavies were clearing up the mess of three houses down. I saw Philpot who had been out in it all night. He looked utterly whacked and had blood on his sleeve – soaked in it.

'Potts!' I grabbed his arm. 'Are you all right?'

He nodded. He hadn't heard me.

'Are you hurt?' I yelled into his hearing aid.

'No. I'm O.K. Some poor blighter had his hand blown off – all over me!'

He and some of the others were still searching the debris for more casualties under collapsed floors and ceilings. He went on with what he had been doing when I came up to him. I hardly liked to ask him, so tired he was.

'Have you your car handy?'

'In my garage.'

He had a flat in New Cavendish Street just round from where we were.

'Could you get me to – or drop me near – Piccadilly?'

'Sure, and I'll give you breakfast at my place en route.'

'No, thanks awfully, but if you'll just drop me as soon as you're off.'

'I was off hours ago but I stayed on to help clear up here.'

So I went with him to Sinclair's flat. Potts, as did everyone at the post, knew about us.

'Anything else I can do?' Potts asked, after dropping me. 'Shall I wait?'

'No, don't – I can have breakfast with Sinclair. He – he's expecting me. You go back and have yours.'

As he drove off the sirens started again.

Non-stop, I thought. The anti-aircrafts were banging away from the docks and in Hyde Park.

No further entry here.

Extract from her memoirs

. . . I had a latchkey to his flat. A haggard, dead-beat porter came to take me up in the lift.

'Did you have much of it?' I asked him.

'One in Bond Street, but the worst of it is north of the Park.'

He knew me, had seen me often, may have known everything and had probably been questioned by Marcia's Private Eye.

The lift sighed down again. I let myself in.

Just at that moment came the screeching whistle of a near bomb and its thunderous explosion as it fell and shook the whole building. I heard a sound as of a gun-shot, but there was such a conglomeration of noise, ambulances arriving, cascades of glass and falling flak one couldn't distinguish any particular sound. Other residents came out from their flats on that floor, all men, no women. Those that had wives had probably sent them away out of London. They were in their pyjamas or dressing-gowns.

'It's not on us,' I told them, 'but pretty close. It's chiefly blast.'

'I was in the bath,' said one wrapped in a bath sheet, 'and the window is blown out. Luckily not in the bath.'

'I think there's some damage in here,' I said. 'I'm going in to see.'

Letting them think I was on duty there, being in my uniform.

The anti-aircraft were still banging away, but the roar

overhead of the enemy had lessened; the Jerries were being driven off.

'They were probably after the Palace,' I said reassuringly to one old grey man who was looking rather shaky, 'but we're after them – they haven't got anything much.'

'Good thing it was a close shave to us and not Buck House,' said another.

They dispersed severally; the old one was fetched by an equally old grey manservant. 'I've got your coffee ready, sir,' he told him and to me:

'There's some windows gone, Miss, if you could come and see and report to your post when you've finished with Mr Sinclair's flat.' He too thought I was on duty in that area.

A cursory glance at Sinclair's large, oak-panelled hall showed nothing much of damage, only some plaster fallen from the ceiling. And then I heard what might have been another shot and the familiar sound of splintering glass – and Colin's voice . . . Oh, God! His voice!

'Got you this time, you bloody sod of a spy! You Hun! I've killed one of your kind, and I'll kill again – you – *you*! who've stolen my woman – my wife! Caught you at it and signalling to guide them to the Palace – Yes! That's your game —'

And again a gun-shot and a yell – 'Got you!' from Colin.

I rushed into the room. He was standing there with a pistol in his hand. There was glass all over the floor from the shattered pane of a bureau bookcase and J. L. S. had fallen against it. I flew to him and raised his head. There was blood seeping through the neck of his pyjama suit.

His eyes were closed. I felt his pulse; it was slow but sure. I turned to Colin. He stood there staring down at us, and then – he threw up his arms. The revolver clattered to the ground and he fell, writhing, convulsively, foaming at the mouth.

J. L. S., raising himself on an elbow, said:

'Darling, he's only grazed the collar bone. I knocked my head as I fell in the blast . . . Let him alone. He'll pass out of it. Get hold of the gun and give it to me.'

I obeyed blindly, thankfully. His voice was stronger with each word. I picked up the gun, avoiding the sight of that pitiable writhing figure with blood and foam on his mouth. I handed the revolver to J. L. S. who had got to his feet. He took it from me and emptied it. 'Only one left,' he said. 'Better get a doctor to him.'

'No, not to him, to you!'

Colin had staggered up. He passed a hand across his face, staring dazedly round the room.

'What? . . . What happened? How did I get here?'

* * *

She gave account of what happened in her journal, but how she dealt with Colin afterwards is reconstructed from her verbal reminiscences.

As always after an attack he remembered nothing of it, nor how he came to be in Sinclair's flat until memory returned. But her first concern was for Sinclair and relief at finding him unharmed other than that the bullet had grazed his collar bone, 'a mere surface scratch', Sinclair told her when she brought bandages and iodine to treat it. The first and second shots had gone wide and lodged in the bureau; the last, the one that caught him, had shattered a pane of the bookcase.

'It was the blast that knocked me out for a minute,' he said, 'and I banged my head against the bureau.'

She was for ringing a doctor. He would not hear of it. 'It's nothing, I tell you. But you can get us all some coffee.' His manservant had been called up and the daily woman would not be there till later. 'Better make him lie down here and fetch a doctor to him when you go home. I'll drive you back presently.'

. . . . .

According to Noel's account of it Colin refused to rest in Sinclair's flat; he took a cup of coffee, and allowed himself to be driven home, not by Sinclair. Noel told him he must not drive with that arm. She would get a taxi.

A taxi was available, and during breakfast, 'I know what happened,' he told Noel. 'I had to see him and have it out with him about you and – him, and what he is. I'll report him to the police. I'd have done so before but I wanted to be sure. And now that Hess has also come down by parachute – they're all in it together – a lot of damn Nazis.' He looked up from his plate of that week's bacon and egg. 'Aren't you having any of this? Or have you given me your ration?'

'No, it's not my ration but I'm too tired to eat anything. Go on telling me what you remember of last night – or this morning?'

As soon as she had spoken she realized her mistake. She should not have pressed him to talk more of that which he had temporarily forgotten and had now volunteered to recall, speaking naturally and normally of it.

A change had come over his face. He pushed away his plate and started up from the table.

'I'll tell you! . . . I didn't do it – I *meant* to! But I didn't. I by-passed him – the blast – just at that moment. My arm swerved. I'd have killed him. Not the first German I've killed – but I didn't do it, I did *not*!'

She would never forget how he looked as he said that while fear and a kind of triumphant self-complacency struggled with the shock of memory returned in brief kaleidoscopic glimpses.

Then he sat down again and resumed his breakfast saying, as his pallor receded and was replaced by his usual healthy colour, 'It doesn't do to keep it bottled up too long. You thought I didn't care. I know we agreed not to care about each other's – affairs.' He reached for the toast rack. 'You didn't mind about Barton or Viola . . . Won't you have some toast? You ought to eat something. Up all night . . .

236

But I did care. I had dreams of him – and you. It wouldn't have been so bad if he hadn't been German passing himself off as one of us. It got worse as time went on. I kept dreaming of him and you – he having you – and then that voice.'

He buttered the slice of toast, smiling to himself. A coldness crept over me. I asked him, although my tongue seemed to stick to my palate: 'What voice – whose?'

He was still smiling, dreadfully.

'His voice, of course. Reminding me . . . So I had to put a stop to it.'

Mrs Hodson came to clear away the breakfast things. 'If you've finished, ma'am?'

'Yes, or will you have some more coffee, Colin?'

'No.' He passed a hand over his chin. 'I must have a bath and a shave. I'm on duty today.' And to Noel, 'You look all in. You'd better go to bed.'

She waited until he left for the post before she telephoned his uncle.

'Archie – I'm terribly worried.'

She told him all, quietly. He heard her out and then:

'I will speak to Jeremy Gore and arrange what is to be done. I'll call you later.'

*   *   *

During the following week Noel sought Sir Jeremy's advice as to Colin's condition. She went by appointment to his Harley Street house, and described in full detail her husband's most recent attack and her fears concerning him.

'He was nothing like the famous medical consultant I expected to see,' as her memoirs gave it. 'He was short, stocky and much younger than I imagined him to be. He wore a lounge suit, his hair almost flaxen fair; his face round and cherubic, he had a high-pitched voice and his consulting room was crammed with objets d'art, a few pictures and those mostly sporting prints and photographs of his bulldogs. He bred bulldogs at his country house, Archie told me, and has three champions, no wife, had never married and is, or had been, one of the final judges for the supreme champion at Cruft's. I found it difficult to reconcile his private life with that of the famous neurologist who had among those photographs of his bulldogs, signed photographs of crowned European heads who had been his patients.'

'Archie Tarrant,' he said, offering her a cigarette, 'has told me something of your husband's history. Can you enlarge on that?'

When she had finished telling him all she knew of Colin's childhood, their marriage and his recurrent and more frequent attacks, 'It is evident,' he said, 'from what you have told me that he suffers from a state of acute mental and emotional tension resultant upon the quarrels – those violent quarrels he witnessed between his parents. There is also a deep-seated aggressive inherited compulsion.'

'Yes,' she nodded. 'But where does his compulsion lead or how does it affect him? He spoke of hearing voices – or a voice. I wondered is that' – she faltered – 'could it be a symptom of – derangement?'

He gave her a quick smile.

'Joan of Arc heard a voice or voices and they burned her for a witch and canonized her five hundred years later. Your husband is neither a wizard nor potentially a saint, and as for deranged, aren't we all deranged at some time or other, especially now when killing or being killed is the order of our day? Your husband is suffering from an obsessive fantasy but this need not necessarily confine him to a mental home.' He handed her a silver ashtray with the head of a bulldog engraved on it. 'This chap for instance,' he flicked the ashtray with a fingernail, 'he was my first and foremost champion. He had an obsessive fantasy about me. He thought I was God.' He gave a cherubic chuckle, 'and to him I *was* God. Your husband has an obsessive fantasy about the German whom he legitimately killed in the First World War and he believes every man with a German name is an enemy agent. Your

238

husband's condition is a reaction to what he and thousands of others did in the trenches of the last war to their fellow men who were their enemies. The German he killed is resurrected in the person of the man he believes to be your lover and was one with his obsession to destroy.'

'But does it mean,' she asked faintheartedly, 'that he is dangerous? That he might attempt – again?'

'No,' he shook his head. His high-pitched voice rose a tone higher. 'That he told you he meant to do it and didn't yet made the attempt, has rid himself of his fantasy – gone. Vanished with his dreams.'

A sigh of relief escaped her, but there was still a lurking anxiety.

'His attacks of' – she hesitated to use the word – 'His – epilepsy. Is there any cure for it?'

'It can be kept under, but the prognosis is usually un-favourable.'

She gazed at him imploringly.

'No hope?'

'In his case a possibility. His attacks, as I gathered from his history, are associated with an aggressive instinct against his father, and his childhood's memories are revisualized in assaults upon the mother whom he loved and whose love was denied him. He has nurtured a vengeful impulse against the father whom he held responsible for alienating his mother from him, having witnessed those fights between his parents, this has been stimulated, as a spark to a powder magazine, by his killing of a German. Hence his aggression which preconditioned him to this act of violence against Mr Sinclair whom he believed to be an enemy. The horrors perpetrated by Hitler and his murderous associates, that have seeped through from Belsen and Auschwitz have compelled him to seek relief from his bottled-up tension —'

'Yes,' she interrupted eagerly, 'he spoke of being bottled up and couldn't stand it any more.'

'Exactly.' He rose from his desk and took a photograph

from a Chippendale cabinet. This, a beautiful country house. 'It is,' he said, 'of Tudor origin, restored in the reign of Anne. I suggest he should go there for a holiday and complete rest. He will be among his own kind, officers from the last war and this war. It is my own clinic where I send neurological patients suffering from shock, neuroses, due to various surgical conditions. He will receive treatment there and will find active employment. They have a small theatre, and one or two who have been on the stage produce and act in plays. They have their own garden if they want to do gardening and can make themselves generally useful, in fact do anything they like within reason.'

'He was sent to a psychiatric place in Paris when he was there with his – with a friend of his, and he hated it,' she told him.

'He won't hate this place. What I suggest is that you arrange for him and Sinclair to meet socially, and ask Sinclair to show him his birth certificate which will once and for all prove he is British, entirely British, born of English parents and of British birth.'

'You think that will make him realize how he has been mistaken?'

'It will help.' He held out his hand. 'Cheer up. And let me know how he gets on.'

She reported this consultation to Sinclair. He agreed that Colin should act upon Sir Jeremy's advice and be persuaded to take sick leave and go to the clinic to aid, if not to complete, a cure.

'And as for us,' he said, 'we must go on as we are, unless he recovers sufficiently to want you back as – his wife.'

'As his wife,' she told him, 'that can never be.'

'Then,' he said, 'you must be *my* wife, for I shall be free to marry you when the divorce comes through.'

'I can't. You know that while he lives I cannot leave him. The chances of a cure are virtually nil. Must he grow old and older without me or anyone to care for him?'

240

'And must you be martyred, sacrifice your life and all that could make your life bearable – for him?'

Then, seeing her face close up and the sound of a choked sob in her throat, he took her in his arms.

'I have no right to suggest it, nor have I any right to you, but all I ask and crave is – that we may not be divided.'

She shook her head. 'We can never be divided while we live, either together or apart. Love, if ours is love or if there is any such thing as love which is not just a wishful thought, a fantasy, then we are together now and for ever even if we never meet again or if one of us dies, killed any minute, any day – as thousands are killed here and everywhere, all over Europe. But if we live, as God or whoever is Almighty in this miserable world, *meant* us to live and do His Will, not yours, not mine, but His, as He said when He knew what was coming to Him, then we may hope we shall be for ever undivided.'

'I don't,' he said brokenly, 'deserve you, my Caro, half girl, half Ganymede, and so utterly and hopelessly desired.'

'Not hopelessly – with hope of the hereafter.' She laid her mouth for an instant to his and went from him blindly.

Extract from Noel's journal June 1941

Last evening we dined with J. L. S. at his flat. He had ordered dinner to be sent from Fortnum's as his man has been called up and he can't get a cook, only dailies. Colin who has accepted the doctor's advice and says he will go to that clinic which is somewhere in the New Forest, has been very subdued since that ghastly night when he was unloosed from the 'bottling up' of himself and what Sir Jeremy called his 'fantasies'.

It was like a flashback on a film to see him as he was before the war, and on normal friendly terms with J. L. S.

Fortnum's had done us proud with salmon mayonnaise, chicken suprême and a bombe (an iced one!) which had been kept in the fridge. We had a bottle of Mouton Rothschild and those two had Napoleon brandy. There were no alerts and after dinner we listened to Churchill's speech telling us that Hitler invaded Russia yesterday. He said how Hitler had observed all his usual formalities of perfidy after having solemnly signed a non-aggression treaty with Russia and then suddenly, without any declaration of war, he rained down bombs upon Russia – another Warsaw, Rotterdam, Belgrade!

'We', Churchill said, 'are out to destroy Hitler and every vestige of the Nazi régime. And now this blood-thirsty guttersnipe must launch his mechanized armies upon new fields of slaughter . . .'

Colin roared with laughter at that definition of Hitler as a guttersnipe, but he didn't laugh when Churchill went on to say, 'Any man who marches with Hitler is our foe . . . This applies to all representatives of that vile race of quislings who make themselves the tool and agents of the Nazi régime against their fellow countrymen and the lands of their birth . . .'

J. L. S. got up soon after that and turned it off.

'Why?' Colin asked him. 'I want to hear more of this.'

J. L. S. didn't answer. Instead he went to his desk and took something from a drawer in it.

'And I,' he said, 'want to show you *this*. The P.M.'s speech comes aptly since it gives me this chance to have out with you what you've had against me.'

He spoke lightly, half jokingly, as he handed him the paper he had taken – his birth certificate.

I watched Colin read it . . . and then.

'My God,' he gasped, 'what can I say – or do?' He got up from his chair, and in a voice a bit slurred, for he was already half loaded when we left home having taken a couple of whiskies on the rocks and the better part of the Mouton Rothschild followed by brandy, he said, 'I deserve everything you want to call me, or horsewhip me if you've a whip or shoot me if you've a gun.'

'I have both but I wouldn't use them on you. It is quite understandable that you took a shot at me for suspecting me of being what I am not, neither I nor our Number One operative, von Steinvort.'

What followed is rather awful.

Colin dropped down, he didn't fall, he just dropped on to his knees, and his hands went to his face, covered it and he shook – with sobs, I thought at first, but it was laughter . . . He rocked with hysterical laughter. And then he got up, held out his hand to J. L. S. and said chokingly:

'I'll let my wife divorce me and you can have her so soon as your wife has got *her* divorce. It's the least I can do for what I did or – didn't do to you !'

Before J. L. S. could answer or cope with that came the alert. It was past 22.00 hours and Colin was on duty at 23.00.

'I must have a taxi,' he said, 'and get to the post.'

'I'll drive you,' J. L. S. told him.

I said: 'No, you mustn't drive through this.' He was only just better of the flesh wound that he called a scratch from Colin's bullet, and had not yet driven because it was in his right arm. But he insisted, and back we went. I got into my uniform although I wasn't on duty because I knew from the incessant anti-aircraft that it would be a heavy night. I would be wanted on the telephone to relieve Mountie.

J. L. S. got us there in good time and he dropped Colin at his action station and drove me on to the post.

The wardens who had been waiting in the post were surging up the steps and I told J. L. S., 'Don't go back in this. Stay in the post till the All Clear.'

'All right, but I won't stay in the post. I'll go out and lend a hand. They'll be wanting anyone who can help with casualties, being short-staffed.'

'You wouldn't, would you,' I said hurriedly, detaining him, 'take Colin at his word about – divorce ?'

'Of course not – in his state. But it's a good thing he got that off his chest, and a brainwave of Jeremy Gore to have

him see my birth certificate. And Churchill's speech was a
– God's Truth! Here we go!' as the shrieking whistle of
a near falling bomb preceded its seismic explosion.

'You go below to your telephone,' he said. 'And take
this.' He thrust my tin hat at me.

'No, you take that. I'll get another one from equipment —'

But he was off, hatless, unprotected, right in the thick
of it.

I took the phone from Mountie and heard from Control.
'Incident in Harley Street.' I called the nearest action
station and told Mountie to lie down on the truckle bed.
He looked absolutely done in.

Later

All clear but still at the post. The P.W. has been out in
it and the deputy P.W. took over. 'Hell of a mess out
there,' he said as he came in.

This entry ends abruptly here but from what she recalled of that night's raid, Colin, who had gone out with
the other men including Habbabuck – (she said she could
never get his name right) – was reported wounded and had
been taken to hospital.

'Mr Sinclair,' Habbabuck told her, 'went with him in the
ambulance. The top floor ceiling came down on your
husband before I could get to him. He saved Mr Sinclair –
he deserves the G.M.'

Sinclair came to her at the post when he had seen Colin
attended to and got him a private room in the hospital;
and from him Noel learned:

'He risked his life for me. The whole of the first floor of
the house divided into consulting rooms was ablaze with
incendiaries. I had gone with him who had been ordered
to fight the fires – the other chaps and the Heavies were
hard at it salvaging casualties, luckily none of the doctors
was in their rooms, only the porter and housekeeper in the

244

basement and two secretaries who were fire-watching. No serious injuries – except Colin. He saw,' Sinclair said quietly, 'that a bath from the floor above us had been dislodged with the blast and was coming down on top of me – I was just under it. Lame as he is he rushed at me yelling: "Get out of the way," and had the ceiling and the whole thing down on him. He was pinned beneath it.'

She went with Sinclair to the hospital and was allowed to see Colin.

'How bad is he?' she asked the Sister in charge of the private wing.

'Not too bad,' evasively. 'He has slight concussion and suspected spinal injury, but the X-ray result has not come through yet. Doctor will let you know as soon as the radiologist has made his report.'

'I'll wait for you here,' Sinclair told her when the Sister, starched, blue-belted, full-bosomed, efficient, ushered her into the room where Colin lay.

His eyes were closed; his forehead bandaged where the fire had caught him, his hands also bandaged, but as she knelt beside him, whispering his name, his eyelids fluttered. His eyes opened to show a faint streak of blue and his lips moved; she caught the words, 'Sinclair . . . is he . . . did he . . .'

'No, you saved him, my darling . . . you saved him.'

'The . . . least I could . . .' he tried to say before those eyelids sank.

ELEVEN

The weeks dragged on through the summer months while Colin hovered between life and death, and Noel watched, waited and prayed . . . 'If he lives let him be *able* to live . . . not to be helpless . . .'

The surgeon and Sir Jeremy had pronounced a spinal injury that could render him permanently disabled. His mind, however, was clear; there had been no recurrent attacks, and she thankfully saw that he welcomed Sinclair's visits. So it would seem the past was forgotten.

'There is hope,' Sir Jeremy told her, 'that the epilepsy, if not cured, may be manifest in less frequent attacks, and partial mobility cannot be ruled out.'

She had to content herself with that.

And now with Germany's heavy concentration of troops threatening Russia without any preliminary warning, and ignoring the non-aggression treaty, a state of war had been declared between the two countries.

This, as Churchill gave it in one of his world broadcasts, marked the third climacteric of the war. The first was when France fell and abandoned us to face alone the Nazi attempted invasion of our island while still unprepared and insufficiently armed. The second turning point was when our R.A.F. beat the daylights out of Hitler's raiders in their holocaustic batterings of London; and the third was when the President of the United States passed the Lend Lease Act with the loan of two thousand million sterling towards the defence of our liberties.

The result of Germany's invasion of Russia meant that, for the time being, the German air force had been temporarily diverted from their chief objective, the bombardment of London. But while the Civil Defence units stayed always at the ready for attack, Noel could now afford to take more time off from her voluntary hours on duty.

These hours were devoted to Colin whose improvement, though gradual, was heartening. He had now been allowed an invalid chair and could wheel himself along the corridor of the hospital's private wing.

'It is wonderful,' she wrote in her journal, 'to see how he has taken this disaster. I have never known him so interested in the war news, so alive – so much himself as when I first knew and married him. It is as if something had been purged out of his subconscious, and has given him a new horizon, a new – almost a new life . . .'

Sir Jeremy's suggestion that he should take a course of treatment at his clinic was no longer practicable in that it would, he said, disturb him to be among mobile companions. 'The majority of my patients there suffer from various forms of neuroses. Some have been wounded, deprived of the use of a limb but are not paraplegic. Better he resume a normal life as far as possible. He mentioned to me when I visited him in hospital that he wished to go back into Civil Defence. He quite accepts that he is out of active service, but he could, he told me, take over the telephone, which is sedentary, as you have been doing. The main thing for him is occupation.'

'What I cannot understand,' she told him, 'is that he has never had an attack – or none has been reported to me – while he was on duty. He was quite splendid in the raids and seemed to be unhampered by his leg; he has become quite used to it all these years. It is only under emotional, not physical, strain that he has a – a fit, and then he forgets all about it.'

'There are forces at work,' the doctor explained, 'that produce, as it were, a war in the mind when the physical body is static or inactive. He took an active part in our present war as he did in the last, but in this case he had no personal contact with the enemy, yet it has lain deep in his consciousness – as he has spoken of it to me while in hospital – of how he "murdered", as he put it, a German in trench warfare. But now that he takes an active part in Civil Defence and runs every risk to save others from being victimized, or as he calls it "murdered" by the savagery of enemy bombardment, the mental strain he has suffered as a result of the last war has been relieved. And his assault, of which you have told me, upon Mr Sinclair has appeased his deep-seated urge for aggression, and his courageous attempt to take upon himself that which might have caused death or a serious injury to another, such as he now suffers, was – expiation.'

When after several weeks Colin was able to leave hospital, though still confined to a wheel chair, to which he had soon become adapted, Miss Penfold offered, in fact commanded, that Noel should take Colin to The Chantrey. 'I still have a modicum of domestic help and you can attend to his other needs. I presume he can manage to go to the bathroom, if not to bath himself.'

'He can do everything,' Noel said, 'except walk, and perhaps he'll be able to do that in time. After all if the President of the United States can attend Congress, make speeches and travel all over America in a wheel chair, Colin can manage to go to the Y.M.C.A. without help from me.'

'To the where?' magisterially demanded Miss Penfold.

She bit back a giggle.

'We used to call it the Y.M.C.A. at the Tree.'

'H'm.' Miss Penfold meditatively plucked at her chin, which had now sprouted a greying miniature cornfield. 'You see now,' she averred, 'the necessity of a medical examination prior to marriage or, as yours must be, a life-long union. Had I known of his disability I would never have countenanced such a marriage, nor would I have credited him – considering his condition – with the courage he displayed on taking it upon himself to save your friend

248

or publisher, or – whatever he is to you,' she said markedly, 'from possible death. Wonder he is alive to tell the tale.'

'He would never tell the tale. Others tell it for him. What he did was witnessed and I have reason to believe it has gone to higher command for recommendation.'

'That's all to the good, and as much or no more than he deserves. But I have seen courage greater than or equal to his, not only in our men in both wars who have won recognition for bravery. And they who have won medals, even the V.C., may have deserved it no more than some of our women who fought for their Rights, so hardly and courageously won. It took Emily Davidson courage enough to throw herself in front of the King's horse at the Derby. George the Fifth's horse that was.'

'And lost him the race, I suppose.'

The outcome of all this was that Noel and Colin, conducted by Miss Penfold, to whom Noel naughtily alludes in her memoirs as 'their commanding officer', arrived at The Chantrey in the middle of September. And it was while they were there that a review of six thousand men and women was held in Hyde Park.

Noel read extracts of the Prime Minister's speech to the assemblage in which he paid tribute to those who had just come out of one long hard battle and might at any moment enter upon another . . . 'In this war, so terrible in so many aspects and yet so inspiring, men and women who have never thought about fighting or being involved in fighting —'

'What's he mean?' interrupted Colin. 'Half of the men in Civil Defence are over age for the Army and fought in the last war as I did, and some of them, like Mountie and others, in the Boer War.'

'He is being polite to all of us . . . He goes on to say we must prepare ourselves to receive other visits in the future – I've skipped the part about the way we and all Londoners have stood up to the enemy's bombardment and he says that we are now bombing him – he means Jerry – at a heavier discharge in tons of bombs than in any monthly period he has discharged on us . . .'

'That's something,' said Colin glumly, 'but just how many tons *has* he discharged on us? And he hasn't done with us yet. Goering will be thinking up something a bit more blastable to hurl at us.'

'Blastable's good,' laughed Noel, rejoicing to see him more his normal self.

It was during this visit to The Chantrey that she saw in *The Times* the announcement of the death of Lord Aviemore.

She immediately telephoned Sinclair.

'Was it sudden?' she asked him.

'Yes, in a way. He had a cold – as usual. He always seems to get a worse cold in the summer than in the winter, and he finds it difficult to shake off. He went for a walk in the Park, it came on to rain. He got drenched, went home, and then it went to his lungs. Pneumonia.'

'There was quite a bit about him in *The Times* and it names you as his heir. Are you?'

'Yes, but only for the title. Anything else goes to his granddaughters with the estate. The property near Deal is not entailed. Can I come down? I'm missing you like hell. Or will the aunt object?'

'Probably, but it doesn't matter. Colin would like to see you.'

'How is he?'

'Much better. More as he was when I first knew him – and no sign of the "legacy".'

Sinclair arrived the next evening at The Chantrey, was coolly received by the aunt and warmly welcomed by Colin.

'Did you see,' Colin asked Sinclair, 'the review of the Civil Defence units in Hyde Park?'

'I did – a pity neither of you were there. Churchill paid tribute to you all for what he rightly called the courage of Londoners and the Civil Defence services under tremendous strain and gained us scores of millions of friends throughout the whole of the United States.'

'Friendship from the States,' Miss Penfold sourly supplemented, speaking for the first time with more than one word, 'has not shown itself in action so far. It will take more than the bombing of Britain to bring them in.'

'But they've loaned us the money to carry on, otherwise where would we be?' put in Noel.

'Just where we are,' said Sinclair. 'Not all Hitler's fury and his thousands of tons hurled down on Britain, and the U-boats' torpedoes shattering our convoys, will crush us. We'll go on to the end with Churchill's V sign – for Victory.'

Miss Penfold, rising from the table, asked him:

'Are you staying in Canterbury?'

'Yes, I have booked a room.'

'Cancel it. There are spare rooms enough here.'

'You've won her over,' Colin said grinning, when the three of them were left in the drawing-room after coffee while the aunt went into the garden to spray the roses. 'The greenfly,' she announced, 'are a menace this year. High winds.'

And out she went.

Sinclair turned to Noel.

'Can you make my apologies to your aunt? I have given the address of the hotel to my secretary at the office in case she wants to get in touch with me for the next day or two. There may be messages waiting for me already.'

'Can't you ring her up,' said Colin, 'and tell her you are here?'

'Sorry, old man, it would be too late to get her now and I haven't her phone number with me. I'll be over here tomorrow.'

Colin wheeled himself to the door with him and stayed talking outside for a while. When he came back, 'I've had a word with Sinclair about the divorce.' He moved to the table where the coffee pot and empty cups remained. 'He says it is going through undefended and is a certainty she'll get it.'

'Yes, we know.'

'Well —' he poured himself a cup from the coffee pot.

'No,' she started up, 'don't have that. It will be cold. I'll ask the cook to get you some fresh.'

'This is all right and it's your cup I'm using, the only one with lipstick on it.' He smiled round at her and wheeled himself back to her side. She sat down again on the sofa looking up at him and he looked down at her with a brightness in his eyes reflecting the light of the dying day through the uncurtained windows. 'Well, I've just told Sinclair to go ahead and get rid of his adhesion as soon as possible. The *decree nisi* is a cert as you are not defending, then you can have each other for better and not for worse as it is now.'

'Darling,' she put her hand over his, 'don't.'

'I mean it. I've told him I'll give you a divorce from me rather than I should divorce you to be dragged through it twice. There's evidence enough with Viola in Paris even if there is a time lapse. I've kept her up my sleeve in case she was wanted, knowing how it is between you and Sinclair. She's game. She'll do it. I've written to her. She heard I'd been knocked out and wrote to me from Liverpool where she's doing censor work. So Bob's your uncle. Give me a cigarette.'

The next morning Noel wheeled Colin into the orchard, where apples hung like little rosy moons on the filled branches. Hogg's dog followed them.

'That dog,' said Colin, 'has been here before.'

'You mean —' She stroked the silken head on Colin's knee, Bob gazing up at him with melting soft brown eyes.

'I mean that he has come through several incarnations and next time he will be one of us, only much more so. *He* would never harm a soul living or dead. Not he. Made

252

in God's Image – which we are meant to be and aren't. What are we? Sons of Belial.'

'No, foster sons of God and handed over to the wrong foster parents.'

'Such as Hitler – a false prophet come among us and with half the world for his disciples.'

The sound of a car in the lane that led to The Chantrey caused the dog to prick his ears, nose pointed.

'That's Sinclair,' said Colin. 'You go to him. I'll come on later. And,' he called after her, 'tell him what I've told you. It's up to you both now.'

She met Sinclair before he went into the house.

She took him by the arm.

'Let's get away from here. I have to tell you —'

And she told.

'Expiation,' he murmured.

'That's what Sir Jeremy said when he saved you from being killed.'

'Do you think he wants to marry this Gibbon person?'

'I'm sure he doesn't. He never wanted to marry either of them – Barton or his gibbon. No, what he wants – has always wanted – is a mother, not a wife. I couldn't be either satisfactorily for him, but the gibbon would mother him. She'd probably make him take up the antique business again, after the war, of course, because of bombs and having to pay the earth for insurance of the antiques. Archie would finance him and she could be his manager, boss, and maternal mistress – not that he is inclined that way, he never really was, and anyhow that isn't what he wants from her. He wants me. No' – she took his hand to her lips – 'not as you want me and as we want each other, but just to have me there in his possession like a Ming vase, and yet he will hand me over to you for keeps . . . more expiation, as I see it.'

He was silent for a minute; then slid his arm round her shoulders. 'It's as I see it too. Not that it would make any difference to us – or would it?'

'Every difference.'

She turned her eyes from his that held hers in a long, close look.

They had come to a boundary of The Chantrey's land that marched alongside a field where two Jersey cows, mother and daughter, grazed. Here a stile led to a footpath down to the village.

'Let's sit here. Those two,' she pointed to the cows, 'so sweet and gentle. Awful thought that they have to be killed and eaten when too old for milk.' She shuddered. 'Cannibalism.'

They sat together on the stile watching the slow munching of the grazing cattle; one raised her head and leisurely advanced. Noel held out a hand to her.

'I often come here. She likes to have her nose stroked. I can't bear the thought of her being butchered and rationed for dinner.'

The howl of a distant siren came over the air. The cow moved quietly away to join her daughter.

'More butchery,' Sinclair said. 'He's over the coast. One of us will get him – unless he gets us.'

The sky was a blue transparency, cloudless, bees hummed in the lush grass; the air was laden with Indian summer warmth. Shadows slanted through dappled sunlight, honey-gold.

'Such a lovely world,' she whispered, 'to be destroyed . . .'

From Noel's journal October 1941

We are fed up with this lull. Far better to be doing something – out in it rather than sit here in the post waiting for an alert that never comes. But it will any day or night. It's the waiting for it that is so sickmaking. It is awful for Colin not being able to get to the post for the telephone, which he wanted to do, because of the steps down to it but the Chief Warden is going either to remove him to Post 4 which has a cement ramp down to the basement, or else he will fix up a temporary ramp at our post. But I think we shall get over that difficulty because Sir J. says he is so much improved that with help he can get out of his chair and manage to walk down the few steps to the telephone room.

Yes, he is so much better now, particularly since he has been awarded the B.E.M. It was Buckie who reported to the Chief Warden that he had seen Colin risk his life to save J. L. S.

Hitler is so busy strafing Russia that for the present he is holding his Blitz from us to concentrate on them. I hear we are getting our own back on Germany with devastating raids.

She says nothing in this entry of the latest development concerning Marcia's action for divorce, but retrospectively she recounts what brought about an apocalyptic climax.

I had to let J. L. S. know that I would never desert Mr (Colin) Micawber. It was so awful a decision to have to make that I couldn't think or write of it, not until it had lain forgotten in the dust of years so that I can bring it out again without a wrench . . . Time *does* heal. Not for some, and for me it will always leave the scar of it.

'You must understand,' she told Sinclair when, after those three weeks at The Chantrey, she and Colin were back again in London, 'you must *see* that we can't go on as before. Not now. It will have to be all or nothing for us, so it must be – nothing.'

She could not meet his eyes. 'I felt,' she said, 'as if I had stuck a knife into him and was watching him bleed.'

And as if he took that thought from her, 'Don't,' he said, under his breath, 'cut me off. We belong to each other.'

'Yes, but supposing you had to go to – to Australia or somewhere the other side of the world, thousands of miles away, we would know we were together even though apart. It would be the same as if one of us were dead. We would still belong to each other.'

A bitter laugh escaped him.

'Geographically? As a minor island of the Dominions never visited by the King but belonging to the Crown?'

She noticed lines beneath his eyes she had not seen before, engraved as on a fine etching, and a deeper line from nose to mouth. The crisp lion-coloured hair receding from his forehead showed a few threads of grey. It gave her a pang to see him older than she had thought of him; but she knew he must be rising fifty. It would hurt more at that age, the older one is.

'But you wouldn't,' she said pleadingly, 'want him to suffer – as if he hadn't suffered enough already?'

Her upturned face was under his. He took it between his hands.

'My love,' he whispered, 'my dearest absurd little love, how do you know that this maternal-mistress of a gibbon is what he really wants and needs? Not you, but a manageress of his life.'

'And that,' she said, 'is just what he wants of me – now. He didn't before. Not ever. He didn't want me at all really, not as' – she made her lips firm to say – 'not as you – if you want me. Do you?'

'Want you? God!' He let fall his hands. 'More than ever in your life you could want me.'

'And so does Colin, but not in the same way. I – I'm trying to make you understand. It is what he felt for me the first time we met at an art students' revel and he told me all about himself. He talked on and on. He said I had a listening face. He said he had known me for ever and he has always felt like that about me. He must have me with him whatever happens – always.'

'Like one of his precious Ming vases, not to be sold at Sotheby's or given away to me. Darling,' he caught her to him. 'I'm sorry, but I'm no sentimentalist. I face facts realistically. One has to be a realist in my job, both as publisher and – the other thing. Colin's Quixotic gesture in offering his Dulcinea to me is all part of his life's drama,

256

making amends for what he calls the murder of a fellow man, the German he killed in the last war. And then to get it out of his system he takes a shot at me. He deliberately fired two shots wide and the third also, only it just grazed me. And so by doing that he got rid of his guilt complex of murder. Yet aren't we all murderers, we who fought in the First World War and are fighting in this? War *is* murder. It is going on every day, every hour here, there, in Germany, Russia – the Middle East, wherever there are fighting forces fighting – for what? Freedom, justice to end tyranny, to bring sanity and unity between nations, or for love? Love of their country, love of their fellow men or love of themselves – to *save* themselves? I wonder. But what Colin is prepared to do for you – and me – is sacrificial. The "far, far better thing", but it doesn't come off. I hate to disillusion you, my darling, but the gibbon is still in Liverpool, censoring away like the efficient well-meaning manageress she is, and has no intention or knowledge of allowing herself to be cited in a divorce case.'

'How' – she drew herself sharply away from him – 'how can you possibly know that?'

'You told me her name and what she is doing as war work in Liverpool. It was easy to get on to the censor's office. She wrote to Colin, as I ascertained, to congratulate him on getting the B.E.M. and that gave him the idea of using her.'

'How awful of him!' she gasped.

'Not at all. A wishful thought to offer you a divorce, although it wouldn't have mattered how or because of whom or where. In spite of his present disability he could pass the night in an hotel with a paid woman to do or not to do what evidence requires. And so long as they spend the night in a bedroom playing poker or rummy or whatever, then you can have your, or his, divorce.'

'Yes,' she said with ice in her voice, 'I see you *are* a realist. I can be a realist too, without prejudice or sentiment. I cannot leave Colin to fend for himself and get

257

divorced from me by playing poker all night with a – a woman unknown. No names mentioned and a fee paid for services *not* rendered. I can't —' and then she thawed, melted, and was wrapped in his arms. 'I can't – I must – we mustn't —' her face was buried against his chest. She heard the beating of his heart. 'How it hurries,' she murmured. 'Is this hurry all for me?'

'Until,' he said unsteadily, 'it stops beating for ever.'

'But never again to be together,' she tried to tell him. 'Never again – as we were.'

There are no more entries of significance in her journal for the next several weeks. Desultory jottings mention that the full strength of Germany's Air Force was still heavily concentrated on Russia, and that the United States rallied to Russia's aid with supplies of much needed armaments and munitions.

At home austerity had been strictly enforced. Personal extravagance must be subdued if not entirely eliminated. Clothes were rationed and petrol for pleasure motoring forbidden; meals in restaurants were limited to five shillings a head. By the end of the year 1941 Japan, already harassing the Far East, declared war upon Britain and the United States. And even while the Emperor of Japan's emissaries were conferring with Washington on the situation, Japanese aircraft swooped down upon the great American naval base of Pearl Harbor and put out of action many of the United States fleet stationed there . . . 'So this means,' Noel's entry gives it, 'that America is bound to come in with us and we are at war with Japan.'

And now the United States was our sworn ally against Nazi terrorism, with a vanguard of American forces pouring into Britain.

It was towards the end of that year that Noel still stoically refused to see Sinclair, nor when he telephoned would she speak to him.

Colin, meanwhile, continued to improve, and although

258

it was not yet advisable, according to Sir Jeremy, that he should attend the Wardens' post as a telephonist, he was now able to help himself out of his wheel chair and with the aid of crutches move about the room.

While he still tentatively alluded to divorce she continued to insist that she would never allow him a divorce. 'For,' she said, 'I am your wife and will remain so, as long as we two shall live.'

Poor comfort for him who said his life was a living death.

'Stuck here between four walls . . .' He brooded silently, listened to the wireless and Churchill's world broadcasts, while now, with the temporary cessation of raids, she needed to give only her part-time thirty-six hours to A.R.P. She would wheel him out to the High Street when she went shopping for their weekly rations, or into Regent's Park; but this enforced inertia was taking its toll of him.

She came back from the post one evening, having left him for four hours with two of Gavin Johns' spy thrillers from the Times Book Club, to find him just recovering from an attack.

He had left his chair and was struggling to hoist himself up from the floor. There was blood on his lips.

'I got up to get a cigarette, and came over faint,' he told her.

She telephoned Sir Jeremy.

He came as soon as he could that same evening, examined him and pronounced:

'I want a screening of his heart. I will arrange for him to see —' he mentioned the name of an eminent cardiologist.

The report from the heart specialist diagnosed that there had been a slight coronary thrombosis but no immediate reason to anticipate a recurrence. Complete rest and continued immobility. No attempt to leave his chair for the time being unless accompanied.

'Is it likely to recur?' she asked Sir Jeremy.

'At any time and without any warning, yet one can live a life's span without a recurrence; but three recurrences could be fatal.'

So now there was more to watch and wait for, and fear. And he became impatient, fretful, unable at the present to go to the post since it meant he must leave his chair to be helped down the steps to the telephone.

But as those few weeks passed and he strengthened physically, the doctors agreed he could return to telephonic duties at the post. This, on condition he take no undue exertion.

'Fat lot of exertion,' he grumbled, 'being wheeled about like a baby in a pram . . . I see,' he was reading *The Times*, 'that the age of national service for men has been raised from forty-one to fifty-one and that those in Civil Defence can be excluded as on work of national importance, but if over forty-one they will not be posted for the more active duties with the forces. As for the women' – he grinned round at her – 'they'll be called up for active service. It says here, reporting Churchill's speech of yesterday, that women between twenty and thirty will be required for the A.T.S. or the other fighting forces. So that lets you out. You are over thirty.'

'I'd have to be let out because of my back but in any case all our full-time men and women of the right age groups will be called for active service now.'

'So I'll be some use,' said he, brightening. 'The A.R.P. will always need telephonists.'

It was a few days after this that, having wheeled him back to the flat one afternoon, she told him, 'I must get to the shops before they close. Mrs Hodson was going to bring me our butter ration but she forgot to take our books, and we've no spam and only one egg. I'll have to get some offal. I believe oxtail is offal and unrationed. I shan't be long.'

She was gone almost an hour because long queues had formed and she had to wait her turn.

She let herself in with her latchkey and went to the sitting-room; his chair had been brought from the floor above to avoid the stairs. She called to him:

'I've brought our sweet rations too. We haven't had them for three weeks, so —'

As she entered the room the words froze. She saw that he had slid sideways from the chair and that his mouth was a little open, his jaw a little dropped. One of his hands hung down, the other was pressed to his chest.

Panic seized her . . . So motionless, no sign of an attack. She felt for his pulse; not a flutter. She put her lips to his, not a breath, and his hand was cold.

She rushed to the telephone and rang the doctor. His receptionist said he was on his rounds but would ask him to call so soon as he —

She replaced the receiver and rang Sir Jeremy's number. He too was unavailable but would come when he —

She returned to the chair and that unmoving figure in it. She raised his head; it was limp and heavy on her arm; so chill and waxen his face, and those eyes so wide unblinking . . . O God, no! Not this!

At any time and without warning . . .

'He could not have wished for a better end,' said Archie Tarrant.

*   *   *

Extract from her journal December 1941

Well, it's all over . . . Lots of flowers, a wreath from the Post. Barton sent a heart of red roses. J. L. S. sent the loveliest cluster of spring flowers flown from the Scillies, and there was a spray of snowdrops and violets from the gibbon.

It is in his Will that he wished to be cremated. I asked the verger if I could have the flowers to take to a hospital

261

rather than leave them there to die in the Garden of Remembrance.

So I took them away and J. L. S. drove Aunt Rhoda and me to the military hospital at Milbank where I left the flowers. And afterwards he dropped us at Archie's flat where we were to have lunch. His cook had prepared a pheasant, don't know how Archie got it as there are no shoots now.

I couldn't eat anything. I just sat there, dumb.

'You don't have to grieve,' Aunt Rhoda said. 'He is to be envied. Millions today don't go so peacefully and painlessly. It is how I would wish to go, but none of us goes till we're invited.'

I thought but didn't say that I hoped my invitation would be a long time coming, because that very morning I had a letter from Faith, Hope (and no Charity) the solicitors dealing with the undefended case of Sinclair v. Sinclair that it was due for hearing on January 21st, 1942. The New Year and it would be the happiest of all New Years for us. No obstacles now against our marriage. I know it is as Colin would have wished, and J. L. S. knew it too.

He came back to the flat after we had taken Aunt Rhoda to her house. It is still there in Fulham that used to be open country more than a hundred years ago. There had been a bomb at the corner and the pub demolished and some windows in her house were broken in the blast.

I wanted her to stay at The Chantrey for the duration but she won't hear of it. She said, 'I'm not going to be left out of this. I'm fire watching and can give first-aid.' I'm not surprised that she and her lot won the vote.

And a week later:

J. L. S. telephoned me today to tell me Marcia has withdrawn her petition. There will be no divorce, and for us . . . no marriage.

Thirty years on

'You see,' she said to me, 'she wanted to be a peeress. I remember he told me long ago that she was keen on titles. At that time there was not a chance he would inherit. His cousin had teenage daughters but his wife could still have had a child as she was not past child-bearing age. And although she could have used his name even had she divorced him it wouldn't have been the same as if she had remained his wife. So,' a whimsical smile came and went upon her little old-young face, 'I was never his wife. Not that it made any difference. We were together and that was all we wanted. We were,' that smile fluttered up again, 'quite shameless. She is still Marcia, Lady Aviemore, and I'm still Noel Harbord. Nobody minds about that sort of thing these days and they didn't mind – much, then. The few friends we had accepted the situation, especially Birdie. She lived to be ninety.' The smile faded. Her blunt-cornered mouth quivered to the words: 'I hope I don't go on living to be – older. I always dreaded being left. It is so lonely. Abysmal loneliness sometimes . . . But,' she brightened, 'I ought not to complain. We had twenty lovely years together, not under the same roof but near enough. And he made me art director of Marriott's art department and so we shared our lives.' Her eyes, unfaded with faint coin-like markings under them, gazed into the distance. Her hair of silvery cropped curls was reminiscent of the Caroline Lamb portrait in her page's costume. I understand why he called her Caro . . .

She said: 'I stayed on in A.R.P. during the war. As I was living in Piccadilly (for he took a flat for me in the same building as his), I was moved to a post in Westminster. I quite missed it when it was all over . . . But there had been one thing none of us could stand. The Blitz was nothing to it. The first time we heard it was about eight o'clock one morning. It sounded like an express train flying overhead because the thing *flew*! I thought of what he had told me years ago that Hitler was planning "quite something". They came two years later – the doodle-bugs. My back wasn't too bad then. It has got worse with old age and arthritis . . . I remember being called to an incident on a Sunday just off Oxford Circus. The thing had cut out, that was the beastly part of it. We had no warning. It just went silent and then – the bang! Had it been a weekday the casualties would have been . . . But there were thousands who got it other times, especially when followed by the long-range rocket. A forerunner, I suppose, of the moon rockets today.' Her eyes left the distance and came back to me. 'I wonder – if we have it again – of course it will be different, worse if anything, just the press of a button hundreds or thousands of miles away, and then, total destruction. Perhaps it will be the end of this civilization. All civilizations have had to end since the beginning of world with*out* end. But if it should come, I wonder how this generation will stand up to it.'

I said: 'I think they will, just as you and all of them stood up to it . . .'

* * *

Obituary from The Times

Mrs Noel Harbord, widow of Colin Harbord, on July 24th, 1974, at 100a Piccadilly. One time art director of Marriott, publishers.